It was hard, Kendall thought.

She didn't want to see a father and daughter curled up on the sofa, reading books and playing board games. She didn't want to bond over a roaring fire or hot soup or cuddle up against the storm. She didn't want to remember. Kendall tipped her head back and let the rain fall on her face. She didn't want to forget. She wanted to just stay here, in this spot, and let the rain and wind take her away.

"Kendall." Hunter's hold eased. He stepped back, offered his hand instead. "Please."

Kendall looked over her shoulder to where Phoebe stood in the window, her tiny nose pressed against the glass in between splayed hands. Kendall couldn't do this. She couldn't spend endless hours looking at a little girl who reminded her so much of the daughter she'd lost. She couldn't...

She took a deep, shuddering breath, looked down at Hunter's hand.

And placed her trembling one in his.

Dear Reader,

From the time Kendall Davidson walked onto the page in *Always the Hero*, I could not wait to tell her story. Writing about a female veteran of the Afghan war was a responsibility I took very seriously; so seriously, I second-guessed myself, hoping I was doing my fictional military heroine a fraction of the justice so many of our servicemen and servicewomen deserve.

I knew it would require a special man to convince Kendall love was worth taking a chance on, but other than that, he was a blank slate. Correction: I knew Hunter MacBride would need an advantage in his fight to win Kendall's heart—his niece Phoebe, a child in need of the kind of help only Kendall understands. The more books I write, the more I realize just how resilient the human heart is.

This story, like all the Butterfly Harbor romances, is about the healing power of love and acceptance, friendship, community and hope. Here's wishing that Kendall and Hunter's (and Phoebe's) journey to their happily-ever-after finds a place in your heart.

Anna J

HEARTWARMING

Safe in His Arms

Anna J. Stewart

Recycling programs for this product may not exist in your area.

ISBN-13: 978-1-335-51083-9

Safe in His Arms

This edition published by arrangement with Harlequin Books S.A.

For questions and comments about the quality of this book, please contact us at CustomerService@Harlequin.com.

Printed in U.S.A.

Bestselling author **Anna J. Stewart** was the girl on the playground spinning in circles waiting for her Wonder Woman costume to appear or knotting her hair like Princess Leia. A Stephen King fan from early on, she can't remember a time when she wasn't making up stories or didn't have her nose stuck in a book. She currently writes sweet and spicy romances for Harlequin, spends her free time at the movies, at fan conventions or cooking and baking, and spends most every night wrangling her two kittens, Rosie and Sherlock, who love dive-bombing each other from the bed...and other places. Her house may never be the same.

Books by Anna J. Stewart

Harlequin Heartwarming

Return of the Blackwell Brothers

The Rancher's Homecoming

Butterfly Harbor Stories

Holiday Kisses
Always the Hero
A Dad for Charlie
Recipe for Redemption
The Bad Boy of Butterfly Harbor
Christmas, Actually
"The Christmas Wish"

Visit the Author Profile page
at Harlequin.com for more titles.

For Aimee Costa-Schmitz.

Cousin by birth. Friend by choice.

CHAPTER ONE

"WELL, PHOEBE?" HUNTER MACBRIDE stopped his decade-old motor home at the turnoff for the Liberty Lighthouse. "What do you think?"

Hunter's seven-year-old niece turned her doll-wide gaze out the bug- and grime-encrusted windshield to get her first glimpse of Butterfly Harbor and California's historic lighthouse. He powered down the windows and let the roar of the ocean welcome them. The faint sound of rattling pebbles cascading beside the lapping waves and late-winter wind reminded him of the carefree summers he'd spent at his grandparents' beach house growing up. For the first time in a long time, Hunter felt as if he could breathe.

The coast had always brought him a sense of peace. In his experience, there wasn't a problem that couldn't be solved by the roar of the water and the sheer power of Mother

Nature crashing against the rocks. He could only hope this place would do the same for Phoebe. It had to. He'd bet everything—including his career—on it.

"I've always loved lighthouses," Hunter said. "Used to explore them whenever I could." He cast an eye on Phoebe. "Nothing better than climbing to the top, around and around that spiral staircase—"

Phoebe looked at him and frowned, her brows knitting into a perfect V over her little nose.

"That's right, a spiral staircase." He wound his finger in a circle and drew it up. "Your mom and I used to have races to see who'd make it to the top first. One time I went so fast I threw up on her."

Phoebe's skeptical stare went blank at the mention of Juliana. It had been six months since her parents—Hunter's sister and brother-in-law—had been killed in a car accident. Six months since he'd become sole guardian to his niece.

Six months since Phoebe had changed from a rambunctious, energetic chatterbox to a child of few words.

Hunter's heart constricted as he rubbed

the back of Phoebe's hand. Thick dark curls framed her face and tumbled around her shoulders. There were times he swore he was looking into Juliana's face, but with far wiser and more guarded eyes. What he wouldn't give to take away the trauma and pain his niece had been through. What he wouldn't give to have his sister back.

"You want to know a secret?" He leaned close and whispered, "I haven't eaten a corn dog since."

Phoebe's lips twitched.

Hunter's spirits soared. Earning a smile from Phoebe was tantamount to scaling Mount Everest. She was so guarded now. So controlled. It was all he could do not to jump out of the motor home and do a little dance of joy. Instead he gave her the warmest smile he could and continued his observations.

"I used to call lighthouses soldiers on the hill." Hunter pointed at the tower stretching toward the sky. "They always look like they're standing guard. Which they are, in a way. There's a light up there, in the lantern room just inside the catwalk. It would glow and shine its light into the ocean and guide ships safely to the shore."

Phoebe pointed to one of the smaller buildings surrounding the lighthouse. From a distance he could see the keeper's cottage attached to the base with a roof in dire need of repair. Across the way, closer to the cliff line on its own rocky little hill, sat the carriage house that would serve as their home while Hunter researched and wrote the book—literally—on the Butterfly Harbor lighthouse and its restoration efforts to be used for publicity purposes.

He kept a slow pace as he maneuvered his oversize motorized baby down the dirt road. His smile widened as the white cottage with empty, weathered window boxes came into sight. "Yup. That's our house."

A quick glance at Phoebe, and he saw her mouth form a perfect O before she bit her lip and sat back in her seat.

"We're going to have to set up some ground rules, kiddo."

Phoebe sighed.

"Until I get the lay of this place and figure out where everything is, I don't want you wandering around on your own. You stick by my side or by the house, okay? Phoebe?" He gave her a look that told her he expected an actual answer. "Either by the house or here in the motor home."

"Okay."

"It's going to take a few days to get used to everything. It's okay to be scared of new places, Phoebs. But I won't let anything happen to you. This is our big adventure, right?"

Did she have to look at him as if he was losing his marbles?

"Right. Maybe it's just my big adventure. Let's check this place out and find the keeper." He shoved open his door and dropped to the ground. He grimaced as he realized thirty-two wasn't nearly as young as it had felt a few weeks ago. Hunter pressed his hands into the base of his spine and arched his back, shook out his legs and tried to remember what it felt like for his toes to move. "Maybe I shouldn't have taken those last six hours in one stretch." He swore he even heard the motor home sigh in relief as he slammed the door and headed around to help Phoebe out. First things first, unload then get something to eat. Preferably something that didn't come out of a box or a can.

As he rounded the front of the white-and-gray motor home, he saw a woman striding around the side of the lighthouse. A woman who made him stop in his tracks. As a photojournalist, he was an observer by nature. He found people fascinating. The way they moved. The way they didn't. But there was an aura about this woman, a power—the way she stood under the midafternoon sun, her dark hair pulled severely back into a ponytail, wearing worn, snug jeans encasing long legs and a gray sleeveless tank that made him shiver in response.

How was she not covered in goose bumps in this cool ocean air? Because the goose bumps would have been chased off by the muscles on this woman's arms. *Toned* didn't have anything on her. Neither, it seemed, did pain. Even from a distance, he could see the scars. Scars that marred her left arm and shoulder and reached up the side of her neck. Angry scars. But ones that spoke of strength and resilience.

"We aren't open to tourists." The woman's voice danced along the wind, strong, clipped, no-nonsense. She planted her hands on her hips and pinned cool silver-gray eyes on him.

"I know. I'm Hunter MacBride." He glanced back at the motor home before walking toward her, hand outstretched.

The caution in her eyes as he approached had him slowing.

"We aren't open to hunters, either."

Hunter grinned. Was that a joke? "Ah, good to know." He chuckled and made sure to keep his distance. She was a woman alone out here. He didn't blame her for being suspicious. "I'm a friend of Gil Hamilton's from college. He's hired me to write a book." He jerked a thumb toward the carriage house. "Said I could stay here while I work."

"Gil hired you to write a book?" She couldn't have sounded more dubious if he'd told her he was a fairy-tale prince. "About what?"

"Butterfly Harbor. The Liberty here." He inched his chin up to get a closer look at the lighthouse tower. "You must be part of the restoration crew."

"I am the restoration crew." She dropped her hands to her sides. "Gil didn't tell me anything about this."

Hunter winced. This was going so well. "Don't know what to say. I'm a little earlier than expected. Maybe he hasn't gotten around to it. You, ah, living in the carriage house?"

"No."

"Oh. Well, great. I guess we won't be putting you out, then. I'm sorry, I didn't catch your name."

"I didn't throw it." She looked over his head, scanning the motor home as a door slammed. "You here with your wife?"

"I'm not married." First time that statement didn't come with a ping of regret. He was one of those men who'd expected to be married and well into a family the size of a softball team by now. But with his on-the-road job, the right woman had never presented herself. "I can't just yell *hey you*, can I?"

"I've been called worse. If you're not here with your wife, who—"

Had Hunter not been watching her, mesmerized with the way the light played against the odd color of her eyes, he would have missed the color draining from her cheeks and lips. Shock drifted across her face before tipping those eyes of hers into pools of misery.

Hunter felt Phoebe grab hold of one of

the loops of his jeans as she circled around him. "Well, there's my girl. Hey there." He bent down and hefted Phoebe into his arms, not too difficult given she was such a little thing. Her jeans and dark T-shirt were warm from the sun. "This is my niece, Phoebe." He took a step toward the woman.

The woman took a step back. And stared unblinking at Phoebe.

Unease uncoiled inside him. "Phoebe, this lady is refurbishing the lighthouse. I'm guessing we're going to be seeing a lot of each other."

Phoebe clutched the back of Hunter's neck and met the woman's gaze.

"It would help if we knew your name," Hunter pressed. What was wrong with the woman? Hadn't she ever seen a single father before? Why was she looking at Phoebe as if she were an alien who'd landed from outer space? Her expression made him grip his niece tighter.

"Kendall," the woman choked out. "Kendall Davidson." And with that, she walked toward the keeper's house, opened the weather-beaten green door and closed it firmly behind her.

KENDALL PRESSED HER back against the closed door and slowly slid to the floor. The scarred wood welcomed her as it always did, with firm support and splinters to spare, absorbing the trembling she had no control over. She drew her knees into her chest so tight and so hard she could barely breathe. She didn't want to breathe. She didn't want to feel. She didn't want to… She squeezed her eyes shut until she saw stars. She didn't want to see.

A tiny sob escaped her lips. She slapped her hand over her mouth and rocked until she banged her head against the door.

In the past six years, Kendall had faced down terrorists in Afghanistan, watched most of her squad get blown into the afterlife and survived thirty percent of her body being lit on fire. She'd walked among others who'd been harmed or killed with bullets and hate, heard the screams of terror and grief of families suffering. Every day she got out of bed was a gift.

But put one little girl in front of her, a little girl with big brown eyes and even bigger dark curls, and Kendall wished Matt Knight had never rescued her from that burning SUV in Afghanistan.

She knew what it was like to be bone-shivering cold. But that wasn't why her arms and legs were shaking. She couldn't feel anything—hot or cold—as the image of a little girl in her uncle's comforting arms burned through her mind.

Even as the thought of another little girl—one she couldn't save—singed her heart.

Hunter MacBride and his niece, Phoebe. They were going to be staying here. In her sanctuary, where for the last seven months she'd finally found the peace and solitude that had eluded her since she'd come home. Where she'd finally begun to put the past behind her as she fixed the lighthouse and surrounding buildings stone by stone, shingle by shingle.

This Hunter man would have been intrusion enough. Him she could have managed. But the idea of Phoebe popping up around every corner, her laughter coating the air, little girl squeals of excitement and happiness—that was going to take some getting used to. If she ever could.

She rubbed a hand against her chest, hard, shoved herself to her feet and went to the small shuttered window above the mattress in the corner. She lifted up on her toes and popped open the shutter, just an inch or so, and watched Hunter start unloading bags and a backpack. She could hear him humming as he handed a bright yellow bag to Phoebe, who hauled it up the little hill to the carriage house.

The house she'd finished restoring just last month. The only thing left was to fill the window boxes with something bright and cheery like red geraniums, but she figured she'd ask Matt's wife, Lori, to do that in the spring. Lori Knight could just look at a window box and fill it with color and life, whereas Kendall…well, Kendall killed everything she touched.

"Just leave things by the front door, okay, kiddo?" Hunter called before stretching his arms over his head. He turned suddenly, his brown-eyed gaze landing firmly on the house. Kendall ducked out of sight, both mortified and irritated at her reaction.

She scrubbed at the paint splotches on her fingers to give herself something to do as she waited for them to go inside. Bracing herself, her heart hammering as she listened for Phoebe's voice, her laugh, an excited squeal at the majestic image of the ocean mere feet away.

Their front door closed. Kendall finally let out a breath that didn't feel tinged with fear. In the next second, she grabbed her wallet and her sweatshirt and headed out, ready to take the two-mile hike into town at a far brisker pace than usual.

It didn't dawn on her until she was halfway there that she'd never heard a sound from Phoebe.

Not one little sound.

CHAPTER TWO

FOR ONCE IN his life, Gil Hamilton had not exaggerated. Hunter unloaded the last of his and Phoebe's bags into the cottage, and only then did he take the time to stop and look around. It was small, cozy, but the perfect size for him and Phoebe. Especially with the two small bedrooms separated by an updated bathroom complete with a claw-foot tub. He'd bet Phoebe could deep dive in that thing.

He thought the white walls would be blinding, but the starkness was broken up with splashes of blues and greens reminiscent of the sea. As promised, Hunter found a desk situated beneath a window that overlooked the ocean and updated outlets in the walls. The perfect writing location once he got his laptop set up.

The kitchen lined the wall closest to the door, a galley style that more than suited their needs for meals at the square table steps away. He found dishes, pots and pans, and plenty of glasses and flatware. What the kitchen didn't have he probably did in the motor home. A small sofa and two chairs bookended the stone fireplace. The bedrooms each had a small flat-screen television and DVD player, no doubt in preparation for renting this place out to vacationers, Hunter imagined. He'd have to use the motor home for his photography work. He didn't want to clutter the place with all his equipment. He wanted this place to feel as much of a home as possible. For Phoebe.

Phoebe.

Hunter sighed and dragged his hands through his too-long hair. What was he going to do about Phoebe? She should be in school, something he'd argued extensively about with her paternal grandparents, who had taken serious exception to his being granted custody after their only son's death. A bachelor father, they'd called Hunter, and a nomadic one at that. As if he was some throwback character from the '50s incapable of taking care of a child. He'd been as big a part of Phoebe's life as he could from the day she was born, arranging jobs so he could stay with Juliana while her husband traveled for work. Besides, Hunter was the only family Juliana had. Now Phoebe was the only family he had, and he was going to do whatever it took to give her the best life possible.

He knew he had some serious decisions to make, but his niece was doing okay with her homeschooling. She could read better than he could, and she was pretty good at math. He'd done enough research online to know what she should be studying. Socialization was where she was lacking, and that was top of his list now that they'd be staying put for even a short while. Hopefully there were some kids her age in town who would help bring her out of her shell and have her uttering more than one or two words at a time. And maybe remind her that the world wasn't a completely bad place.

Maybe he should have consulted more doctors other than the two who had assured him she'd come out of it when she was ready. They'd told him not to push. To let Phoebe move through her grief in her own time. Or maybe he was second guessing himself constantly because he was terrified of the one thing he couldn't control: a custody battle.

Movement outside the kitchen window, brought his attention to where he could see the lighthouse standing tall and proud against the wind. Kendall Davidson. She reminded him of Phoebe in a way. She wasn't particularly loquacious. A woman of few and bullet-pointed words. But the way she'd looked at his niece… That expression of hers might very well haunt him for a while. He'd bet she liked her space and the peace and quiet, which was why, when he heard her front door slam, he didn't venture outside. Instead, he stood at the window and watched as she headed—on foot—down the road he and Phoebe had traversed moments before.

His stomach rumbled, reminding him it had been a long time since breakfast. He'd been so anxious to get here he'd driven straight through lunch. Phoebe—ever reliable, responsible, adult little Phoebe—had shoved an apple into his hand a little over an hour ago before munching on one herself.

"Phoebe! You hungry?"

She popped up in the doorway of her bedroom almost instantly.

"You want to go into town on our bikes or do you want to eat here? Gil told me about a diner that has milkshakes and hamburgers."

Phoebe's mouth twisted as she considered. "Strawberry milkshakes?"

"I'd bet on it. Get your coat on, okay? It's probably going to get chilly. Don't forget your helmet!"

She disappeared into her room as Hunter stepped outside, scanning the area and deciding once they got back he'd repark the monster in the little grove behind the house. Depending on how long they'd be here, he figured he could buy a cheap secondhand car, but Butterfly Harbor was a pretty small town. Why add to emissions or subtract from his bank account when his feet and bike would do just fine? "All set?" he asked when Phoebe joined him at the monster and hopped on her bike. She gave him a thumbs-up. "Okay then. Our first trip into Butterfly Harbor. Let's do this, kiddo."

KENDALL STOOD OUTSIDE the Butterfly Diner, scanning the booths inside for a sign of Mayor Gil Hamilton. After stopping at the still-under-construction town hall, which was scheduled to reopen later this year, she'd been told by his assistant at the temporary offices that he was out and about. Of course he was, Kendall thought. It was, after all, an election year, albeit late March. Now she'd have to trek all over to hunt him down.

She needed to talk to him as soon as possible. She needed him to change his mind and make Hunter MacBride and Phoebe stay somewhere else. She needed her solitude back.

While there were plenty of people enjoying the homemade offerings at the diner, Kendall didn't find a hint of blond hair and political ego anywhere on the premises. Hands shoved in her pockets, she fidgeted in place, peering at the customers through the large windows.

"Only time you bounce on your toes is when you don't know what to do." The friendly male voice from behind her had her turning. "What's going on, Hacksaw? Take a wrong turn at the hardware store?"

Kendall grinned. There were fewer things on this planet that could make her smile easier than Matt Knight. Make that Deputy Matt Knight, who was looking mighty proper in his khaki uniform. "You seen the mayor anywhere?" she asked.

"Not today. Then again, I've been stuck in the office the whole time. First ray of sunshine I've seen since I left the house." He tilted his scruffy chin to the sky and basked for a moment. "Can't wait for Ozzy and Fletcher to get back from that law enforcement conference so we can resume our regular patrol schedule."

"Taking double shifts so Luke can be home with Holly more was a nice gesture." The sheriff, Luke Saxon, and his wife were expecting. Holly owned the Butterfly Diner but was rarely pulling shifts these days.

Matt shrugged. "Least I can do. I'm hoping to garner some goodwill once those twins arrive. Maybe give them a test run."

Once upon a time Kendall had dreamed of a husband, a family. She and Sam had planned it all out, two point five kids—he'd gotten a serious kick out of the decimal point—beginning with getting married once both their tours ended. But those dreams and plans had died with Sam when he'd been killed during an insurgent attack in Afghanistan. She'd loved Sam. She'd loved only Sam. "You and Lori starting to think about kids?"

"Maybe." Matt probably didn't have any idea just how goofy he looked when asked about his wife. Boy, she and Matt had come a long way from sharing those sand-encrusted camps oversees. "We're exploring our options. Kyle seems to be all for it, which I think is what's finally convinced Lori it's time."

Funny, Kendall thought. Ever since she'd arrived in Butterfly Harbor last fall, she'd heard talk about how Matt had changed Kyle's life, but the teen he'd adopted had been good for Matt, too. The experience had turned him into the stellar father and parental figure Kendall suspected her friend was always capable of being, despite his own troubled childhood. Add Lori to both their lives and, well, that was as close to a perfect match as Kendall had ever witnessed.

Kendall probably should have reassured him with platitudes and words of encouragement, but neither were her style. Besides, she and Matt knew, better than most, that life was completely unpredictable. Luck and hope had nothing to do with an outcome. It could turn—and devastate—on a dime.

Instead, she cast a forlorn look back into the diner. "I really need to talk to Gil. Any idea where he might be?"

"He and Jake are scouting out locations for the new community and teen center. They could be anywhere. What's going on?" Matt leaned against the lamppost as if he had all the time in the world.

She appreciated his friendship more than she could say. And he'd slipped right into Butterfly Harbor as if he belonged here—which, after more than three years, he did. The big, burly soldier she'd served with hadn't brought the darkness home with him, despite the war taking his leg. Sure, he'd had his struggles, but he'd set his mind and gotten what he wanted. Now he was married to one of the nicest—too nice, sometimes—women Kendall had ever met and had adopted a teenage foster kid who was making a name for himself around town as an up-and-coming handyman. She'd even hired Kyle to help out on some of the bigger jobs she'd had with the lighthouse. Life was sweet for

Matt Knight. One of the few things that did her heart good.

"Kendall, what's wrong?" Matt asked again when it was clear she'd gotten lost in thought.

The last thing she wanted was Matt getting involved in her problems. Again. He'd spent most of the last few years looking after her in one way or another. She'd finally gotten on her own two feet, and no way was she turning back now. "You know anything about Gil hiring some guy to write a book?"

"Um, yeah. Something MacBride. Photojournalist from back east. Went to college with Gil, I think. He was looking for a change, and the town council wants to produce a travel book for visitors. Can't promote the gorgeous place too much, right?"

"Yeah, right." Kendall winced. Darn it. Not that she expected to hear different. Keeping herself as far away from the town hubbub as possible meant being out of the loop. "The guy's early, it seems. He's staying at the carriage house."

"Up where you are?" Matt's eyebrows went up. "That going to be a problem?

I thought you were living in the keeper's house."

"I am. And he is." Her hands came out of her pockets and started flailing about the way they always did when she was on edge. "It's just… I'm used to being alone. I like being alone. I need to be."

"I know you like it, but whether it's what you need?" Matt shrugged. "Not going to agree with you there. What's the matter with the guy? Is he a creep? Need me to give him a talking-to?"

Kendall rolled her eyes. "Like I couldn't handle a creep. And no, I don't need you to give him a talking-to. I need him to… leave." Even as she said the words, she spotted two figures—a larger man and smaller girl—riding toward them on bikes. "I can't believe this. Is he following me? Does he have radar?"

"He's here? MacBride?" Matt spun around before Kendall could stop him.

"Don't stare. Oh, shoot, Matt. Behave yourself."

Matt looked at her over his shoulder, an odd expression blanketing his dark-haired features. "What's this all about? You're almost flustered. You don't fluster."

"No, I don't," Kendall snapped. "But what I don't need is someone getting in my way up there. I work alone. It's just how I do things. Can you just help me find Gil so I can explain… Hello." She locked her lips into a tight line as Hunter MacBride pulled his bike to a stop beside Matt.

Kendall's heart hammered against her chest as she did everything she could to avoid looking at Phoebe. Phoebe in her little jeans and jacket and cute little shoes and big brown eyes…

"Hello, neighbor." Hunter unhooked his helmet and draped the band over his handlebars. "Fancy seeing you here. Phoebe and I are dying for some home cooking. Aren't we, kiddo?" He reached back as Phoebe climbed off her bike and pushed it next to his. "Hi, there." Hunter turned that million-watt smile on Matt and offered his hand. "Hunter MacBride. You'd be the sheriff?"

"Heaven forbid." Matt actually shuddered and returned the greeting. "Deputy

Matt Knight. Kendall and I go way back. She was just telling me about you."

"Was she?" Hunter grinned.

Kendall's stomach did a double tuck drop to her feet. She'd been so distracted by Phoebe earlier she hadn't registered just how good-looking the man was. Not Hollywood handsome, but head-turning nonetheless. Dark brown hair, amber-specked brown eyes and a dimple in his chin that made her fingers itch to check how deep it went.

He was taller than she was, almost as tall as Matt, and his chest and shoulders were broad enough that she didn't think Phoebe would feel anything other than safe and protected.

Phoebe. Kendall shifted uneasy eyes to the little girl, who was peeking out from behind her uncle, staring wide-eyed and cautiously at Matt.

"This is Phoebe," Hunter introduced Matt to his niece. "I'm guessing you're one of our go-to people if we're ever in trouble."

"Absolutely. Nice to meet you, Phoebe. Are you going to be here long?" He glanced at Kendall with an all-too-knowing smile on his face. Kendall recognized that expression.

It was one he'd learned from his wife, who had developed a propensity for matchmaking now that she was submerged in happily-ever-after.

"A few months," Hunter told him. "Depends how long it takes me to write the book on this place. Here, you need help with that?" He reached down and unhooked Phoebe's helmet.

Kendall kept her eyes pinned on Matt as the little girl pulled her head free and shook out her curls.

Matt's jaw locked, and Kendall ducked her head. But not before he saw the sorrow she was unable to hide. It was then she knew she wasn't imagining things. He saw what she did.

Panic and dread piled like rocks in her chest. How was she going to survive this, them, for months?

"Well, aren't you pretty," Matt said after he cleared his throat. "I, um, need to get back to the station, but feel free to drop by anytime. I'm sure you'll have plenty of questions about..."

"I have to go." Kendall spun on her heel and headed away from them. It didn't matter which direction she went. She didn't care. She just needed to get away. From the man who made her think of the future that would never be hers.

CHAPTER THREE

"HOW BIG ARE your milkshakes?" Hunter asked the attentive, sandy-blond-headed waitress once they were seated at a booth. Phoebe had barely glanced at the menu before she'd scrambled onto her knees and looked over the back of the booth to where a group of kids had gathered at the end of the counter.

"Quite big. Big enough to split." Their server, who wore a pink T-shirt, inclined her head toward Phoebe. The woman's long ponytail fell over her shoulder as she flipped her pen in her hand, making the small diamond solitaire wedding set twinkle on her finger. "Or I can whip up a mini one just for her."

Phoebe turned a big-eyed grin back at him, then up at their server.

"Would you like your own shake, sweetie?"

Phoebe nodded.

"Got it. So that's two burgers, one mini. And two milkshakes. One mini." She pointed to Phoebe. "Side order of onion rings and...a green salad." She ticked off the items on her pad. "That do it?"

"And coffee, thanks." Hunter handed the menus back. "Busy place." Not overly crowded, but full enough he could tell it was a favorite go-to spot for locals and tourists alike. Not that this time of year was tourist season, but it should be given the beautiful weather. Gil had told him the town was slowly becoming a year-round go-to destination. He liked the throwback feel of the diner, from the black-and-white tile floor to the orange-and-black vinyl stools and booths, no doubt a decorating homage to the town's namesake monarch butterfly.

Speaking of butterflies. They were everywhere, in every form, dangling from the ceiling of the diner, attached to the walls. Even perched perfectly on the edge of the windowsills. Children's renderings, artist offerings and even a few scribbles on napkins.

"Saturdays have become nonstop. I'm Paige, by the way. Paige Bradley."

"Hunter MacBride." Hunter offered his

hand and cast a quick glance at Phoebe. "This is my niece, Phoebe."

"Nice to meet you both." Paige looked over her shoulder to the group of surprisingly quiet kids. "My daughter Charlie's somewhere in that pack. And that's Simon with the glasses." Paige shifted toward Phoebe and crouched down, pointing to each child as she referenced them. "There with the brown curls? That's Marley O'Neill. And Stella Jones. She wears bells in her hair sometimes. She jingles when she walks. Would you like to meet them, Phoebe?"

Phoebe looked at Paige for a long moment before she shook her head and scooted back in the booth.

"Maybe another time." If Paige was put off by Phoebe's reluctance, she didn't let on. She pushed to her feet. "You staying long or just passing through?"

"We'll be here for a while," Hunter said. "I'm writing a book on the lighthouse."

"Oh, you're the photojournalist we've heard about." Paige seemed to bite the inside of her cheek. "Have you, um, been up there already?"

Sensing where this was headed, Hunter

nodded. "We have. Just finished unloading the motor home."

"Ah." Paige nodded. "So that must mean you've met Kendall."

"We have had the pleasure." Questions flooded his mind about the odd, quiet, apparently easy to offend woman. Hazards of the job. He always had questions. But experience had taught him barreling in demanding answers was rarely the way to glean accurate and helpful information. "She seems nice."

"She is," Paige said with an apologetic shrug. "She's just..."

"No need to explain," Hunter assured her. "We all have our stories. Speaking of which, I'd love to start talking to residents, get a feel for the place. Really get to know what makes Butterfly Harbor tick."

"Oh, well, I'd be happy to participate, but Charlie and I haven't been here that long."

"Long enough?" He pointed to her ring and smiled at the pink rising to her cheeks.

"How do you know this is recent?"

"Intuition. Plus you keep turning it with your thumb, as if you're still getting used to it. I tend to notice things like that. I bet there's a great story behind it."

It occurred to him the book could take a more personal spin rather than having a focus on purely historical information. The lighthouse would be the perfect starting point, but it was obvious there were a lot more stories to be found in this town. More than the buildings and the restructuring—it was about the people, as well.

"Hmm, you could say that. If you're looking for a newcomer's perspective, I'm your girl. But Holly, Simon's mom—she's the owner—she's lived here her entire life. As has her father. Holly's home today, but she should be in for a few hours tomorrow morning. She and her husband are expecting twins in a couple of months."

"Oh, wow. Well, I wouldn't want to bother her right away."

"Doesn't mean you wouldn't like to talk to her, though, right? Don't worry. I'll hook you up. You have a cell number?"

"Absolutely." He pulled out his wallet and handed over a business card. "My schedule's open."

"Well, I might just be using you in the

coming weeks then. Talking to you would be a good excuse to get Holly off her feet if I can't at least get her out the door. I'll put your order in with Ursula. She's our mainstay at the grill. And your shake is coming right up." She winked at Phoebe.

"Everyone seems so nice here." Hunter folded his hands on the table and looked across at his niece. "You like it so far?"

Phoebe nodded and rearranged herself on the seat. The top of her chin almost brushed the table, but as was her routine, she placed her napkin to her right and arranged her fork and knife and spoon, making sure they were aligned properly. Above the din of conversation and childish laughter, the milkshake machine rumbled to life. A grumbling voice added to the noise as it echoed from beyond the pass-through window.

"Maybe after lunch we can walk down to the beach," Hunter suggested. "Get our feet wet in the ocean?"

Phoebe knocked her head to the side. *Maybe.*

"Or we can take a walk around town. See what stores they have here? Maybe there's a bookstore." Hunter grinned when Phoebe's eyes widened. "Yeah, I thought that might get your attention. I have to admit, I did a bit of checking, and I know for a fact there is a bookstore. But you know what else it has?" He leaned forward and lowered his voice to a secretive whisper. "Cats."

The skepticism on Phoebe's face shouldn't have been possible, not in a child so young. But there it was. She thought he was joking.

"I swear." Hunter made a crisscross gesture over his heart. "Cats and books. Might be a nice way to spend the afternoon, right?"

"Are you talking about Cat's Eye Books?" Paige asked. She set a small pink-filled glass topped with a cavity-inducing swirl of whipped cream and a solitary cherry on top on the table and followed it with Hunter's coffee. "One of Charlie's favorite places to go. You'll love it. Both of you. Just be sure you always look up." Paige laughed at Phoebe's expression. "You really don't have to say a word, do you? Your face says it all. Trust me. Look up."

Phoebe watched Paige walk away before she picked up her straw, unwrapped it and slid it carefully into her glass. Hunter's heart had become immune to the little daggers of despair that struck whenever he noticed how precise and careful Phoebe was. It was as if she considered everything around her to be temporary. To end at any moment. But pushing her out of her comfort zone, one that seemed to give her some solace and security, didn't seem right.

"How is it?" he asked after she took a dainty sip.

Phoebe nodded, her lips twitching before she drank again. Then pointed to Hunter's messenger bag. "Do you want your book?"

Phoebe nodded.

Hunter retrieved the tattered copy of *Charlotte's Web*. The same book she'd read over and over for the past six months. The same book her mother had been reading to her just days before Juliana and Brent had been killed. Phoebe settled in, book on the table, fingers pressing the worn pages open, and pursed her lips as she dropped into the story.

Hunter took the time to catch up on his emails before pulling out his own notebook. He'd already taken a few pictures of the town with his phone during their ride into town, initial images that, when assembled, would give him a bit of a roadmap of what to concentrate on when he brought out the big guns. While camera phones were fabulous, they didn't capture everything for him. Not the way a big, need-two-hands device with a long lens tended to. There was something about hefting that camera in his hands, feeling the weight of it, knowing the power it possessed to capture a moment, a fragment of time that never got old.

He loved the smell of this place. The hot, steamy grill. The promise of fried onions with a hint of bacon. The aroma of coffee wafting its way around the sugary sweetness of a cavalcade of pies lining the case by the register. Made him grateful they had their bikes. Too much time in Butterfly Harbor and he was going to gain fifty pounds.

And that was just the diner. Hearing former celebrity chef Jason Corwin had opened a restaurant at the historic Flutterby Inn, a building he was certain would take days to investigate and photograph to its fullest potential, had gotten his salivary glands going. The restaurant, Flutterby Dreams, wasn't exactly Phoebe friendly, so he'd have to play that one by ear.

Scrolling through the city's website, Hunter made note of the different businesses, the mentions of historic buildings that could be contemporaries of the lighthouse. He had a full day planned tomorrow at the library, searching through the archives for any events that might have included Liberty Lighthouse. Phoebe could get started on that new math unit he'd showed her.

He felt she should be back in school by now, but every time he even broached the subject, Phoebe resisted. No doubt the idea of being in a classroom again took her back to that day—the day when the police had come to collect her from school after the accident. Just that morning Phoebe had had parents who adored her, doted on her. Hours later, thanks to a drunk driver, her entire world had vanished.

No wonder she didn't want to go back. But Hunter knew the time was coming when he wouldn't have a choice. She couldn't stay out of school forever. Something Phoebe's paternal grandparents had begun to convey through their recently obtained lawyer. It was one more strike against him, the first being his job and the fact that he didn't have a permanent address that wasn't a PO Box. An uneasy nausea churned low in his stomach. He knew Eleanor and Stephen meant well and that they were concerned about Phoebe—not that they'd shown much interest in her before their son's and daughter-in-law's deaths. It hadn't taken them longer than the reception after the funeral for them to suggest to Hunter that his rootless lifestyle wasn't conducive to the raising of a seven-year-old. Their claims seemed bolstered by the fact that Phoebe had become withdrawn, but the therapist he'd consulted with shortly after the accident had given him the reassurance that it would just take time and encouragement from him to help her move beyond the loss.

Bringing up her parents in regular conversation didn't illicit the hostile reaction it once had; Phoebe was getting used to hearing the stories or comments, and while she didn't necessarily contribute to the conversation, he could see she was listening, processing. All positive steps toward healing.

Shaking himself out of his reverie, he blinked and found Phoebe watching him. Those brown eyes of hers seemed to see so much—far more than his jaded ones ever could.

Hunter gave her one of his trademark "everything's great" smiles, and she returned to her book. The little tyke picked up on everything. Every mood he had. Every thought that passed through his mind. It was almost… spooky.

"Okay, here you go. One cheeseburger, one mini burger, a side order of onion rings and one green salad."

Hunter scrambled to clear his stuff off the table as Paige set their food down. Phoebe shifted onto her knees and tucked her napkin into the collar of her shirt.

"Such a little adult," Paige murmured, then turned surprised eyes on Hunter as Phoebe claimed the bright green tomato-and-cucumber-topped salad for herself. "I'm guessing the two of you have been through a lot."

"A bit." Hunter kept his tone upbeat. "But we're doing okay, right, kiddo?"

Phoebe stuffed a grape tomato into her mouth and gave them both a thumbs-up.

"Yeah, well, you've definitely come to the right place. Just keep your eyes open for butterflies, Phoebe. They're everywhere in this town."

"Even now?" Hunter slopped ketchup onto his burger. "I thought monarch season wasn't until—"

"Monarch season is all year round here in Butterfly Harbor. Trust me. It's the magic of the place. And you know what they say about butterflies and luck, don't you?"

She'd clearly caught Phoebe's attention. Paige bent down. "It's said if you whisper a wish to a butterfly, it'll carry it on the wind and deliver it. But you have to be very careful and catch a butterfly right here." She tapped the tip of one finger. "The butterflies will come when the time is right."

Phoebe's brows veed. Hunter had no doubt, if she'd been a teenager, she'd have rolled her eyes and muttered a bitter "whatever." Instead, she smirked and returned to her salad.

"Well, it was worth a shot." Paige pushed back to her feet. "Butterflies aren't my specialty. Although my daughter Charlie's becoming an expert. If you want the real skinny, head up to Duskywing Farm one morning and talk to Calliope Jones. Now she's magic with those creatures."

Phoebe stabbed her fork hard into her salad and looked out the window.

"I think we're a little leery of magic right now," Hunter explained. "But I appreciate the advice. I'm up for anything since we're here."

And if that happened to include a bit of magic, all the better.

KENDALL HAD SPENT the better part of the afternoon searching out Gil Hamilton. Granted, it wasn't how she'd expected to spend the day, not when she had plastering and sanding to do on the exterior of the lighthouse. But at least, in the meantime, she was able to submit her new order for supplies to Harvey Mills at the hardware store and check the community bulletin board for any side jobs she could knock out quickly.

Abby Corwin's grandmother Alice, who ran the Flutterby Inn before Abby took over, was looking to do an upgrade on the backyard patio she shared with her roommates before summer arrived full-on. Meanwhile, Mrs. Hastings, the former school principal, wanted shelves built for her dining room. A handful of other tasks ended up in Kendall's phone, enough that she abandoned her original goal of hunting down the mayor and headed off to make contact with her new clients.

At some point the lighthouse was going to be finished and Kendall would be out of a job—and a place to live. The more money she could bank, the easier it would be when the time came. Not that she charged much beyond supplies, but every penny helped.

In the years since she'd been discharged, she'd lived in her car, in shelters and, for a few months that Matt didn't know about, on the street. She'd been lost without Sam, without the life they'd planned. It was as if she'd been left utterly rudderless in an unending storm on the ocean. Those days, when the darkness got so bad, when everything above, around and beneath her felt too big to escape, there was little more she could do than just sit and breathe. And even then, breathing was an effort. So where she lived hadn't meant a lot to her. She could have been in the most palatial of homes, surrounded by the best of friends, and it wouldn't have made a difference.

But the medication had. Eventually. The

therapy had. Somewhat. And she'd vowed to never have another day like those when the darkness had almost won.

Now, she knew as long as she remained in Butterfly Harbor, she would always have a place to rest her head. Or stash her duffel bag. Thanks to Matt, and everyone, in fact. Heck, Matt was even talking about constructing a tiny house for the back portion of his land. Not that he'd said specifically that he was thinking about Kendall. But she knew him well enough to guess the thought had crossed his mind. Matt Knight never did anything randomly. There was always a method to his…madness.

Madness. Kendall almost laughed as she bade goodbye to Greta Bundy, a former council member who was looking to have her bedroom repainted. Her little cottage-style house looked like it had been plucked from the pages of Mother Goose, with the white picket fence, lattice trim around the windows and roof, a lush green lawn and an arched front door that had forest animals carved in the stained redwood.

Kendall wouldn't wish her familiarity with the opposite of the picture-postcard scene on anyone; it wasn't as if she wore her issues like a badge of honor or even a shield. If anything, dragging her past with her was part of what kept her quiet most of the time. Not having the ability to see the bright side of anything for so long, she'd learned it was better to simply stay quiet and observe. And gradually, eventually, that silence had, in a way, set her free.

She wasn't meant for a life other than the one she had now. Simple, careful. Alone. That's where she had to keep her focus. And leave the past in the past. The panic attacks had subsided, and she knew to plan well ahead of time should any fireworks or other large noises happen around town. And she'd been doing okay. Better than okay. She'd been doing...good.

Until Hunter MacBride and his niece, Phoebe, had arrived.

Kendall stopped walking, that familiar lack of air pressing in on her. The more she tried not to think about the little girl, the more she was all Kendall could think about. Images of another little girl, laughing and tumbling in the air, her face alight with promise and hope despite her family's difficult circumstances. Until those circumstances were ended. For good.

She needed to get back to the lighthouse. Back to where she felt safe. She could track Gil down later today or even tomorrow. But for now…

No!

Kendall snapped herself free. One hard shake of her head, one forced push of relaxation through her body had her looking at the peaceful sight of the blue ocean mere blocks away. From where she stood at the top of the hill, it felt so close. The water, the crashing waves. The feel of the damp sand between her toes. That was all she needed.

"My kind of therapy, here I come." Kendall slipped her phone into her back pocket and zipped up her sweatshirt. Keeping the ocean in focus, in sight, in mind, she walked forward.

And longed for peace.

CHAPTER FOUR

"REMEMBER WHAT PAIGE at the diner said, Phoebe." Hunter pushed open the door to Cat's Eye Bookstore and ushered her inside. "Look up."

Phoebe's chin shot up, and she turned in circles. Hearing Phoebe's soft gasp before she pointed a finger up at the ceiling had Hunter doing the same. Amid the chin-high polished wooden bookcases filled with tomes, an intricate maze of wide shelves, cubbies and platforms had been built into the walls for three, no, five cats of varying ages to enjoy. A yellow-eyed tabby blinked down at them from its regal perch, reminding Hunter of the Cheshire cat in *Alice in Wonderland*. "Well, hello there." Hunter couldn't stop the smile from forming.

"That's Zacharia." A man emerged from around the corner, his arms loaded with a stack of hardcover books. "And don't worry, he's not a leaper. He prefers to sit and rule over us from above."

"Good to know." The last thing Hunter wanted today was for a cat to land on his face. "Paige over at the diner told us to be sure to look up when we came in." He trailed his gaze around the room, shaking his head at the cats darting in and out of sight. "This is amazing. How many cats do you have?"

"Officially? One. Zacharia there." As if the books weighed no more than a bag of feathers, he stopped beside them. "We're fostering four others at the moment. My daughter, Mandy, and I rotate them so they don't get bored at the shelter. Also gets them acclimated to interacting with people and each other. Sorry. I'm rambling. What brings you by? Anything in particular?" He headed to the new releases table, placed the books he was carrying on the nearest shelf and started reorganizing the selection. "Or just browsing?"

"Phoebe's in need of some new books." Hunter took a long moment to appreciate the larger-than-expected store that stood on the corner of Monarch Lane Whispering Wing three blocks from the diner. "And I suppose

I am, too. Especially anything having to do with Butterfly Harbor and the surrounding areas. I'm doing research for a project."

"You must be Hunter MacBride. I'm Sebastian Evans." The man offered his hand to shake. "Gil said he thought you might be stopping by. Welcome to Butterfly Harbor. And hello to you, too, Phoebe." He bent down just as Paige had to meet Hunter's niece eye to eye. "What kind of stories do you like?"

"She reads widely," Hunter said when Phoebe looked up at him. "And she's…shy around strangers."

"Totally understand. Wish my Mandy had been shy at that age. Would have made things a lot easier." Sebastian laughed. "She'd talk nonstop to anyone and everyone. Still does. That said, she's thirteen now, so you must be seven? Eight?" he asked Phoebe.

"Seven," Hunter confirmed.

"Right. I have a special going today on children's and YA books. Buy three books, get the fourth for free. How about you and your uncle look around for a bit and if you have any questions, you can let me or one of the cats know?"

Phoebe pointed up as a sleek black cat emerged from a cubby.

"That one's Ruby," Sebastian told them. "And over there we have Bella. My daughter named her that because she's so poofy and pretty. Not the sharpest crayon in the box, though. I can't tell you how many times she's mistaken a fur ball for a mouse. But a kind soul nonetheless."

Phoebe looked confused.

Hunter wasn't sure he'd ever seen a cat with so much fur. Almost pure white with a collar of gray, Bella had bright blue eyes that almost glowed even in the daylight. "What is she, a Ragdoll?" His great-aunt Eunice had had a Ragdoll cat when he'd been growing up.

"We think so. Part, at least. Mandy's been looking into it. She's hoping to be a vet, which explains the menagerie around here. The ones you have to look out for are Chuck and Lilith. They're barely a year old and love little girls especially. Careful or they might try to follow you home."

Hunter recognized a barely restrained plea when he heard it. "I'm not sure a cat is in the cards for us right now. We aren't staying very long, and being so close to the cliffs—"

"That's right. You're staying up at the Liberty, aren't you? Mandy and I have been dying to see how it's coming along, but we're trying to be patient while Kendall finishes it."

Phoebe wandered down the aisle toward the children's section.

"So there's only one person working on the lighthouse?" Hunter asked.

"Yep. Kendall's a bit of a one-woman miracle construction crew. Not much she can't do on her own, but when she needs help, she knows who to call."

"You?" Hunter picked up a new mystery by one of his favorite authors he hadn't realized was out yet.

"Oh, no. There's a reason I own and operate a bookstore. Mandy's more handy than I am. No, the deputies help Kendall out from time to time, as well. And some of the local teens. And Frankie Bettencourt, of course. You meet Frankie yet?"

"Afraid not. We only just got into town today."

"Butterfly Harbor's first female firefighter.

Also been a pain in my backside for going on thirtysomething years."

At Hunter's curious look, Sebastian grinned. "She's my best friend's sister. Twin, actually. Older than Monty by three minutes, but you'd swear it was three years the way she talks. We grew up here together."

"Then I'm definitely going to want to talk to you in the future. All of you," he added. "For the book."

"Yeah, sure. Whatever you need." Sebastian finished adding the new books to the display and moved behind the counter that had a selection of hand-carved wooden bookmarks, hand-turned pens and butterfly-topped pencils. The glass case beneath the register displayed a sign signifying locally made jewelry, some of which were miniature books with real leather bindings. "I know a lot of people haven't been happy with some of the decisions Gil's been making, but we can't argue with results. The town's coming back to life. Should make a good angle for your book."

"How close was it to dying?"

"About as close as you'd want to get. A little over two years ago, I was considering leaving. Would have killed me to give up this place. Starting over with a new store in a new town wasn't financially feasible, not with Mandy so close to college. Gil's revitalization plans, the building of a new butterfly sanctuary, bringing a national TV crew out here to cover one of our food festivals—it's all helped. It's helped a lot. Given us store owners some breathing room."

"Gil's never been one to let protests or detractors get in his way." Not that Hunter knew Gil that well. To say he'd been surprised to get Gil's call a few weeks back was a massive understatement. He hadn't seen or heard from his friend in almost a decade, but while Hunter had lost touch, obviously Gil had kept tabs on Hunter and his career.

"We'll see what happens come election time. If things keep running smoothly, he should keep his job."

"And if things don't run smoothly?" Hunter asked.

"Good question." Sebastian shrugged. "Other than politics or banking, not exactly sure what the Hamiltons are made for."

Hunter felt a tug on his shirt. When he turned and looked down, he saw Phoebe, clutching a hardbound book against her chest as if it were gold. "What do you have, kiddo?" He bent down, held out his hands and felt his heart break a little more when she handed over a brand-new copy of *Charlotte's Web*. Her eyes shone, and it wasn't the first time he had a difficult time deciphering grief from hope. "Well, this is lovely." His smile made his cheeks ache. "We can add this to the stack, okay? How about we go explore together? I bet there are some math puzzle books around here somewhere? We've been homeschooling," he explained to Sebastian.

Unfazed, Sebastian tapped his hand on the counter. "Then I have just the thing. Follow me."

A little over an hour later, the sorrow over Phoebe's main choice of book had been tempered by the half dozen other books Sebastian had talked her into trying. A few were ones Hunter never would have considered, given they were far above a seven-year-old's reading level, but Sebastian had sat on the floor with Phoebe and explained each one, encouraging her by letting her know his daughter had loved these books at her age.

The science and math workbooks were a pleasant surprise and included lots of fun experiments they could do together.

"Depending on how fast she goes through these," Sebastian told Hunter as he accepted Hunter's credit card, "you might want to start visiting the library. Phoebe's old enough for her own card."

Gripping the edge of the counter, Phoebe's eyes went wide, and she bounced on her toes.

"Won't that cut into your profit margin?" Hunter joked.

"It's good business sense. A reader like her is hard to find, and we want to keep readers interested. Alternating between will keep things fresh. You'll find the library two blocks north from the elementary school."

"Good to know."

Phoebe inched closer to him at the mention of school. Hunter laid a hand on her shoulder and squeezed, their silent sign that he understood and she could relax.

"And, because I expect you'll be repeat customers, here you go, Phoebe. Your very own Cat's Eye book bag." Sebastian placed a few of her books into the drawstring bag, then stepped around the counter to help her slip it on like a backpack. "You bring this with you whenever you come in, okay?"

She nodded so hard she almost tipped over. "Thank you."

Hunter felt a burst of happiness at Phoebe responding without prompting. She must have decided that Cat's Eye Books was a safe place.

"You sure I can't interest you in a cat?" Sebastian asked. "Or maybe two? Two is always better so they each have a companion. I'm sure Chuck is around here—"

"Nice try." Hunter chuckled and purposely did his best not to look anywhere near Phoebe. A pet might be a good idea, but maybe something smaller. Like a goldfish. "Appreciate your help. And the information. I'll be in touch about talking to you and Frankie and her brother. I bet you guys can give me some insights into this town few others can."

"Count on it."

Hunter held out his free hand once they were back outside. "Well, Phoebs. I have to say that's the most fun bookstore I've ever been to."

People roamed the street, darting across the road toward the beach. Seagulls cawed in the distance as the scent of briny seaweed coated the air.

"I'd say we've had a good first day in Butterfly Harbor. How do you want to finish it? The beach or…"

"Ice cream!" Phoebe tugged hard on his hand and pulled him to the next shop. Harbor Creamery.

"You sure?" Hunter feigned disbelief. "I don't know. You had a big lunch."

Phoebe scrunched her face, dragged him closer and jabbed a finger against the menu displayed in the window.

"Oh, they have kiddie scoops." They also had gelato, which Phoebe pointed to next. Even at seven, she knew his weakness. "Okay, one scoop. But that means broccoli with dinner."

Phoebe shrugged and led the way inside.

IF KENDALL WAS LUCKY, and had Frankie's help, she'd get the scaffold erected on the west side of the lighthouse this week. She had a lot of painting to do. As the sun began to dip for the day, Kendall gathered up her tools, stashed them in the rebuilt shed and pulled down her makeshift workstation.

Kids got into everything, and the last thing she wanted was anything enticing Hunter's niece. Hopefully school would keep Phoebe occupied and away from…her.

She didn't need, didn't want, a daily reminder of little-girl needs and wants. That everything and anything that went wrong with the world could be solved with a mother's hug.

She wasn't a mother, though, Kendall reminded herself. She'd quit that dream when she'd lost Sam. She'd only come close when she'd all but adopted Samira and her family in Afghanistan.

Samira's father was a translator, looking after his two sons and daughter along with his late wife's parents. Samira, at ten, had become a bit of a caretaker, always helping her father. But she'd loved soccer. And soon, she and Kendall had a standing practice session that gave both of them something to look forward to.

"Stop it." Kendall lugged one of her sawhorses back into the keeper's house when Hunter's and Phoebe's bike tires crunched on the dirt and gravel road. Their bike baskets were filled to overflowing, and Kendall noticed Phoebe was wearing a familiar amber backpack. Obviously they'd found their way to Cat's Eye Books.

Apprehension tugged at Kendall's stomach as she quickened her pace in the hopes of finishing for the day before Hunter thought to…

"Hello." Hunter steered his bike to the lighthouse rather than the carriage house and dismounted with that now familiar, friendly, if not quirky grin on his too-handsome face. He engaged the kickstand and plucked a small paper bag out of the front basket.

Because she wasn't a complete curmudgeon yet, she gave him a quick chin jerk. "Hi." She pushed the air out of her lungs to dispel the cloud of melancholy.

"This is for you." Hunter offered her the bag.

She blinked at the bag as if it were filled with snakes. "Why? What for?"

"A peace offering of sorts. And a thank-you. For sharing this with us." He motioned to the view of the ocean alight with the flame of the sunset.

Kendall needed him to understand she was not up for any social interaction where he or just about anyone was concerned. She shrugged and turned away. "Not necessary. This wasn't my choice." And the man whose choice it was had been dodging her all day long.

If anything, her refusal seemed to encourage him. Hunter darted over, stepping in front of her before she reached her door. "It would be rude not to accept. And even though you're trying your best, I don't think you're inherently rude."

Kendall shot him a humorless smile. "Guess again."

"I know we're intruding." He tried again and moved between her and the refuge she sought. "And if you're like most people, you don't like change. But change happens. And we're here. We need to find a way to get along. If not for each other, certainly for Phoebe. She's been through enough this year. I don't want her being scared of the person we live next door to."

Kendall resisted the pull to look over her shoulder. She would not look. She would not… She glanced back to where Phoebe stood astride her bike, tiny hands clutching the handlebars with white-knuckled uncertainty.

Stiffening her spine, bracing herself, Kendall faced Hunter again, opening her mouth to argue. But when she found herself looking into determined eyes, she saw the one thing she knew she could lose to: a father's resolve.

Her heart nearly seized. "I like my solitude." Like? More like she needed it as much as she needed air to breathe and water to drink. Small doses of interaction were fine. Doses of her choosing, but knowing this man and his little girl were steps away from the one place she'd been able to feel free again? Why was the universe playing with her again? "She doesn't have to be scared. I might not be here much longer, anyway." It was the first time she'd considered it, dropping everything and leaving town. But avoiding Hunter and Phoebe might be the simpler solution.

"Oh." He looked surprised at that tidbit of information. "Well, for as long as you are here, I'd appreciate it if you didn't glower at her."

Kendall frowned. "Glower? I didn't mean

to hurt her feelings." Something akin to guilt wrapped itself around her.

"Prove it. Accept this from us, please." He lifted the bag again. "We guessed. Phoebe did, anyway, at the flavor. At least pretend to appreciate it."

Kendall accepted the package, peeking inside. If she'd had a heart left to break, it might have shattered into a million pieces. "Strawberry." The tears came, even after all this time. "Thank you," she finally managed. At his arched brow, she took a deep breath, glared back. Then turned to Phoebe. "Thank you, Phoebe."

Phoebe's mouth curved up at the corners before she climbed off her bike and steered it toward the guest house.

"Thank you," Hunter said. "Have a good evening."

Kendall nodded, because she couldn't speak. She waited until she heard the door close behind him before she hauled the sawhorse into the house, set the bag on the table and finished cleaning up outside. When she literally had nothing left to distract herself with, she went inside and dropped the bag of ice cream into the sink.

After taking a shower and changing her clothes, she returned to the one-room dwelling, knotting her shoulder-length hair high on her head. The newly restored electricity and lighting flickered and bathed the space in a dim glow. Even though her stomach growled, she didn't feel like eating. That said, she hadn't eaten since breakfast, and even that had been a scrambled egg and the last of the scones Abby Corwin had sent home with her last week.

Kendall opened the small fridge and stared at the assortment of fresh vegetables and eggs that local farmer Calliope Jones insisted on personally delivering every few days.

Kendall sighed. Salad didn't appeal. Veggies were never her first choice. She'd eaten enough eggs lately she should be clucking. Surrendering, she plucked up one of the three spoons out of the crooked, handmade mug and pulled the pint of ice cream from the insulated bag.

She popped open the lid and looked down at the creamy, soupy, almost completely melted concoction. One dip of the spoon had her mouth watering. She could smell the fresh strawberries mingling with the cream and sugar. She took a bite and nearly swooned.

She walked over and sat cross-legged on her sleeping bag–covered mattress, making her way through the ice cream one soft, blissful, sorrowful bite at a time.

Closing her eyes, she accepted the truth. Her stay in Butterfly Harbor had come to an end.

"COME ON, PHOEBS. Finish up your breakfast." Hunter sorted through his satchel to make sure he had everything he needed for the day. After getting into a solid routine over the past week, he was anxious to get to work and put his extensive internet notes to use.

Laptop, map of the town, cell phone. Notepad. His excessive purchases of legal pads probably qualified him for some sort of support group, but there was nothing he liked better than scratching pen or pencil against paper the good old-fashioned way. "Phoebe?"

He glanced over to the table and found Phoebe, *Charlotte's Web* open, pushing half a bowl of cereal around in the milk with her spoon. "Not hungry?"

Phoebe shrugged.

"If you're done, please take your bowl to the sink and rinse it out." Mornings like this he remembered how his sister had been with Phoebe. His niece wasn't a voracious eater. There were times she just didn't want to eat or wasn't hungry. Juliana hadn't fretted over it too much. Neither did Hunter.

Phoebe did as he asked then returned to his side, tugged on his sleeve.

"Yeah? What's up, kiddo?"

She just blinked up at him.

"Well, I need to get a good look at this town, but first I have a meeting with the mayor." One that had already been rescheduled twice.

Phoebe's eyes went wide.

It was all Hunter could do not to suggest she not be that impressed. But while Gil Hamilton might not inspire his admiration, their first nights in Butterfly Harbor certainly did. He couldn't remember the last time he'd slept so well, but he shouldn't have been surprised. He loved the ocean. Always had. And being this close to it, hearing every sound it made, settled his soul in a way he'd been hoping to find.

"Unless you've changed your mind about school, looks like you'll be tagging along with me. Have you?"

Phoebe shook her head.

"Okay, then. Load up that new bag of yours. Choose one of your schoolbooks and one new book we bought at Cat's Eye. And grab us each a bottle of water from the fridge." He'd unloaded the last of their gear from the motor home last night. And caught himself once again stopping to look over to the keeper's house that lay almost dormant against the darkness, its flickering light a reminder of the woman who lived inside.

Hunter had to have been blind not to see the sense of grief that surged into her eyes as she'd looked down at the ice cream. The same grief that flashed the first time she'd set eyes on Phoebe. The possibilities running through his mind about the source made his heart ache for her. Nonetheless, he wasn't about to enquire further.

She didn't have to tell him she enjoyed her solitude—that was as clear as a spring morning every time he caught sight of her.

This morning was no different than the past few. He'd purposely tried to keep his distance and certainly didn't want Phoebe getting under her feet, but honestly, going out of his way to avoid Kendall Davidson was becoming a full-time job. One he didn't have time for. Not if he was going to get that new book proposal off to his agent and come up with a decent draft of the Butterfly Harbor manuscript for Gil sometime soon.

When Max Miller, literary agent to the semi-famous, had suggested he spread his wings and try his hand at fiction, Hunter had thought the man might have finally slipped his tether to reality. Hunter dealt in facts, facts caught by a camera and detailed by the words that flowed out of him as a result. But the challenge of doing something new had intrigued him. Even better, it excited him. Of course he'd locked in that promise seven months ago; three weeks later his entire life had been flipped upside down. His rather carefree, go-anywhere, film-anything lifestyle had ground to a screeching halt when Juliana and her husband had been killed. Now he was a single father living on the road, taking every freelance job he could in order to build up the coffers he suspected he was going to need in the very near future.

Coffers that could do with the serious dose of coinage a solid new publishing contract could bring.

Hunter's chest tightened. The money was one thing. Time was another. He was down to one month. One month to deliver a saleable proposal to Max who, now that he was getting up in years and was culling his client list, was getting more difficult to please. So yeah. Hunter had four weeks left. And not a single, solitary idea.

The job offer from Gil had been a lifesaver, and while the project itself was going to take a tremendous amount of work, he knew one thing for certain: Butterfly Harbor could very well be his last chance for inspiration.

Phoebe was struggling with the strings of her new bag, trying to get her arms into them. Hunter quickly got her situated, then himself, and they headed out for their bikes.

Phoebe came to a stop on the top step, thumbs hooked in the straps of her bag. As she did every morning, she watched as Kendall reassembled her sawhorses and worktable and unloaded tools.

Phoebe pointed at Kendall and looked up

at Hunter. "Yeah, I see her. Morning, Kendall." He doubted he'd ever sounded cheerier in his life as he waved at their neighbor.

Kendall gave a quick wave before returning her attention to the plank-and-pipe scaffold erected around the lighthouse.

Why the gesture felt like a massive triumph, he couldn't say. Still, she'd waved. Progress.

It wasn't long before they reached the mayor's office, currently housed in a two-story old saloon-style building that soared to the top of Hunter's must-photograph list. Butterfly Harbor was fully awake. People strolled up and down the streets. Cars carrying daily tourists slid into parking spots as families and couples unloaded beach chairs, coolers and jackets to keep off the morning chill of California air. Personally, Hunter loved the brisk coastal mornings. It got his blood moving.

His cell phone rang after he'd checked in with Gil's assistant. Hunter glanced at the screen, felt his body tighten at the familiar number. With Phoebe settled in one of the lobby chairs, he stepped outside to take the call. "Good morning, Lance."

"Hunter. I believe you were supposed to check in once you and Phoebe got settled."

Hunter wasn't a man normally quick to temper, but Juliana's in-laws' lawyer had a way of triggering even the most calm of pacifists. "We only arrived in town a few days ago, so you saved me a call." As if he'd been champing at the bit to report in.

"Is the child adjusting adequately to her new surroundings?"

"*Phoebe* is doing fine," Hunter explained. "As the court-appointed social worker stated in an affidavit only three weeks ago." A social worker he'd driven half a day out of his way to meet with.

"Has she returned to school?"

"Not yet, no." But she would. Soon. At least he hoped she would. Otherwise her paternal grandparents were going to have even more ammunition to use against him. "But other than that, she's functioning as she should be and within expected parameters."

If Lance Dunbar, Esquire, picked up on Hunter's sarcasm, he didn't let on. "We would like the address of where you're staying on record."

Hunter rattled off the oddly structured

address; it wasn't as if the carriage house at Liberty Lighthouse had a street number.

"And how long will you be staying at this address?"

"For as long as the project takes me," Hunter said as Gil's assistant poked her head out of the door to wave him inside. He held up a hand and nodded. "I'd guess about two to three months."

"And where will you be going next?"

"To be determined," Hunter said. He could recite these questions in his sleep. When he could sleep. These questions, which were posed to him each and every time he took a new job, were what kept him awake most nights. "There's a video-chat session scheduled for tomorrow evening with Stephen and Eleanor," Hunter reminded the lawyer. "Can I assume this is a confirmation call for that?"

"My clients see no use in video chatting with their grandchild who refuses to speak to them. It's a waste of everyone's time."

Hunter cursed himself for not having the forethought to record the call. "They could see her. She speaks just fine." To people she trusts. When she feels like it.

"As I said, a waste of time. Please be sure to notify us of any location change as soon as it takes place."

"Noted," Hunter grumbled into the already-disconnected phone. These conversations were getting more abrupt and more disconcerting. Not for the first time, Hunter wondered how Stephen and Eleanor Cartwright had raised such a likable son. Brent had become one of Hunter's best friends almost as soon as it became evident he and Juliana were serious. Hunter had served as one of his groomsmen at the wedding, and it had been Brent who had asked Hunter to be Phoebe's godfather a few seconds after the little girl had entered the world. Losing both his sister and his friend had gutted Hunter, but he hadn't been able to give in to the grief—not when Phoebe needed him. And she did need him.

No matter what Stephen and Eleanor might think.

Doubt crept in. A very small part of him wondered if she'd be better off with them, living a more traditional life with a home, school, friends, never wanting for anything because she'd have financial security. But then he remembered how Brent's face would darken whenever the topic of his parents was raised, and how he'd say money didn't equate with love and if it was the last thing he'd do, he'd raise Phoebe knowing she was utterly and completely accepted.

Which was why, no doubt, he and Juliana had designated Hunter as Phoebe's legal guardian should anything happen to them.

Shaking off the unease that always descended after one of these calls, Hunter headed inside. "You okay, kiddo?"

Phoebe gave him a thumbs-up without even looking up from her book, the latest *How It Works* on astronomy.

"She's good as gold," the assistant told him. "I'll keep an eye on her."

"Thanks, I appreciate that. I'll be back in a bit, okay?"

Another thumbs-up. Hunter headed up to the second-floor landing and the mayor's office.

Had Hunter forgotten about Gil Hamilton in their years since college, it would have all come rushing back the instant he stepped into Gil's space. The sports awards and medals lined highly polished redwood bookcases. Certificates of achievements, letters of commendation, photographs of Gil and his father shaking hands with some of the biggest political names of the time spoke of a life dedicated to…well, Hunter wasn't entirely sure what. Clearly Gil had been busy in the last ten years.

But it was the sight of Gil Hamilton himself that had Hunter doing a double take. The man hadn't aged a bit since they'd graduated college. Same sandy-blond hair, same classic polo shirt and khakis, although Hunter would bet he wore a suit more often than he'd be willing to admit. They'd cut classes a lot to surf, as the beach had only been a hop, skip and a jump from campus, and judging by the look on Gil's tanned features, including that same self-assured grin, his old friend still found time to catch some waves. Chilly waves, but waves nonetheless.

"Hunter. It's good to see you." Gil came around the desk, hand outstretched. "Thanks so much for taking the job. And for going along with my schedule. I didn't expect it to be so long before we met."

He returned the greeting, then slung his bag from around his shoulder and set it on the floor next to the chair across from Gil.

"Can I get you coffee? Tea?"

"Ah, no, thanks." Hunter smiled.

"I appreciate you coming in."

"No problem. Phoebe and I enjoyed the morning ride."

"Ride?" Gil's eyebrows disappeared beneath the sweep of hair that barely missed his eyes.

"Yeah, bikes. Easier to tote around than a car. I left the motor home up at the lighthouse. With Kendall Davidson," he added just so he could watch Gil's expression.

As predicted, Gil Hamilton did not disappoint.

"Ah, right. Kendall." He scrubbed a hand against the side of his neck. "Probably should have given you a heads-up about her."

"You should have given her one about me and Phoebe," Hunter corrected. "Look, I'm used to being a surprise to people. Part of the job. But that woman looked positively spooked when we arrived."

"You're right. I messed up with that. I'll head up there and apologize. Easy fix."

Hunter bit the inside of his cheek. He didn't think anything with Kendall Davidson would be an easy fix, but it would be a testament to Gil Hamilton's people skills. "She's interesting. Been here long?"

"A few months. She's a friend of one of our deputies. Matt Knight. They served in Afghanistan together."

Afghanistan. Explained the burn scars, Hunter supposed. And probably more. "I met him at the diner our first day in town. Seems like a good guy."

"He is. So I made up a list of people it would be good for you to talk to about the history of the town." Gil handed Hunter a file folder. "Most of them have lived here all their lives."

"This is a start, thanks." Hunter wasn't about to tell Gil he preferred to move organically through a place, talk to people on their own, see who they thought was worth his attention. "I know what you're looking for in this book."

"Do you?" Gil's bright eyes dulled a bit. "I don't want a hatchet job, that's for sure. It's mainly for tourists and for promotion. Encourage people to move here. It's a special place. You know, sell self-published copies in the stores, send them out to the media who might be interested in covering upcoming events or holidays. A press package on steroids."

Hunter settled back into the conversation he'd been expecting, the same conversation he'd had with countless others in his career. "I don't go looking for dirt, if that's what you're worried about."

"I wouldn't say worried, exactly. The town has a colorful history."

"If you mean what happened with your father, I already know about that." And Hunter had no plans to include any of those controversial details in his manuscript.

Gil's normally open, friendly expression did a vanishing act. "I'm sure you do. This is about the rebuilding of a community, the coming together of a town. The way we've banded together and saved it."

"Then that's where I'll start." He was definitely going to be spending a lot of time at the library. "I appreciate having the place to stay while I'm working. Phoebe loves it up there."

"How's she doing?"

"Fine. I think." They'd discussed, peripherally, at least, Phoebe's issues since the accident. “Emotionally, she has her good days and her bad. I’d say I was hoping a change of scenery would help, but she gets a lot of that.”

“There’s a lot to be said for silence.”

“True enough.” Hunter’s lips twitched. “Still, I wouldn’t mind hearing a bit more about what she’s thinking from time to time. There’s nothing wrong with her. She’s grieving. It’ll take patience on both our parts.”

“Sure. It makes sense.” Gil nodded. “We all handle grief in our own way. She’s got someone who cares about her looking after her. That’s what makes the difference. Still a few months left in the school year in case you’re worried about her not hanging out with kids her own age.”

“That would be nice. But she’s not budging on that.” Hunter shook his head. With respect to that subject, Phoebe had not remained silent.

“Then maybe check the events at the youth center for her.”

“A youth center, huh? Your idea?” Once upon a time Gil had considered running charity organizations for a living—until Gil’s father had gotten wind of that and put his foot down and insisted he follow him into local politics. One thing Gil had always had problems with was stepping out from under his father's shadow. Even now that Senior had been gone a good few years, Hunter could still see the specter hovering not only in this office, but over Gil himself.

"The former sheriff's actually. Jake Campbell. He and Luke Saxon, his replacement, worked on the project together. Been doing pretty well so far, well enough that they're looking for a new, larger space. In fact, they're also looking for new instructors. If you're still as handy with that camera as I'm hoping you are."

"Not a lot of call for photography classes that don't include a cell phone, but I'll check it out." It was on the tip of his tongue to ask if the position would pay, but given it was a community center, he already suspected the answer. Didn't mean he wouldn't be willing, though. "Well, I'm sure you have a lot of work to get to. I'm heading to the library to get a jump on my research." Hunter got to his feet.

"Sounds good. Oh, and here. This should help settle you in." He handed Hunter an envelope. “It’s half up front, as we discussed. Other half on delivery. You said maybe two or three months?”

“Should be,” Hunter confirmed. Gil was right. The check in his hand would absolutely ease a bit of the burden weighing on him. He’d played a bit of hardball with his old friend, but given he’d had to make a cross-country drive to get here, he didn’t feel too guilty about it—and if he had, that phone call from the lawyer would have tipped the balance. “I’ll be in touch in a few weeks to let you know how I’m coming along.”

CHAPTER FIVE

WITH PHOEBE ENSCONCED in bed, Hunter slipped out of the carriage house and closed the door behind him. He found the darkness both captivating and intimidating with only a solitary light burning in the window of the cottage breaking through the night. He shivered against the cold, and considered going back for a sweatshirt, but the ear-thrumming pounding of the waves at the base of the cliffs pushed his discomfort aside. It was too late for coffee if he hoped to sleep tonight, and he was not a tea kind of guy, but a steaming mug of hot chocolate sure sounded good about now. He made a mental note to add some to the grocery list.

His shoes crunched along the gravel path. He was amazed at how the spinning thoughts that kept him awake faded into silence beneath the sound of the ocean breaking against the shoreline.

There was little, he supposed, more powerful than nature at its freest. His fingers itched to return for his camera, but photographing at night took a bit of preparation and planning. As he stood there, above the crashing waves and beneath the steadfast lighthouse that had overseen this shore for longer than he'd been alive, he knew this would be the perfect shot, the perfect image for the story he'd been hired to write. And the emotion he hoped to convey with his words. He stooped down, scooped up a handful of pebbles and let them trickle through his fingers. Hunter could barely hear them drop back onto the ground above the waves, but there was something connective about being out here, in the darkness, seeing this scene in the same way as people had decades before. No blinding lights to distract, no sounds of technology blaring in his ears. Only the water and the rush of wind and the smell of the sea to fill his senses.

He felt her presence before he spotted her, that spark of energy that crackled whenever Kendall was around. Hunter looked over his shoulder as she stepped out of the grove of trees on the far side of the cottage.

He couldn't explain it. He hadn't tried to, but that energy called to him, perhaps even more strongly than the tide had called to him tonight.

Hunter knew the instant she noticed him. She hunched her shoulders, tipped her chin down and huddled into the thin zip-up gray hoodie she wore, as if she could withdraw like a turtle into her shell.

She could have gone around him; he half expected her to when she missed a step and almost stumbled. But she kept on her path toward the keeper's house. "Nice night for a walk," he called out to her when she drew close.

"Yes, it is." She offered a quick smile before glancing at the carriage house. "Is Phoebe…?"

"She's asleep. Or she's supposed to be. I'd lay even odds she's huddled under the covers with a flashlight and her book." Growing up, his sister used to do the same thing, which was one reason he didn't make a fuss about it. "She thinks I don't know she does that most nights."

Kendall lifted her face into the moonlight and he caught the flash of what wasn't exactly humor, but understanding. "She thinks she's putting one over on you."

"Probably." Hunter dusted off his hands and stood. "The last thing I'm ever going to be upset about is her reading." Even if it was the same book, day after day, night after night. "Do you walk out here every night?"

Hands shoved deep into her pockets, Kendall rocked back on her heels. How was she not shivering to death? he wondered.

"Most nights. I'm not the best sleeper." She winced as if the conversation took effort. Still, she didn't seem in too much of a rush to head inside and he took that as progress. "There's an outlook about a mile and half that way." She jerked her chin in the direction she'd come from. "I found it a few days after I got here. There isn't a path or anything to it, it's just one of those places that helps shake loose the day."

"Sounds like you had the kind of day I did. My mind won't turn off." He didn't approach her, didn't make any move other than pushing his hands into his own pockets to stop them from stiffening up. "I met with Gil today. To talk about the book."

She nodded, looking past him to the ocean beyond.

"We talked about you a bit," he added.

Now that caught her attention. His eyes had adjusted to the dark and he saw the flash of irritation in her eyes, saw her spine stiffen, only to soften moments later. "What about me?"

"Only that our arrival caught you by surprise and that I thought he should have given you some warning. He agreed."

"Did he?" Kendall's eyebrows lifted.

"He'll be by to apologize. He should, anyway. I would if it were me."

"You're not Gil Hamilton," Kendall said with a quick smile. "You were right the other night. I've been rude to both you and Phoebe, so it's me who owes the apology."

"Accepted." The unspoken truce between them felt like the biggest hurdle he'd jumped yet. "We don't want to get in your way, Kendall. I'm just here to do a job and hopefully show Phoebe there's more to life than grief."

"I know. It's just..." She hesitated. "Children make me uneasy. I—"

"You don't owe me an explanation, Kendall." Although he was curious. *Uneasy* seemed an odd term to use. She hadn't said she didn't like children, or that she didn't want to be around them. "On the bright side, you don't have to worry about Phoebe talking your ear off." His heart twisted. What he wouldn't give to hear Phoebe's nonstop chattering once more.

"Maybe it's that she just waits until she has something important to say."

"Maybe," he agreed. "Would you like to continue this conversation inside?" He pointed to the carriage house. "I don't know about you, but I'm half frozen."

"No, thank you." Kendall took a step around him and shook her head. "Maybe another time. I've got a big day ahead of me tomorrow and I need to try to get some sleep."

"Fair enough." Disappointment he didn't expect slid through him. He couldn't explain it, but he liked being around her, liked talking with her. "Maybe next time then. Good night, Kendall."

"Good night, Hunter."

"YOU JUST COULDN'T wait for me, could you?"

Kendall looked down from the second

story of the scaffold she was building and found Frankie Bettencourt looking up at her, shielding her eyes against the morning sun. A sun that turned Frankie's tied-down, fire-red hair to a color resembling molten lava. "Sorry. Got an earlier than expected start. Come on up."

"Surprise, surprise." Frankie set her coffee cup down, unzipped her sweatshirt and shrugged free, tossing it onto the workbench before she scrambled up the side rungs to join Kendall. "Nice job so far. Feels sturdy."

They could have been twins, Kendall thought with something akin to humor shifting through her. Jeans, sneakers and tank tops were both their preferred attire. But while Kendall gravitated toward the grays and blacks of the spectrum, Frankie was a rainbow of contradictions. Even the bra strap that peeked out from under her sunshine-yellow tank was fluorescent pink. By comparison, however, Kendall looked as if she needed half a year's worth of good meals and twice that much sleep. That said, Frankie was toned, muscular and more fit than most athletes. She had to be, given her job as a captain in the Butterfly Harbor

Fire Department. She was also a good three inches taller than Kendall. So…maybe the twins idea didn't fit, after all.

"How far up do you want to build this thing?" Frankie's feet landed solidly on the plank platform. She gripped and shook one of the pipes and gave a nod of approval.

"No more than five, I think." Kendall had been debating that for the last half hour. She had a sixty-foot extendable ladder she could use as backup to do the plastering and priming, but the idea of a scaffold made more sense. She could get more done in less time. "I've put braking wheels on the bottom so I can move it around easily. The connections are holding well, but I don't want to stress it out."

"We won't. But given we don't have this property marked as a construction zone, let's not borrow trouble." That was Frankie. Safety first. Well, prevention first. Chances were she'd seen a lot of preventable accidents as one of the town's first responders. "So okay, boss. Put me to work."

Kendall relaxed. This was why she liked working with no-nonsense Frankie. With little small talk and a make-the-most-of-every-moment attitude, jobs usually got done faster than expected.

With two of them now, they were able to alternate handing up the pipes and connectors, and within the space of a few hours, Kendall had a working, movable, practical device to reach all the cracks and wear on the exterior of the lighthouse.

"At this rate you're going to be done with this before they even pour the first layer of foundation on the butterfly sanctuary." Frankie grabbed a bottle of water from her backpack and drank. She fanned herself as Kendall climbed down and joined her.

"Have you been up there yet?" Kendall asked.

"Nope. Thought you might have been, though. You know, you could probably run the project yourself."

"I work better alone." Kendall grabbed her own bottle and toasted Frankie. "Present company excluded, of course."

"Appreciate that." Frankie took a deep breath and wandered over to the edge of the cliff. "I don't know how you don't just stand here every moment of every day." She shook her head. "I'd forgotten how beautiful this spot is. Such a shame the Liberty has been practically hidden all these years."

Kendall agreed. To a point. That the overgrowth of trees, shrubs and various other fauna had obscured the initial view of the lighthouse from anyone driving past certainly didn't pay this area justice. But from a purely selfish perspective, Kendall was grateful it was still private. She glanced over at the motor home wedged between the guest house and the grove of eucalyptus and redwoods. At least until recently.

Coming back from her walk last night and finding Hunter standing on the cliff edge, looking as if he belonged there, had thrown her off-kilter. The peace she'd found during her walk and contemplative mingling with the elements had been replaced with a bout of nerves that she'd struggled to get under control. It had been so much easier, Kendall thought, being rude. But since when did Kendall do anything the easy way?

"You have company?" Frankie gestured to the motor home.

"A writer of some kind. Hunter Mac something." The sound of his name on her tongue gave her chills. "I guess Gil hired him to write a book on the town's restoration process."

"Wait, Hunter MacBride?" Frankie grabbed Kendall's arm like a besotted schoolgirl spotting a crush. "*The* Hunter MacBride?"

"Um, yes." Kendall frowned. "Should I know who he is?"

"Only if you paid attention to the news about three or four years ago. Let me get my phone. Hang on."

The past reached its clawed talons up around Kendall's throat and squeezed. Three or four years ago the last thing she'd been doing was paying attention to the news. She'd still been reeling from Sam's death and dealing with injuries that had left her laid up in the burn unit of the VA for more than four months. Whatever professional sweet spot Hunter had hit had coincided with the worst time of her life.

"Here. Look." Frankie returned with her phone, tapping through images as she held it out for Kendall to see. "He got the cover of *America News* for this photo of our soldiers on the ground in Syria. And here, from Afghanistan. People thought he might get the Pulitzer for his piece on Sudan. He should have, if you ask me. The guy's got a good eye and even better voice when it comes to telling the real story behind the images."

Kendall shoved her hands deep into her back pockets, hating to see but unable to look away from the black-and-white photograph of a Syrian mother clinging to her severely injured child, and the American Marine huddled around them trying to protect them from an attack.

Above the roaring of the waves and the constant cawing of seagulls, Kendall could feel the ground shaking beneath her feet as dirt, shrapnel and blood rained down around her.

"Hey, you okay?" Frankie tucked her phone away and laid a gentle hand on Kendall's shoulder. "I'm sorry. I should have remembered—"

"No, you shouldn't have." Kendall winced and cleared her throat; if only she could clear her mind as easily. Even now she could feel the sensation of flames licking at her skin as she'd clung to life. "It's fine, Frankie. I didn't realize he'd done something so..." So what? So affecting? So dangerous? So...

important. That mental door she'd slammed shut creaked open ever so slightly.

"You know if you ever want to talk about anything, I've got pretty good ears." Frankie released her hold. "I can shut up better than a lot of people, too."

"I know." But the truth was she'd never been able to talk about what had happened to her with anyone. Not even Matt, and he'd been a big part of her time in Afghanistan. In an odd way, she'd been prepared for that kind of tragedy; it was part of the job.

"So what's next on the agenda? You get started on the inside yet?" Frankie turned back to the lighthouse with what even Kendall could see was forced cheerfulness.

"Some." But she was going to have to kick things into high gear soon. "I keep meaning to visit the library and do research on the place, but so far I've had other things to keep me busy."

"Probably have a good chance to do that later this week." Frankie had another long gulp of water. "Storm's coming in. A big one. Sweet time to hunker down and chill."

"Now?" Kendall glanced toward the horizon.

"Soon. You know what they say about April bringing showers. Gonna tick Xander off to no end. His company is ready to start on the sanctuary's foundation later this week. Now they'll have to wait until they know it'll be dry conditions for a bit. Hey, you wanna play hooky for a few hours and go see what's happening up there? It's not often I get a full day off and I want to make the most of it."

It was no secret Bud Granger, the fire chief, was getting ready to retire. As Frankie had been his number two for the past year and a half, she was at the station almost 24/7 gearing up to take over the position. On more than one occasion, Frankie had told Kendall it was the only job she'd ever wanted since she was a little girl. And finally, after all these years, she was getting her shot.

It was on the tip of Kendall's tongue to say yes to the idea of checking out the property, but her new timetable didn't allow for slacking. "I really can't. If a storm's coming in, I should get those cracks plastered and sealed sooner than later." And now that she had a stable scaffold, she could do just that.

"Your loss. Xander Costas does make for a beautiful view." Frankie grinned and waggled her eyebrows, teasing.

"Don't let Calliope hear you talk about her husband that way," Kendall warned. "She'll sic her army of bees after you."

"Would be totally worth it. Besides, he has a construction crew, too. You need anything?" Walking backward, she retrieved her sweatshirt and empty coffee cup. "I can stop by again later."

"I'm good, thanks." The sooner she started putting some distance between herself and the friends she'd made here, the easier it would be to leave. "Have fun ogling the architect."

Frankie zipped up her sweatshirt and gave Kendall a fingertip wave as she left.

HUNTER WAS SO immersed in old issues of the *Monarch Gazette* that when Phoebe tugged on his sleeve, he felt as if he were being dragged up from the depths of the ocean. "Hey, kiddo." He reached for his pen to make some notes, then clicked a picture of the paper's article with his phone. "What's up?"

"I'm hungry."

"Hungry? So soon after—" He glanced at the clock situated above the checkout desk and inwardly cringed. "Oh, wow. Okay. Definitely time for lunch."

More like almost time for dinner, Hunter had to admit. He'd fallen in love with the library the instant he'd stepped foot inside. The building itself was one of the town's oldest, with magnificent architectural touches and attention to detail. He'd started making a list of the other buildings from around the same period so he could get an idea as to a timeline of the town's creation. Special touches and details weren't only reserved for the exterior of the building but had been carried inside, too, with intricate crown molding outlining the ceiling and an enormous carved ceiling plate depicting images of the ocean and seafarers of old. He'd have to ask about getting permission to come in either before or after hours to photograph the place in different types of light. The shadows cast by the giant arched pane-glass windows made him feel as if he were in one of the old British college libraries. And don't even get him started on all the books.

Near as he could tell, Phoebe was in seventh heaven with a stack of books on either side of her chair on the long, sturdy, hand-carved table.

The library had a steady of stream of customers throughout the day, keeping the two women wielding the computer wands busy and entertained.

"You want to hit the diner again?" he asked Phoebe as he began gathering up his things.

Phoebe shrugged.

"We can play it by ear. You should have reminded me sooner about eating. Sorry about that."

Phoebe shrugged again before her attention was pulled toward the double glass doors at the far end of the room. The same kids who had been at the diner last week warmed inside, with a little redheaded pigtailed girl in the lead. She hitched her backpack higher on her shoulders and waved enthusiastically to the librarians. She and her friends claimed a table near the front, keeping their voices respectably low. Then they each boomeranged out in different directions in the stacks.

Hunter noticed his niece, who once again seemed intrigued by the group of children.

But not, Hunter realized with a sigh, enough to make an effort to speak to them.

"You want to check any of those out?" Hunter asked as she retrieved her bag. Phoebe's big eyes considered the stacks of books, placing some gently aside and making another, then she handed a pile of four to him. "Let's see what we have. *Little Women. A Little Princess. The Secret Garden*... Hey, I know these books." Clearly she'd found the classics section. "Don't you think they're a little old for—"

Phoebe folded her arms across her chest and huffed out a breath.

"Okay, okay," Hunter chuckled. "You know what you can handle. *Tom Sawyer.* Kiddo, you are a girl after my own heart. This was one of my favorite books when I was your age. Well, I was a little older than you. A lot older than you."

Phoebe grinned and puffed out her chest.

"I think Sebastian was right." Hunter helped her with her bag again and handed her the books. "It's time you got your own library card. We'll be here long enough for you to enjoy it."

A few minutes later, stomach growling,

Hunter watched as Phoebe carefully filled out her own application, guided by a patient and impressed Mrs. Bumble, aptly named with her round figure and beehive hairdo.

"Hi!" exclaimed the pigtailed little redhead in overalls grinning up at him. "Are you the man writing the book on Butterfly Harbor?"

"I am. Hunter MacBride." He held out his hand, and, after a minute and an incredibly cheeky grin, she shook it.

"I'm Charlie Bradley. We've all been talking, and we wanted to make sure you knew about the magic wishing box."

"The wishing box?" Hunter's interest piqued. "I don't think I've heard about that."

"Charlie's the resident expert," Mrs. Bumble told him. "Nearly drowned herself trying to find it."

"Well, that part was an accident." Charlie's face scrunched with something akin to guilt, but the way her green eyes sparkled, he suspected there wasn't much. "But it worked! I got my wish. I wanted a dad. Now I have one." She grinned up at Hunter. "He's a deputy."

"Matt Knight?"

"Nah. Fletcher Bradley. He adopted me. Just like I wished for. So I know the magic is real."

Phoebe stopped writing and turned around, backing up closer to Hunter.

"There are magic caves down at the ocean," Charlie went on. "We can show you sometime if you want."

"I'll check my schedule. But that sounds like something I should absolutely include." He made a mental note to do an online search. "What do you think, Phoebe?"

Phoebe looked as if she wasn't entirely sure what to think.

"Hi." Charlie moved in closer to Phoebe. "I'm Charlie."

Phoebe raised her hand in a bit of a wave.

"Phoebe doesn't like to talk," Hunter explained.

"Oh." Charlie shrugged. "Okay. Mom says I talk enough for everyone, anyway, so that's cool. Maybe we'll see you around sometime."

Phoebe grabbed hold of Hunter's jacket and snuggled closer.

"Maybe," Hunter told Charlie. "Thank you for introducing yourself."

"No problem. I know everyone in town. It's kind of my job. I'm gonna be a deputy like my dad, so I need to pay attention. But don't tell my mom. It's a surprise."

"I'll bet it is." Hunter tried his best not to laugh, especially at Mrs. Bumble's overarched brows.

"'Kay, bye." Charlie returned to her friends, and they immediately bundled their heads together to talk.

"That one," Mrs. Bumble said with a shake of her head. "On the go with one adventure after another, from sunup to sunset and the sweetest heart in town. But she's right about the caves. They'd be worth a look. I'd take one of the deputies or the sheriff with you, though. The tide down there's unpredictable. And maybe not safe for everyone." She angled a look at Phoebe, who was torn between watching Charlie and her friends and finishing up her application.

Hunter and Mrs. Bumble chatted awhile longer, and he got some leads on who he should talk to first about the town, beginning with BethAnn Bromley, the wife of a late state senator who had returned to Butterfly Harbor last summer. "You'll get an earful of gossip along with the facts, but you'll have far more information than you thought possible," Mrs. Bumble said as she presented Phoebe with her very first card.

Phoebe patted her heart.

"You're welcome," Mrs. Bumble responded without hesitation, then quickly processed Phoebe's books. Soon they were on their way back toward Main Street.

When Phoebe seemed to be steering him toward the ice-cream parlor again, he shook his head. "Not today, kiddo. We'll save that for a special occasion. Let's see. There's a Chinese takeout over there. On a Wing. Clever. Looks new. Want to try?"

Phoebe scrunched her nose and shook her head.

"Right. I forgot. You're not a fan." Proof no child was perfect. Personally, Hunter could have lived on Chinese food. "Hey, I know. How about we get a sandwich and drinks at the diner and eat at the beach?"

Phoebe's brow creased, then after a moment, she nodded.

"Great." Crisis averted. "Let's go see what they have."

Phoebe hugged her books against her

chest and surprised him by skipping beside him. The sight nearly stole his breath. Phoebe had been so controlled these last months, so deliberate even with every step she took, and yet today, she was smiling and skipping like any little girl. But he longed for the day he knew she could be truly happy and carefree again.

His throat tightened. Phoebe's laugh had always been one of the sweetest sounds he'd ever heard. And oh, when she sang, his heart just took flight. He could remember the look of pure joy and pride on his sister's and brother-in-law's faces when she'd performed, by herself, in the first-grade talent show. Brent had presented her with a bouquet of six roses afterward and hoisted her into his arms, declaring her to be the next Broadway sensation. Phoebe had laughed and squealed, clutching her roses to her chest, just as she held on to her books today.

She tugged on his hand. "Sad?"

"I'm not sad, kiddo. Not really. Just remembering something." He had to blink quickly to force the tears back.

Phoebe looked up at the sky above them and pointed.

"Yeah. I was thinking about your mom and dad and how much I miss them." He bent down when tears pooled in her eyes. "I was thinking about your talent show, remember that? How beautifully you sang?" He swiped a thumb across her cheek before he tweaked her chin. "They were so proud of you. And they'd be so proud of you now, Phoebe." He willed her to feel the pride and joy she brought to him. "They loved you more than anything in the world."

She nodded, her chin wobbling.

"It's okay to be sad. You know that. We've talked about that. And you can talk to me about anything. Always."

Phoebe nodded.

"Okay, then. Let's get that lunch."

"LOOKING GOOD UP THERE."

Kendall twisted suddenly and nearly flipped over the side of the scaffold. A container of spackle in one hand, she pressed her free hand over her racing heart. "I should put a bell around your neck."

Hunter had quickly moved in when she'd wobbled and grabbed hold of the crisscrossing pipes as if he'd somehow catch her if she fell. "Sorry. Thought you heard us come back. You going to do this whole thing yourself?"

"Yes." Kendall almost didn't understand the question. "Of course." She'd made good progress today. "Why? You want to help?"

"Trust me." Hunter grinned and shook his head. "You don't want me anywhere near tools or home repair. I'm a menace. Or so my father used to tell me."

"Doesn't take a genius," Kendall said, then realizing how that might sound, she bit her lip. "Sorry. I guess maybe it does take a bit of…"

"Talent. The word you're looking for is *talent*. Have you had dinner?"

Dinner? She hadn't had lunch. She'd zeroed in on the task and hadn't come up for air except for bathroom and water breaks. "No."

"Great." He held up another paper bag, this one larger than the first one they'd presented to her last week. "We brought you a sandwich. And kettle chips. Paige said someone named Ursula was trying them out at the diner. Vinegar flavored. I liked them. Phoebe, not so much."

Kendall couldn't stop herself. She looked past Hunter to where Phoebe's nose wrinkled, and she shuddered. The little girl was so small she almost vanished behind the pile of books in her arms. "You don't have to keep bringing me food," Kendall said. "I can feed myself."

Hunter set the bag down on the bottom plank. "You're welcome."

Kendall took a long, steeling breath. "Thank you." Contrary to what he believed, she did have manners.

"We ate at the beach. Tuna fish sandwiches, chips and a chocolate chip cookie for dessert. I also think we ate more than our share of sand. Stuff gets everywhere."

Kendall stared at him. Did he not get the message? She didn't want to chitchat. She didn't want small talk. She wanted to be alone for her own peace of mind.

"Yeah, well, it does at that. I need to get back to work. Thank you, again," she added at the last second when her stomach growled. "For the dinner."

"We're going to visit Duskywing Farm tomorrow," Hunter called up to her when she turned her back on him. "Can we get you anything?"

"No, thank you. Um. Calliope brings me stuff sometimes." Sometimes? Try every other day. "I was going to fill the window boxes," she called when he started to leave. "If you and Phoebe wanted a project. Calliope can help you choose something. Or if Lori Knight is there—ask her. She works part-time at the Flutterby Inn, but she's a miracle worker with flowers and plants."

"Great info, thanks. Have a good evening."

"Yeah," Kendall said into the wind that was picking up as the day drifted away. "You, too." Confused, unsettled, she abandoned her plastering and descended the three stories to the ground. How could a man be both too pushy and yet not? All day she'd been planning what to say to him when she saw him again. Now that she knew who he was, what he'd done with at least part of his life, she felt she owed him a compliment or at least an acknowledgment, but once again, he'd appeared out of nowhere and thrown her off-kilter. And for a moment, she'd almost smiled at the sight of him. At the sight of Phoebe.

"You'll get another chance. He'll—they'll—be here awhile." She made quick work of the cleanup today, storing and stashing her tools and supplies almost in record time. She plucked the bag off the plank and carried it inside with her for after she showered and changed.

Between erecting the scaffolding, all the climbing up and down and the upper-body stretches as she'd plastered a good third of the lighthouse tower, every muscle in her body ached. But in a good way. In a maybe-I'll-sleep-tonight way.

Tonight she sat at the small square table next to the bare window overlooking the ocean. She needed to replace it with double-paned glass because of the breeze eking through, but there was something oddly comforting about the sound of the wind pushing in that relaxed her. A promise of more work, maybe? Or a reminder that life continued to roar, continued to move forward, no matter how stuck she was.

She popped open the paper container and ran her finger almost lovingly over the soft white bread encasing lush, thick tuna salad. A smile tugged at her mouth as she remembered how, when she'd been in the army, she'd dream of tuna fish sandwiches and potato chips. Once, when she'd video chatted with Sam. The two of them had laughed so hard, Kendall had cried.

She'd cried for almost two days after, the desire to hold her fiancé in her arms so overwhelming she didn't know how she remembered to breathe. It had been Matt who had found her, curled up in her bunk, trying so hard not to let the tears fall she'd almost suffocated herself. Most of the time she was fine. Both she and Sam had known going in that deployment was going to be hard, and they'd done pretty well the first two years. Until a single picture of her childhood-sweetheart made her realize how much of her life was slipping away.

Matt had understood. As much as he could. What he was able to do as a sounding board became as vital to her as the stifling, hot air she breathed every day. The others in their battalion were understanding but tended to try to tease her out of her moods rather than just let her spew. But

Matt, he'd set himself as the target and let her fire. Time after time. Word after word.

She never would have made it back if it wasn't for him. And sometimes, when those voids had gotten so dark and the depression so deep, it was only the thought of her friend that had kept her from sliding into the abyss.

But now, today, for the first time, she found herself smiling at, of all things, a tuna fish sandwich. And for the first time, it felt okay.

CHAPTER SIX

"PHOEBE!" IN THE darkness of the night, Hunter raced around the tiny cottage, flipping on lights. He checked under her bed, the bathroom, even the closets. It had been months since she'd done this, taken off in the night in search of her parents who were never coming home.

Panic seized him around the chest and squeezed, slowing time to the point where he felt as if he were slogging through mud. He'd walked through minefields, hunkered down in foxholes with dedicated soldiers, even stared down the barrel of a gun when he'd snapped the wrong photo. But the abject terror over not being able to find his niece erased all reason and rationality from his mind.

"Phoebe!" he called again as he ripped open the door and raced to the motor home, looking in every nook and cranny he could think of. He found nothing.

The door to the keeper house swung open, and Kendall stepped out. Her long legs were bare beneath the snug black shorts and tank she wore. Her hair was loose and flowing around pale, scarred shoulders accented by the moonlight as she strode toward him, barefoot.

Only then did he feel the rocks and dirt beneath his own bare feet. The pajama pants he was wearing did little to keep the chill of the night off his skin as he shivered. Why wouldn't his brain work?

"What's wrong?" Kendall demanded in a tone he'd never heard from her before.

"Phoebe. I woke up to check on her. Sometimes she has nightmares," he explained as he turned around, searching the darkness for any sign of his niece. "And she sleepwalks. She's not inside. She's not in the motor home. What if… Oh, God." His gaze froze on the edge of the cliffs. "What if she fell? What if…"

Guilt and dread slithered down his spine. He took a step away from Kendall, toward the cliffs.

Kendall caught his arm, stopped him. "I'll get a flashlight and look. You wait here."

"But—"

"You. Wait. Here," Kendall ordered, her eyes flashing in the dimness of the porch light. She raced back inside and returned seconds later with shoes on her feet and an industrial flashlight in her hand. She was already scanning the beam in every direction.

She detoured around him, heading to the cliff's edge. Hunter tried to make his heart beat again as she scanned below. "She's not down there." She headed back, aiming the light high and over and around and… She stopped and let out a breath he could actually hear. "There she is."

"What? Where? Where is she?" Hunter raced over and stood behind Kendall as she arced the light up to the top of the scaffold. "Phoebe." If the sight of his niece sitting there, her favorite book clutched in her hand, was supposed to make him feel better, it didn't. If anything, the fear surged again.

"Don't." Kendall reached back and gripped his arm. "Don't yell. Don't get mad. Not yet. Not until I get her down."

"I'm not mad, I'm terrified."

"I know." She squeezed his arm. "I can feel it. Let it go, Hunter. It's not going to do either of you any good, and I need to focus. Here. Take this." She pushed the flashlight into his hand. "I'm going to get her."

"What? No, wait, you can't—I mean, of course you can. You're…capable." More than, he acknowledged. Having served in the military, she knew what pressure was, and she knew how to process fear probably better than most. But that didn't make the idea of Phoebe being where she was any easier.

"Hunter, pull it together," Kendall snapped. "I get you're scared. And believe me, Phoebe and I are going to have a long talk about what's permissible around this area and what is not. But we aren't going to do that now. Right now I'm going up there and I'll bring her down to you. Okay? Nod for me, Hunter."

"Yeah. Yeah, okay."

"I need you to trust me." She grabbed his other arm and gave him a good shake. "I won't let anything happen to her."

"Yeah." He nodded again.

Kendall stepped back and headed to the scaffold. She stood there for a moment, hands on her hips, and looked up at Phoebe. "Hey, Phoebe. You doing okay up there?"

Hunter flashed the light up and caught Phoebe's nod. Near as he could tell, she wasn't scared at all. If anything, she looked as surly as Kendall had the day they'd turned up unannounced.

"Is it okay if I come up?" Kendall called. "I bet the view is pretty great up there."

Phoebe turned her head toward the ocean, shifting a little.

"I can feel your fear from here, MacBride. Suck it up." Kendall glanced over her shoulder at him, but where he expected to find anger and irritation, he saw understanding. Compassion. And, thankfully, a bit of terror, too. "Phoebe? May I come up?"

Phoebe nodded and tucked her hair behind her ear. Hunter made sure he kept the light on Kendall as she climbed up the side of the scaffold, the pipes and planks creaking as she did. The muscles in her arms and legs strained as she moved effortlessly to the top of the structure. She walked carefully across, speaking to Phoebe in words he couldn't quite hear. The wind had picked up and Hunter considered going back inside for a jacket for his niece. By the time he aimed the light upward again, he saw Kendall and Phoebe weren't climbing down as he'd expected.

Kendall had taken a seat beside her.

"WOW." KENDALL TRIED to sound casual beside Phoebe and not to appear as if she was assessing the young girl's condition. Physically she appeared to be fine. The hem of her sky blue pajamas ruffled in the night breeze. Her hair was loose and tangled around her bright but sullen face. "I was right. The view's pretty great." Not that she could see very much in the darkness, but the moon was full enough to cast a glistening sparkle against the ocean. "You do know you shouldn't be up here, right?"

Kendall leaned back against the lighthouse and drew one leg up, hooked her hands around her knee and closed her eyes.

The plank creaked a bit as Phoebe shifted, probably, Kendall thought, to look over at her.

"Can't say I blame you, though." Kendall took a long, deep breath. "It's not just the view, is it? It's the sounds. The way the waves crash against the rocks and the wind rushes against your ears. It's like the higher you go, the more peace you can find. Or the closer to heaven you can climb." Kendall opened her eyes and tilted her head. "That's what you were thinking, wasn't it? That if you climbed high enough, reached far enough, maybe up here you could see your parents again."

Phoebe blinked, and inclined her head in a way that told Kendall she'd hit the target on the first shot.

"Can I tell you a secret?" Kendall laughed at Phoebe's arched brow. Boy, this kid was old for her age. "Of course I can. You're like the best secret keeper ever, aren't you? I've done the same thing. Still do. I climb as high as I possibly can, hoping, praying that when I get to the top I'll find…" She cleared her throat, still unable to say Sam's name without feeling her heart fracture. "One time I climbed the highest mountain I could. So high there was snow at the top, all hoping I could find what I lost. But I didn't." What she had caught was a nasty case of pneumonia and an extended stay in the hospital followed by a psych exam. "And neither did you."

Phoebe shook her head.

"You put a right scare into your uncle. You know that?"

Phoebe looked down to where Hunter was whipping the flashlight back and forth like he was directing a plane for landing.

"We're fine, Hunter," Kendall called down, but she knew from experience nothing was going to replace the feeling of Phoebe in his arms again. "We'll be down in a minute." She heard him mutter something before the light clicked off. Kendall turned her attention back to Phoebe. "Here's another secret, but it's not mine. It's your uncle's."

Phoebe shifted around, pulled her legs under her and looked at Kendall, all expectation.

"He loves you."

Phoebe rolled her eyes.

"Okay, you know that already, don't you? But there's even more to that. Because when you were born, you became a part of him. Like a little piece of you broke off and lodged in his heart. Just as it got caught in your mom's and dad's hearts. The idea of anything happening to you—" Kendall swallowed the tears burning her throat. "The idea of losing you is literally the worst thing he can think of, and when he couldn't find you tonight, when you took off without telling him, without telling anyone, well, that little piece starts vibrating and telling him something is very, very wrong."

"He's hurt?" Phoebe tapped a finger against her chest, above her heart.

"Yeah." Kendall nodded. "Yeah, I think you hurt his heart tonight. He knows you didn't mean to, and I understand why you did this, but you can't do this again, Phoebe. Will you promise me that? If you want to climb high, then you need to tell him. He'll walk right alongside you because that's how much he loves you. And he will always, always understand."

Phoebe reached over and poked Kendall in the arm.

"What?" Kendall looked down, her skin warming where Phoebe had touched her, and traced her scars. "Oh, those. I was in an accident. A bad one, and I got burned. But they don't hurt. Not anymore." Not half as much as the ones on her heart.

Phoebe poked a finger into the sky, touched her lips, then pointed back at Kendall. "Oh, yes, I guess so. Yeah. You can tell me, too, if you want to climb. But someone always needs to know where you are. No running off like this again, especially in the dark." Especially, Kendall thought, around these cliffs.

Only then did she feel the same abject terror slipping through her as Hunter had no doubt felt minutes before.

"Will you promise me, Phoebe? No more running off?"

Phoebe sighed, nodded, then held out her pinkie finger.

Kendall's heart lodged in her throat. For a moment, she saw Samira with her bouncy curls and wide eyes looking up to her with expectant, hopeful promise. The disappointment that such a promise would never be fulfilled made her heart ache.

Phoebe began to frown, her brow wrinkling as she lowered her hand. Unable to bear the hope fading in her eyes, Kendall linked her finger around Phoebe's. "Pinkie promise," she croaked. "Can we go down now? It's getting a little cold."

A little cold? Her goose bumps were demanding their own jackets. Kendall held out her hand. "I can carry your book for you."

Phoebe clutched the book against her chest, paused to look up at the star-strewn sky, then nodded and slowly handed it over. Kendall tucked the book into the back waistband of her shorts and twisted around to start the descent. She got a solid foothold and urged Phoebe to come down in front of her so she could guide her to the ground.

Kendall was pulling the book free again when Hunter raced over and engulfed Phoebe in a hug so fierce, Kendall could feel it.

"You're okay, right?" He knelt down and ran his hands up and down Phoebe's arms, looking for injuries. There was no point in telling him she'd already checked. Kendall knew from experience that until Hunter verified it for himself, there wasn't any convincing him his niece was fine.

Phoebe glanced back at Kendall, who gave her an encouraging nod. When the little girl faced her uncle again, Kendall heard her whisper, "I'm sorry. I shouldn't have gone out by myself."

"No, you shouldn't have. Apology accepted." He took hold of her hand and squeezed. "We're still going to have a long talk about this, young lady."

Kendall smirked at Phoebe's heavy sigh. Nothing like the "young lady" discussion. "Here." She held out Phoebe's book and earned an ear-to-ear smile as Phoebe accepted.

"Thank you." Hunter pulled Phoebe into his arms as he stood, hoisting her against his hip. "I don't anticipate sleeping anytime soon. I can put on a pot of coffee—"

"Um, no—" She broke off when Phoebe reached out with a hooked pinkie finger. It was as if she already understood she'd slipped past Kendall's defenses and wasn't ready to let go. "All right, sure. One cup."

"Decaf?" Hunter asked as he walked carefully, barefoot, over the dirt- and rock-strewn ground.

"Only if you prefer it. Caffeine doesn't keep me up," Kendall said and followed him inside the guest house. "Never has."

"I used to practically mainline caffeine sodas in college. Okay, you. Back to bed." He set Phoebe on her feet, but she clung to his hand, tugged him with her. "Ah, okay. I'll be another few minutes," he said to Kendall. "Coffee's over there if you could get it brewing."

Kendall tried not to listen to Hunter's gentle lecture about not going outside without telling him, but the house was small, and his voice carried. It was, of course, a one-sided conversation, at least as far as she was concerned, but the way he didn't give in to the fear that had almost consumed him moments before was admirable.

What did surprise her was that the coffeepot, one he'd clearly brought with him, was almost as old as she was. No pods or single-serving cups for this guy. He used a stained, overworked and clearly loved machine that almost challenged her. Almost.

The last time she'd stepped foot in this house, it had been empty save for the few pieces of furniture Gil had sent over from the antiques and thrift store. But in the short time since Hunter and Phoebe had arrived, they'd managed to personalize the place with some framed photographs and lots of books and loaded the desk with Hunter's computer equipment. It wasn't just a house any longer. She saw that he'd actually managed to turn it into a home.

Hunter closed the door to Phoebe's room, the coffee was dripping into the pot and the familiar, habit-forming aroma filled the air. Hunter ducked into his room and returned with two sweatshirts, one of which he handed to Kendall. He tugged on his own and sat at the kitchen table to pull on a pair of thick socks.

"Not sure I'll ever feel warm again." He actually shivered. "Like California cold is anything close to freezing. Ha. You know I once spent a winter in the Antarctic photographing penguins? Now *that* was cold."

Kendall gave him a tight smile and tugged the navy zip-up on, trying not to notice the spicy scent of his aftershave or the promise of strong, male comfort. She stood there, wondering where or even if she should sit. This was a bad idea, coming in for coffee. Connections, friendships, even cursory ones, were only asking for trouble.

"Thank you," he said softly.

Kendall could all but see the adrenaline draining from him as his body sagged and his shoulders drooped.

"I thought we were past this," he said. "If you hadn't been here—"

"If I hadn't been here, the scaffold wouldn't have been there, either, and it wouldn't have been an issue." Because she needed to do something, she walked over and sat down across from him. "I should have made it a point to tell her not to go climbing." Instead Kendall had gone out of her way to avoid any kind of conversation with either of them.

"She's a smart girl. She should have known. She did know," he corrected himself. "It just didn't matter. I suppose I should be grateful she has a mind of her own, but then I start panicking about what she's going to be like as a teenager. Or, at this rate, next week."

Kendall nodded. "How long has it been? Since her parents died?"

"A little over six months. Six months." He managed a quick laugh. "Sometimes it feels like six years. Other times, six hours." Hunter focused weary eyes on her. "Sorry. Don't mean to turn maudlin on you. Not the way I anticipated starting my day."

Kendall shrugged and ran a hand up and down her fabric-clad arm. "Any start to a day is good. Means you're still here. Do you mind me asking what happened? With Phoebe's parents?" Because concentrating on Phoebe meant not having to admit to herself how nice Hunter MacBride was to look at and to speak with. He came across as one of those men who had no idea how attractive he was and would no doubt brush aside any mention of his handsome features or well-toned body as easily as he'd brush a speck of lint off his shirt. Until she'd seen him frantically searching for his niece, she'd have considered him unflappable. That he wasn't somehow made him even more appealing. And that idea definitely made her stomach twitch.

"A car accident." Hunter's face went blank for a moment. "They'd been looking for a bigger house—my sister had gotten a big promotion at work. Then, just like that, they were gone. Goes to show you never know what the universe has in store for you." He started to stand, but Kendall beat him to it.

"I've got it." She didn't think her heart could take any more battering, but once again, she was wrong. She pulled two mugs out of the dish rack. "How do you take it?"

"Black and straight. And usually on an IV."

Kendall swallowed hard. She recognized forced defensive humor when she heard it. Sometimes the deflection was the only way to push through the pain. Hunter sounded as if he'd almost mastered the technique. Kendall had never come close.

"They say the loss gets easier with time. It doesn't." Kendall set his World's Greatest Brother mug on the table and curled up in the chair across from him. The sweatshirt engulfed her to the point where she didn't feel quite so…alone. She tugged the hem over her knees. "It gets manageable, and some days are better than others, but there's no erasing the grief. Or the emptiness. It's always there."

Hunter wrapped his hands around the mug and set that assessing gaze on her. "That's the voice of experience talking."

No point in denying it. She sipped the coffee, frowned and looked down at her mug. "This tastes…different."

"It's chicory. I picked up a lifetime supply when I was in New Orleans. Addictive. You like?"

"I do." She sipped again and felt herself finally beginning to relax. "I didn't mean to spook you earlier, staying up there with her for a while. I didn't want her thinking what she thought needed doing wasn't worthy of attention." Double-edged sword, that. Now she'd started bonding with the little girl, and that terrified her more than just about anything. She didn't want to care. About anyone. Because the people she cared about, the people she loved, had a way of leaving her.

"What was she doing?" Hunter asked.

"Trying to get to heaven."

He paused, his gaze shifting briefly to the framed photograph nearby of Phoebe and her parents. "I should have guessed that."

"No reason you should have. Everyone processes grief differently, Hunter. How she misses her parents can't come close to touching how you feel about losing your sister. And vice versa. But tonight opens a new avenue of communication for you both."

"I'm just grateful this happened at night, out here, where no one other than you was witness to it." He cringed, leaned back in his chair and gazed out into the darkness as if he could see the ocean beyond. "Last thing I need is for her grandparents to hear she's playing Houdini and sneaking out and scaling scaffolds at night like some super heroine."

"Grandparents?"

"My brother-in-law's folks." Hunter turned back to his coffee and drank. "Stephen and Eleanor Cartwright. They don't think a single man, especially one without a permanent home, is the appropriate guardian for their only grandchild. And they've had their lawyer tell me so on multiple occasions."

Sensing Hunter needed someone objective and emotionally removed from the situation to talk to, she stepped through the door he'd opened. "Were they involved in Phoebe's life before their son died?"

"That's just it. No. In fact, Brent and his parents had been estranged for a number of years." In that moment, Hunter looked defeated. "At the funeral, Brent's father told me if I didn't give them complete custody, he'd ruin me. Professionally, financially. He said he'd make it so no judge would ever consider me fit to raise her."

Kendall's stomach roiled in disgust. "What did you tell him?"

"Considering Phoebe was in the room, not what I wanted to. As politely as I could manage, I told him to get lost. That hasn't stopped them from asking for a court investigation and threatening me with a custody battle. It doesn't help that Phoebe hasn't said more than a word or two since the accident. She isn't the same and they need someone to answer for it. Not that any of this is Phoebe's fault."

"Of course it isn't." Kendall tried to keep her frustration in check. If there was one thing she had no tolerance for, it was people who didn't see outside their own circumstance. While she didn't know the details, clearly his sister's in-laws were trying to make up for past mistakes, even if it wasn't in the little girl's best interest. "It's not yours, either. Have you hired a lawyer?"

"No." Hunter grimaced. "Partly because I'm afraid once I do it really will turn into a full-blown custody battle, and that's the last thing I want for Phoebe."

"And the other part?"

"Picked up on that, did you?" Hunter grinned and took a long drink of coffee. "I don't have the money for a lawyer. Not a good one, anyway. Not yet. But that might change in the next month or so. If I can get this new project off the ground."

"You mean the book on Butterfly Harbor?"

"Oh, that, no." Hunter pointed over his shoulder to where he'd set up his laptop on the rustic desk she'd repainted white. "That's just to get us over the hump. I'm supposed to be writing a book. Fiction. A thriller. Maybe. My agent thinks I should branch out, and it is something I've thought about over the years. If only I had an idea of what to write."

"As I don't have a creative bone in my body, this might be completely off base, but don't they usually say write what you know?"

"Meaning I should try writing about a burned-out photojournalist trying to raise a little girl?"

Kendall shrugged. "Why not? I'd read it."

"Yeah." Hunter's shoulders relaxed. "Yeah, maybe there is something there. And by the way, you have plenty of creativity. You redid this place, didn't you? It's beautiful."

"It's practical," Kendall argued. "But I am going to reach out to Gil about having a fence installed around the perimeter of the cliff line. I think we can both agree it would bring some peace of mind, not just to us, but to anyone else who might stay out here. And on that note." She uncurled and stood. "I'm going to try to get some more sleep. Gonna be a wet and windy weekend."

"So I heard. No, keep it." Hunter stood when she started to shrug out of the sweatshirt. "You always look like you're freezing, and it'll make me sleep easier. As if I'm going to sleep."

"Thanks." She shoved her hands into the deep pockets. "And if you want, I'll install a new security bolt on the door. Maybe one high up enough little hands can't reach it."

"I hate to go that route, but maybe it isn't a bad idea. Sure, let's do it. I'll cover the cost."

"We'll work it out later. So, um. Yeah." She gave him a quick smile. "Good night."

"Good night." He walked her to the door, held it open for her. "Kendall?"

She turned around on the porch step. "Yes?"

"I hope you don't mind me asking, but since you are the voice of experience." He hesitated, as if he regretted saying anything. "Who did you lose?"

The question hit her unaware, but that was her own fault. She should have realized she'd opened her own door by confirming his suspicion earlier. But he'd been honest with her. She owed him nothing less. "Sam. My fiancé," she added, as if she needed to explain. Her fists clenched as she took a deep breath, pushed the words free from the prison they'd been in.

"I'm sorry." He was. She could see it on his face, glittering in his eyes. Sadness and grief, understanding and confusion. But nowhere did she see pity or even sympathy. Just…compassion. Maybe that was why the pain didn't slice nearly as deep as her admission drifted into the night.

"I'll, um, see you around." She resisted the urge to look back to see if he was still watching her. She didn't have to, anyway, not when she could feel his eyes on her as she quickly slipped inside.

Kendall kicked off her shoes and, still wearing the sweatshirt, ducked under the covers before she thought better of it. The familiar fear-induced adrenaline that had surged on her way up the scaffold had long faded. The usual residual shakes had been tempered by chicory coffee and Hunter MacBride's heartwarming smile.

She had lied to him tonight. Any hope

of sleep had vanished with the sound of Hunter's desperate call for Phoebe. She squeezed her eyes shut against the echoes of the past. How many times had she heard similar calls? It didn't matter what country people lived, or what language they spoke, man or woman, young or old; the panicked fear of a parent searching for their child was universal. But tonight, at least, it had resulted in a happy reunion.

And that was enough to keep the tears at bay as she stared up at the ceiling.

And waited for the sun to come up.

CHAPTER SEVEN

"SLOW DOWN, PHOEBE. I don't think the farm is going anywhere."

Phoebe tugged hard on Hunter's hand, dragging him down the hill toward today's excursion to Duskywing Farm. No doubt Phoebe was expecting cows and chickens and a goat or two, but from what Hunter had been able to glean regarding Calliope Jones Costas's organic enterprise, they were more likely to get set on by a couple dozen trees' worth of butterflies.

Despite her excitement, Phoebe had refused to leave the house until she'd finished a supersecret art project, but any irritation he'd felt at having his morning schedule thrown off melted away when he saw the *I'm sorry* card she'd made for Kendall. He'd waited patiently as she'd slipped it under her front door before they left.

The entire pot of coffee Kendall had

brewed early this morning hadn't done its job of keeping him alert as he'd burned their pancake breakfast and accidentally poured coffee in Phoebe's juice glass. He'd practically drowned himself in the shower trying to rev himself up and still he felt sluggish and not quite right. As they rounded the corner, he realized he wouldn't be going anywhere soon, either. Beyond the expansive wooden crisscross fence, acres of well-planted land stretched out in all directions, right up to the tree line. Situated among the lush green explosions of early spring color sat the most perfect stone cottage, complete with a bright red door and a front porch made for sipping lemonade and listening to the crickets jumping through the vegetable patch.

A sleek gray cat sat on the fence post at the gate, looking as majestic and regal as any feline had a right to appear. She blinked lazy eyes at Phoebe, who came skidding to a halt at the sight of the animal. She spun around, her new backpack slapping against her jeans-encased backside as she pointed to the animal.

"I think you're starting to attract them,

Phoebe," Hunter joked and earned a cheeky, dimple-inducing grin from his niece. While he wasn't fully functioning this morning, he had to admit, there seemed to be a remarkable improvement in Phoebe's mood. She still wasn't talking a lot, but she seemed… bouncier. Maybe even happier. She flexed her fingers up at him. "I don't know if you should pet it or not. Maybe we'll wait and ask—"

"Ophelia always likes attention." A gentle, feminine voice drifted across the air as the barefooted woman strode toward them. She was a rainbow of happiness in a dress of rioting blues and purples splashing against one another from the V of the collar to the bottom of the skirt swirling around her bare feet. Her fingers and wrists were almost obscured by a collection of bracelets and rings. "Welcome to my farm and to Butterfly Harbor, Hunter MacBride."

She…jingled when she walked, Hunter noted as she lifted the latch on the gate, stepping back to let them in. As he passed through the gate, in his almost transfixed state, he saw the tiny bells and seashells strung in her long, curly red hair. He recalled a smaller version of her sitting in the diner with Charlie Bradley.

"And you must be Phoebe." Calliope dropped down and rested her arms on her knees. "Aren't you a force to behold? I'm Calliope. You are most welcome here anytime."

Phoebe let out a sound that sounded like a squeaking laugh. Hunter started, his hand tightening around his niece's as he reveled in the sound he'd heard for the first time in nearly months.

"Ah, there now." Calliope cupped a hand against Phoebe's cheek. "I can feel your heart healing already. This place will do that to you, you know."

"The farm or Butterfly Harbor?" Hunter couldn't help but ask.

Calliope tilted her chin up and smiled at him, a smile so bright and open he almost had to shield his eyes. "Either. Both. Come. Have you had breakfast?"

"Ah, not really, no." He still had the taste of burned pancakes in his mouth—pancakes Phoebe had sliced open and scooped out the fluffy center of with meticulous albeit frowning care. "We had a bit of a busy night."

"Yes, that moon does call to us sometimes, doesn't it?" She held out her hand to Phoebe. "I have some fresh-baked blueberry scones in the kitchen, and by now Xander should have brewed some of his toxic coffee. Please, join us."

"Um, aren't you open now?" He glanced at his watch as Phoebe walked forward and accepted Calliope's hand. "The farm, the market. I thought you opened at eight."

"It'll be slow this morning. The crowds will pick up later when people begin worrying about the storm blowing in." She cast somewhat cloudy eyes to the sky. "And it'll be a big one. In the meantime, we'd best get you stocked in provisions for the time being. Come, Ophelia. You and Phoebe can get to know one another inside."

The cat seemed to heave a sigh of irritation before she leaped off her perch and trotted beside her mistress.

"Xander, Stella, we have company for breakfast." Calliope lifted her arm to draw Phoebe into the house. That his niece, normally shy of strangers, followed happily eased some of the tension in Hunter's chest. Maybe things had finally begun to turn for both of them. "Xander, this is Phoebe and her uncle, Hunter MacBride. I'm betting the two of you will have a lot to talk about."

"Xander Costas." Hunter wondered why he hadn't made the connection before. "Of Costas Architecture out of Chicago?"

"One and the same." The dark-haired man turned from a pan of frying eggs on the stove. "We're based here now that the business… Never mind." He chuckled as Calliope sent him a look. "Long story. Heard you were coming to town. I saw your exhibit in New York a few years back. 'War Through Their Eyes.'" He left his post long enough to shake Hunter's hand. "Powerful stuff."

"Thanks." Hunter felt that ping of unease he got whenever he felt himself drifting back to those days. While he was grateful for the opportunity to shine a light on sad yet important events, he wasn't anxious to return there in person or through memories. "Looking to recharge my batteries a bit out here on the coast. Wow. This house is amazing." His photographer's eye snapped to attention at the contrast between the colorful bouquets of drying herbs lined up against the old gray stone structure of the walls. The combination of old world and modern convenience appealed to the photographer in him, as well as the budding novelist.

"We've added on over the years, but it was one of the first homes built when the town was established."

"Telling me that only means I'll want to include it in my book."

Calliope smiled. "Almost like a promotional opportunity. How lovely."

Xander chuckled. "Always looking for a chance to draw new visitors to the nest."

Phoebe was already sitting on one of the wooden benches at the long farm table, licking her lips at the fresh orange juice Calliope poured for her.

"Word's gotten around about your book for the tourists," Costas said. Wearing simple jeans, a bright white T-shirt and, like his wife, no shoes or socks, he didn't look like one of the top-tier architects his family firm had boasted. In fact, the few photographs Hunter had seen of him, he'd been buttoned down from starched collar to wing-tipped toe. Designer, of course. Was this some kind of odd butterfly influence? "Gil Hamilton rope you into that?"

"Sort of. He negotiated a fair but tough offer that I couldn't refuse." Hunter grinned at Xander's snort of laughter. Calliope looked between the two of them as if they'd gone slightly bonkers.

"You know," Xander said, "if you want to get some before shots of the sanctuary site, I can give you a tour. Either later today or…whenever the storm is past. Any ETA on that, Calliope?" Xander carried the cast-iron skillet over to the table and motioned for Hunter to take a seat.

Calliope lifted her hand to his face and gave him a smile that had Hunter blushing. "I'd estimate it'll blow through by Saturday night. I'm anticipating clear blue skies and soaked earth for Sunday."

"Great. How's Sunday then?" Xander offered as Calliope passed out plates. "Believe me when I tell you there's nothing like Butterfly Harbor after a good rainstorm. It's like a rebirth, a new start for everyone and everything."

"And to think less than six months ago you had visions only of steel rebar and cement running through that beautiful head of yours." Calliope brushed her lips against his cheek. "Excuse me. I need to track down my sister. Or we'll be late to school. Again."

"Sister?" Hunter handed Phoebe a napkin as she broke apart a steaming fresh blueberry scone. She leaned forward and breathed in the aroma and actually sighed.

"Stella. She's ten. Almost eleven," Xander explained. "Calliope's… Ah, there's the mini-me, now. Good morning, Stella."

"Hi." Stella trudged in, Calliope nipping at her heels, and sank down at the table next to Phoebe, offering a sleepy smile.

"I like your dress."

Phoebe's unexpected comment had Hunter noticing the dress Stella wore. It was the color of ripe summer peaches and melded beautifully with her bright red hair. "We saw you at the diner the other day."

Phoebe nodded, her attention caught completely by the bells in Stella's hair. The same type Calliope had. No one would ever miss hearing these two coming.

"Stella, this is Phoebe. Phoebe, my sister, Stella." Calliope bent to press a kiss on the top of Stella's head.

"Nice to meet you," Stella said politely and something akin to awe flashed in Phoebe's eyes.

"Do they hurt?" Phoebe lifted a hand to one of the bells, stopping shy of touching it.

"Nope. I love the way they sound. Like fairies whispering in my ear."

Phoebe's mouth made that O of fascination.

Hunter's heart swelled with pride. This was the first time he'd seen Phoebe actively engage with someone her own age.

"It takes a strong will to listen rather than speak," Calliope murmured as she passed behind Hunter. When he balked at the comment, Calliope gave a low laugh. "I'm sorry. I didn't mean to pry. Your concern precedes you. Surrounds you, Hunter. It's difficult to ignore. But you needn't worry. Reflection grows and expands the mind. Silence," Calliope clarified before taking a long, deep breath. "Is lovely. A bit lonely, but lovely nonetheless."

Hunter looked down at his plate of eggs before reaching for the coffee.

"Ah, no. You should drink this." Calliope gently pulled the mug from his grasp and replaced it with another.

He frowned down at the dirty-looking water.

"It's lemon balm and chamomile tea. Good for balance and relaxation. Trust me."

Xander shot him a grin before he asked Stella about whether she'd finished her homework last night, and for once, Hunter was glad to simply sit back, eat, sip on Calliope's tea—which he suspected tasted a lot like her garden—and relax.

Calliope floated around the room and brought an additional sense of peace, a smile lighting her face as she looked at her husband, who was deeply invested in Stella's lamenting of her math class. Stella admitted that no, she hadn't finished her homework because she didn't understand it and Mr. Thewling was tired of trying to explain.

"I always looked at math like a foreign language," Hunter said when Xander urged Stella to pull out her homework so he could take a look.

"A language that doesn't make any sense," Stella mumbled and dragged out a notebook.

"Hunter's right, actually," Xander said. "Math has its own way of doing things. It's a matter of understanding what those numbers are capable of, what pattern you have to follow in order to get the result you're looking for."

"What class is it?" Hunter peered over. "You know, it's the teacher that makes all the difference. My sister always had the worst time in math—she used to have meltdowns doing her homework because none of it made any sense to her. She wanted to quit, and then the next semester she got Mr. Karelius and bam! Something about the way he taught, it finally clicked. That day she brought home her first A, you'd have thought she'd won the lottery."

Unsure why he'd waxed nostalgic this morning around a group of strangers, he shifted in his seat. "Sorry. Not sure where that came from. But that was the happiest I ever saw her, except when she married your dad." He nudged Phoebe gently with his elbow. "And when she had you."

"Nothing makes us happier than when we conquer a challenge or take another significant step on the road of life." Calliope brushed a hand over Phoebe's head as she passed.

The dazed glimmer in his niece's eyes felt like a sucker punch to his gut. It hadn't dawned on him that he'd purposely been avoiding talking about his sister, about Phoebe's mother, in the past few months. He'd been so worried about reigniting Phoebe's grief he'd kept it all bottled up. But if last night proved anything, it was that there wasn't anything he could do to stop the difficult emotions from surfacing and that by stifling them, he may very well be causing more damage.

"Stella needs to leave in a few minutes if she's going to be on time, Xander," Calliope reminded her husband, who gave her a distracted husband wave as he urged Stella to come join him.

"I see some of the problem. And she won't be late. I'll drive her," Xander said.

"Cool." Stella slunk around the table and, to Hunter's surprise, Phoebe followed.

"Hey, Phoebe," Hunter said. "Why don't you—"

"She's fine," Calliope murmured. "Surely you noticed how her eyes lit up at the sight of that page. She's a smart one, your niece. She likes numbers."

"She likes order," Hunter agreed as he polished off some of the best fried eggs he'd ever eaten. "The two normally go hand in hand." A special sense of pride and appreciation swept over him as he watched Phoebe slip between Stella and Xander as Xander slowly reworked one of the equations. Phoebe pointed a few times, nodded when Stella answered Xander's questions, then clapped wildly when Stella wrote down the solution.

"We'll leave you to this. Hunter, why don't you take a walk with me? So you can get a feel for the farm before you start photographing."

"Oh, sure. Yeah, if she's—"

"She's fine," Xander said and shot him a smile. "Quick with this. Here, Phoebe. Let's..." Xander's voice faded as he copied Stella's homework on a separate piece of paper and handed it to her. "You want to try?"

Phoebe's eyes went wide. "Thank you." She snatched the paper and settled herself in, pencil in hand, tiny tongue protruding from her lips. She hunched over and went to work.

"Bring your tea," Calliope urged Hunter and drew him up. The next thing he knew he was outside, the cool morning air wafting over him like a soothing balm. He took a long, deep breath in and, as he let it out, felt the tension leave his body.

"What's in this stuff?" He looked down at his mug.

"Only what you needed," Calliope said and led him along a narrow path between expansive outcroppings of newly grown vegetables.

"Isn't it too early for these?" Enormous bundles of kale and cabbage and red-leaf lettuce sprouted heartily beside crisp-topped carrots and thickly leafed cabbages. The farm was a positive cornucopia of fresh bounty. "I thought you were supposed to plant in the spring for the summer."

"I've never been one to follow a schedule." Calliope bent to pluck a plump strawberry from its vine. "That's not to say some don't struggle, but they bloom in their own time. In their own way. I just provide a little… help." She popped the berry into her mouth. "How are you liking your accommodations?"

"It's wonderful. Perfect," Hunter answered. "Just what we needed."

"Mmm." Calliope began walking again

and he followed. "There is something special about the Liberty. Just when I was afraid the history would be lost forever, Gil surprised me, and here you are. Tell me." Hands linked behind her back, she faced him, the morning sun glinting against her skin. "Have you read the legend yet?"

"About the lighthouse? Ah, no." Hunter shook his head. "I was focusing more on the history of the town first. Wanted to get a good, well, grounding before I moved to specifics. Don't tell me. The lighthouse is cursed."

"Oh, quite the opposite. The lighthouse was actually the first structure constructed in Butterfly Harbor. It was a guide for ships long before anyone, including my great-great-grandparents, settled here. The story goes that one night, during a particularly nasty storm, a newly married couple recently arrived from overseas were lost and looking for shelter. When they found no one about—the former caretaker had passed a few months prior—they settled into the keeper's house. The husband, being a former merchant sailor, went up to the tower to turn the light on to help protect the ships.

Hours later, when he didn't return, his wife climbed up to look for him, but he was gone. All she found was her husband's coat caught on the railing, blowing in the breeze. When the storm passed, she searched the area for him, went to every house, every dwelling, but to no avail. It was believed the wind had caught him in its embrace and carried him out to sea. Since all her hope was gone, the woman climbed to the top of the tower and was about to throw herself into the water, but something stopped her. A fluttering. A moment of clarity. Six months later, she gave birth to a daughter she named Liberty. Named after the promise that brought them to this country. Their descendants oversaw the lighthouse and its land until just a few years ago."

"No wonder I can't come up with a story idea for my book," Hunter joked. "You've got them all. But you said the lighthouse wasn't cursed."

"I did. It's not." Calliope's voice was as soft as the breeze around them. "From that day on, all those who sought refuge from a storm at the lighthouse found their hearts healed. With the bad always comes the good.

Light balances the darkness. Hope always replaces despair. As it will be for you and Phoebe as you deal with your loss."

"And Kendall?" Hunter couldn't help but ask about the woman who had flitted about the periphery of his thoughts all morning.

"Who do you think woke the Liberty up?" Calliope's smile was a bit sad. "Kendall's heart has been more battered than most. But it still keeps beating. And it will, no matter how much she may wish otherwise."

"Otherwise?" Hunter didn't know how to read that. "What does that mean?"

"I don't mean anything serious by it," Calliope said. "But darkness remains and surges around her like the deepest, coldest wave."

"After losing her fiancé in combat, can you blame her?"

Calliope closed her eyes, as if finally she'd heard an answer she'd been waiting for. "Ah. Yes. That makes sense. How interesting that she confided that in you, a virtual stranger, rather than in those of us who have come to love her. I wouldn't mention that to her, by the way," Calliope added with a hint of a smile. "She's not one to accept affection easily, but I believe you are up to the challenge."

"Up to what...challenge? Wait, Calliope—" But his call fell on deaf ears as Calliope swept by him to return to the house, where Xander and Stella were headed off to school.

He stood there, empty tea mug in hand, a bit uncertain about what came next. Before he even thought about taking another step, he caught sight of a fluttering out of the corner of his eyes, a flash of color. Color that was magnifying quickly as a group of butterflies swooped up and toward him, swirling about him in a graceful circle of welcome. A solitary butterfly, its brilliant orange-and-black wings glinting against the sun, landed on the rim of his mug, its threadlike legs itching together as if playing a symphony. He raised the mug, transfixed by the creature that he'd swear appeared to be looking back at him.

And then just like that, the moment broke and the insects flittered away, returning to their home in the eucalyptus trees ringing the edge of the farm.

The regret that he'd not thought to pull out his camera swept over him, but then he remembered the importance of living in the moment, of being present rather than trying to live life through a lens. The butterfly's visit felt like, well, it felt like a gift. One he was exceedingly grateful for.

This had to be the oddest morning he'd ever spent. Anywhere. And he'd been to a lot of strange places.

Phoebe raced out of the house, paper waving in her hand as she headed straight for him. Her curls bounced around her bright face, her eyes sparkling in the sun just like the bells and shells in Calliope's hair. Hunter caught her in his arms and held out the paper to examine it. "You did all this?"

Phoebe nodded. The numbers and equations were definitely scribbled by a seven-year-old, but the logic, the comprehension and the solutions were correct, at least according to Xander's comments.

"You are one smart little girl, do you know that?" Hunter asked. So often, when he looked at his niece, all he could see was Juliana, the sister he'd loved and lost. The woman who had always, no matter what, had his back. But today, all he saw was Phoebe, and the amazing future she had ahead of her. A future he was not going to surrender, but fight for.

He was done running, done hiding. He was done acquiescing to the wants and desires of two people who thought they knew better even though they had no idea who their granddaughter was, who their son had been. Phoebe was his now. His niece. His child.

Which meant it was his job to make her future as bright and as ripe with possibilities as he could. With him.

THE RUMBLE OF a luxury vehicle's engine broke through the crashing of waves as Kendall stabbed the palette knife into the jar of spackle and sighed. Now what? She was in the homestretch and glad about it, already thinking of the next task. She'd made her way around to the other side of the tower, so she couldn't see who was approaching, but if memory served, she had a good idea who it might be.

With only a few hours' sleep, she should have been exhausted, but for whatever reason she was buzzing with energy. Energy that had stalled when she'd spotted the homemade card a little seven-year-old someone had pushed under the front door.

The stars and an I'm-so-sorry-looking moon apologized and said thank you for helping her get down off the scaffold. After Kendall had recognized the kind gesture for what it was, she'd taken the card to the refrigerator and, after digging around in the drawers, found a magnetic chip clip to hold it in place.

Now, Kendall scrambled down the scaffold as Gil Hamilton rounded the bend. His too-long blondish hair blew in the midafternoon breeze that was picking up with every second that passed. "We really need to get you a cell phone," he called to her by way of a greeting.

She didn't respond. Instead she welcomed him with a quick smile.

"It's looking great, Kendall!" Gil stopped beside the worktable and gazed up. "Am I imagining things or are you ahead of schedule?"

"I need to be given that storm rolling in." She pointed toward the horizon, where the gray clouds were gathering.

"Supposed to be a big one. Might need some help with repairs around town after, if you're game?"

Kendall shrugged. "You tell me what needs doing, I'll get it done. Luke back yet?"

"Yes. So are Fletcher and Ozzy, so we've got a full house at the sheriff's station." He rocked back on his heels. "I'm sorry it took me so long to get out here."

"Why?" Kendall used an old rag to wipe down her tools. "I wasn't expecting you, was I?"

"No, not exactly. But I owe you an apology. For Hunter showing up the way he did. I should have respected your privacy more and given you a heads-up. I take it that's why you were trying to hunt me down last week?"

"Oh, that." She had been on a bit of a rampage that day. Not surprising that word had gotten around. Kendall wasn't known for her subtlety at times. "Thanks. I appreciate it. I got over it, though." He was her boss, after all. In truth, she was still getting over it. She really didn't like being sandbagged. "While you're here, I think you need to find it in the budget to install a railing system along the perimeter of the cliffs."

Gil's brow veed. He didn't frown. Not often that she'd seen, but she could tell when he wanted to. "You don't think that would ruin the aesthetic?"

"No more than someone taking a walk off the edge at night." She wasn't about to tell him what had happened with Phoebe. Knowing Gil, he'd start worrying about potential lawsuits, but Hunter had been relieved only she knew what had happened, and there was no reason not to keep it that way. "I'd also recommend some solar garden lights. We can aim them away from the buildings. Check with the insurance agency and the policy. If it fits within code, it might get you a break on the premium."

"Good idea."

Yeah. The fiscal bottom line usually made more of an impact than practicality and safety concerns. "So what did bring you here?"

"I actually wanted to talk to you about what happens after you're done with the lighthouse."

Kendall's body tensed. "Um, actually, I was thinking about maybe moving on." Correction. She should have been thinking *more* about moving on.

"Oh?" Gil looked both surprised and disappointed.

"I don't normally stick around this long, but when I commit to a job, I stick to it until it's done." And while seeing Phoebe every day didn't feel like as much of a gut punch as it once had, her and Hunter's arrival had only reminded Kendall that permanency was an illusion. Better to get a jump on it, before it got a jump on her. She had to cut ties. And the sooner the better. "Not sure I want to take more on, not being sure and all."

"So I guess I'd better look for someone else to head up the restoration project I have in mind."

"What restoration project?" Not that Kendall was a gossip, but she kept her ears open, especially when she was at the hardware store. Harvey Mills, the owner of the store and lumber supply, was a wealth of information on just about every aspect of the town.

"I don't know if I should say anything." Gil suddenly looked uncertain. "If you aren't going to be available, I might need to reevaluate the entire idea."

"Not many people for me to tell, but if that's how you feel." Kendall shrugged, tamping down on the curiosity surging inside her. Or was that excitement? She hadn't felt either for so long it was difficult to tell. She continued to clean her tools, hoping he'd explain.

"There's that string of Victorian homes, you know, where BethAnn Bromley lives. They're some of the original buildings in town, and I was thinking we could restore them, declare them landmarks and open them for tours. You know, deck them out like they were back in the day. Like we're going to do with the lighthouse."

The historic detail of the lighthouse was one of the few parts of this project she was worried about. She did fine fixing things up to within modern standards, but to try to be historically accurate? That came to a level of detail she wasn't quite used to.

"Project like that is going to take some serious time," Kendall said. "Especially if I'm working alone." Or even with the skeleton crew she'd called on from time to time. Frankie and Matt had full-time jobs, and Kyle Winters was doing better in school than he ever had on top of doing part-time handyman work. Beyond those three, there weren't a lot of people she knew she could count on—or who could fit extra work into their day.

"If you're interested, I can look at the town budget, see what there is to work with. Maybe hire a few crew for you. Town could do with some new jobs, don't you think?"

Ah. The light dawned. "I do think." She should have known. Gil was up for reelection soon, and if the rumblings she'd heard around town were true, he was looking for avenues to boost his public image. "And those buildings could definitely use some TLC." Still, committing to the job would mean staying in Butterfly Harbor for, what? Another year or two? Maybe longer? Her heart was already starting to twitch.

"Nothing has to be decided right away," Gil assured her. "You do really great work, Kendall. You're reliable and, well, let's face it, cost-effective."

Meaning she was cheap and easy to deal with. "I'll think about it."

"Great! I'm sure Hunter will be digging up some information on those homes over the next few weeks. Maybe the two of you can work together."

"Like I said, I'll think about it." She gave

him a quick smile. The idea of working with Hunter had her stomach doing that odd little dance she hadn't quite defined yet. She was only just now getting used to seeing him and Phoebe every day. Being around them for more than just a cup of coffee or a trip up to the moon? That might take something she didn't possess.

"Okay, then. I'll check in with you in a few weeks. I'm going to hit the diner on the way home, then Calliope's place to stock up. Town's closing up nice and tight. Ready to batten down the hatches?"

"I will be." Kendall didn't need much more than her coffeepot and whatever leftovers might be in the fridge. Fully expecting the electricity to go out—there wasn't much more she could do to upgrade it other than update the fuses and power box—she planned to start plastering the interior of the four-story tower whenever there was enough light. "I'll see you after the storm."

"You bet."

Kendall nearly rolled her eyes at that cheesy grin of his that flashed. She'd bet he was born with that expression on his face.

From what she'd heard, his father had possessed the same one.

Another job. She took a slow, deep breath and found her attention pulled to the guest house. Phoebe's and Hunter's bikes were braced against the side wall, looking as if they belonged there. The flower boxes remained empty, but there was a feeling surrounding the place now that hadn't been there before. A feeling of happiness and contentment. Feelings Kendall knew she couldn't afford. The second these feelings took hold, that's when life imploded—and Kendall had had enough implosions to last her a lifetime.

CHAPTER EIGHT

"HURRY UP AND close the door!" Hunter, with one of Calliope's baskets looped over one arm and three earth-friendly reusable bags looped over the other, backed into the house with Phoebe right beside him. He should have listened to Calliope and picked up the basket sooner instead of waiting until the last possible moment. The wind was kicking up something fierce, and he and Phoebe were both soaked from the prestorm drizzle.

He dropped his purchases onto the kitchen counter while Phoebe stood where she was and dropped her jacket to the floor and then the bag she'd kept dry underneath. She grinned and flipped her soaked hair off her face.

"Quite a walk back, huh, kiddo?" Hunter teased as Phoebe all but sputtered water. "I think you need a hot bath."

Phoebe nodded, but instead of heading

into her bedroom, she walked to the window and looked out toward the keeper's house. She tapped on the window to get Hunter's attention.

"What's up?" He ran a towel over his face and hair and joined her. "Oh, Kendall? I'm sure she's okay. Snug as a bug in a..." He trailed off at Phoebe's rolling eyes. "Yeah, I need some new material. But she's fine, Phoebe. Come on. Let's get you all dry and toasty." Speaking of toasty, he looked longingly at the stone fireplace between his desk and the kitchen table. He ran a bath for Phoebe, waited until she was safely ensconced, then picked up her jacket and bag, unloading her books and the new stack of math worksheets Calliope had printed off on her computer. With Wi-Fi not being the greatest out here, he'd been stopping at the library most days and, true to form, he'd lost track of time. Calliope had appeared more amused than irritated as they'd sloshed their way up to the farm, then shooed them home with baskets of goodies and brand-new copies of Stella's homework for Phoebe.

Hunter wasn't entirely sure what he'd done in his life to deserve finding people he could immediately call friends, but his gratitude was endless. Seeing the joy on his niece's face, a joy that hadn't faded even while they'd trudged up the hill to the lighthouse, was worth whatever had brought him to this moment. He was beginning to have difficulty recalling what things were like for them before they'd come here. And he was having difficulty thinking about leaving.

Listening to Phoebe hum and splash in the tub, Hunter stood at the window watching as the storm rolled in. Black clouds moved lightning fast, eating away the last of the sun's rays as the waves tumbled over each other in their rush to reach the shore. The sound felt like a pulse, as if the ocean's heartbeat was picking up speed, pounding its way to shore.

He hadn't been worried about Kendall. Not until Phoebe had brought her to his attention. He'd lost track of the number of days he'd take a break from research and drink his coffee looking out the window while Kendall had continued to bring the Liberty back to life. Instead of quelling his curiosity, however, he found himself more and more transfixed. Never in his life had he met anyone so solitary…so determined to keep everyone at a distance.

Beyond her quiet, determined sense of self, despite the obvious grief and sadness she'd experienced, she was strong. Confident. And worked hard every single day. Whether it was the sun that began melting that cool exterior or maybe the tenacity of his niece, Kendall had begun to come around at least to the point of offering a wave, a smile or even a good morning when they were lucky.

Phoebe had taken it upon herself to go out after breakfast every morning and sit on the top porch step, eyes pinned to whatever task Kendall was tackling that day. Being observed like that would have distracted Hunter, and for a while he thought Kendall might not have realized she'd had a seven-year-old for an audience, who could sit as still as stone for hours upon hours and just watch, but he was wrong. She'd realized.

Because one morning after breakfast, he and Phoebe walked out of the house and found a rope-and-plank swing hanging securely from a branch of a large oak situated between the motor home and the carriage house. Phoebe had raced over to it with a soft exclamation of glee, spinning around and jumping onto the plank, kicking her feet ferociously in her silent demand for Hunter to push her.

Phoebe's laughter had chimed through the air then, robbing Hunter of every ounce of breath he possessed and, as he looked toward the lighthouse, stopped Kendall cold.

He couldn't be sure, not from such a distance, but he swore he spotted tears in her eyes before she turned her back on them once more.

That Kendall would have taken the time out of her day to set up that swing for a little girl she was purposely trying to avoid, for a man who no doubt irritated her to no end just by his presence, said more about Kendall Davidson than any conversation ever would. Which was why, he supposed, over the past few days he'd found himself preoccupied with the thought of her.

Strident in how she pushed herself through life when he could understand the temptation to surrender. He wanted to know everything about her—no. That was wrong. He didn't want to know, he needed to. Those scars of hers—how deep did they run? Was there any way to heal them?

The night of Phoebe's nocturnal excursion, she'd listened to him. Just listened, and it wasn't until she'd left that he realized how lonely he'd been. Not that Phoebe wasn't constant company, but he'd kept so much inside, so much that had been set free that night, that he didn't want to go back. With Kendall, he felt safe. Whatever he'd thrown at her, she'd caught and settled right down with it. Nothing, not a runaway child, not his paralyzing panic that had eroded his ego a good amount, had fazed her. She was the kind of woman who did what needed doing when it needed to be done. Appealing to say the least.

Beyond that, however, Hunter couldn't help but wonder about the woman inside. The woman she'd been before her life had turned upside down. The drawn, tense features, the dark hair and intense eyes, the scars she bared to the world as if daring rejection, all hinted at a strength that struck him to the core. She was beautiful, even when—especially when—she pushed through her own sadness to help a little girl trying to communicate with her lost parents, or to listen to a man afraid of failing the only person who mattered in his life. Kendall Davidson, whether she'd intended to or not, had found a way into his life. And, dare he say it, into his heart.

Which brought him back to Phoebe's concern. "Hey, Phoebs?" he called and then knocked on the bathroom door before he pushed it open. "You about done?" He barked out a laugh when he found his niece covered in shampoo soap suds, grinning up at him like a fool. "Okay, kiddo. That brings an end to today's bath. Duck and rinse off." He grabbed one of the fluffy blue towels. When she was dressed and combing out her hair, he told her, "I'm going to run over to Kendall's real quick. Ask if she'd like to join us for dinner. Are you okay with that?"

Phoebe nodded.

"With me going over there or inviting her to dinner?"

Phoebe held up two fingers.

"Right. Both it is. Maybe she can help us get a fire going." If the electricity went out, they'd be feeling the chill soon enough. He left Phoebe munching on carrots from Calliope's garden and working on a new page of mathematic equations as, huddling back into his jacket, he stepped out into the gusty wind and sleeting rain.

Enough people had told him this was going to be a rough storm that he should have believed them. Probably karmic retribution for scoffing at the idea that the Northern California coast didn't really know what a storm was.

He almost slipped and slid in the mud, scanning the area as he hurried toward Kendall's door. She'd put all her tools and equipment away, and knotted a tarp around the scaffold, which creaked and groaned. He knocked three times and called her name, his voice disappearing on the air. He cupped his hand, peered inside. No light. No sign of movement. No hint that she was home.

Great. He frowned and braced himself again as he hurried back to the guest house. He hadn't been worried. Not when he thought she was inside. He couldn't help but worry now…and wonder where she was.

"YOU CANNOT BE serious about walking home in this storm." Lori Knight, Matt's wife and, by default, the closest thing Kendall had to a best friend, planted her hands on her ample hips and glared not just daggers, but scimitars at her.

"A little rain never hurt anyone," Kendall said and earned a grin of approval from Kyle, Lori and Matt's teenage foster son and Kendall's sometimes second assistant. "It's not that bad, Lori."

"Not that bad?" Lori marched over and flung open the living room curtains. "That's not buckets out there, Kendall. It's garbage cans. Dump trucks, maybe. If you don't drown, you're going to get sick."

"I don't get sick." Anymore. Kendall zipped up first the sweatshirt Hunter had loaned her and then the oversize jacket she'd bought at the thrift store. "I'm too mean to get sick. Besides, it's your fault I had to come out here, remember?" She'd patched the hole in the roof just as the first drops of the storm began to fall.

"Oh, yeah." Lori glared up at the water stain on the kitchen ceiling that was only just beginning to dry. "Fixed it in time, so thank you."

"I can drive her home," Kyle offered and slid off the stool at the breakfast bar.

"Park it, mister." Lori tapped her finger against his history text book. "You only just got your license. Let me have my first heart attack over that before you go driving in this kind of weather."

"I appreciate the offer, Kyle," Kendall told him as he sagged back into his seat, his too-long blond hair falling over one very wise eye. "But Lori's right. No one should be driving in this. Which is why I'm going to walk. A walk that might go better with brownies."

Lori narrowed her bright blue eyes and flipped her blond hair over one shoulder. "You never take leftovers. What's going on?"

Kendall shrugged. "Everyone likes brownies." She'd bet Hunter liked brownies. And Phoebe, of course. They'd brought her dinner and dessert. Time for her to repay the kindness with something more than a surly attitude. "Especially homemade."

"Lori's brownies are the best," Kyle agreed as he reached over to grab one.

"Well, I shouldn't be eating any more,

anyway, so I'm happy to have someone else enjoy them." She ducked down to retrieve a plastic container.

"I thought you weren't doing that any-more," Kendall said. "Kicking yourself for eating what you want?"

"I'm supposed to fine her a dollar every time she does." Kyle grinned before he got up to pour another glass of milk.

"I spent a lifetime obsessing about my weight," Lori told them both. "It's going to take at least half that long to make the mental shift. But I'm getting there." She smoothed a hand down the front of her sweater. "Being happy helps." She hooked an arm around Kyle's neck and brought him in for a hug. A hug that turned the teen's face bright red as he returned the embrace. "Can you be-lieve he's finally ours? Officially legal and everything? Is there such a thing as an 'it's a teenager' shower?"

"If there's not, there should be," Ken-dall agreed. There were few people in her life Kendall loved. Down to the ground, would do anything for, loved. For the lon-gest time—years, in fact—the entire list had consisted of Lori's husband, Matt. But last year Lori had slipped right in beside him. Watching Lori and Matt together, seeing how they were building their family with Kyle, a boy who'd had a seriously rough start in life, made her almost believe in happily-ever-afters again.

Almost.

The rain always helped clear her mind. Maybe it was the years growing up when staying outside no matter the weather was better than going home. Maybe it was the year she'd spent in the Afghan desert, where she'd longed for a skin-soaking downpour. Or maybe it was that before today, walking in a rainstorm was the perfect camouflage for a good cry.

But not today. Today, huddled in her double layers, listening to the squish of her work boots, a container of homemade brownies tucked in an inside pocket, the tears didn't fall. They didn't even surge. The wind battered her to the point where she had to catch her balance a few times, but she actually found herself smiling up at the sky and reveling in the sensation of the sharp drops hitting her face.

Houses were locked up tight and, given

what she'd seen on her walk to Matt and Lori's house, some of the stores had taped their windows to be safe. Butterfly Harbor wasn't often a ghost town, not in Kendall's short experience, but today she'd have been surprised to see even a butterfly drifting in front of her.

Normally she preferred to take the long way to wherever she was going, but today she made an exception and cut across the street before heading up the hill to Liberty Lighthouse. She'd almost lost feeling in her toes from the cold rain and was looking forward to a long soak in the tub when a huge gust of wind nearly slammed her into a lamppost. She gave herself a good shake just as the crack split the air, followed by another long ripping sound that echoed in her ears. A thud echoed around her, followed by a crash. The ground trembled beneath her feet.

Kendall pushed off the post and ran full bore down the muddied, sloppy road, slipping and sliding more than once. Breath sharp in her chest, her frozen fingers clenched inside her jacket pockets as she surveyed the damage. The top half of one of the monstrous redwoods standing guard along the perimeter of the lighthouse had landed in the path between the keeper and guest houses. It had missed both buildings by inches, the thick trunk wedging itself firmly against her own front door. The tip-top branches had broken free when they'd scraped against the guest house's windows. Even as she moved toward the keeper house, the door to the carriage house was thrown open.

"Kendall?" Hunter shouted into the rain and the wind. "Is that you?"

"Yes!" She slipped and slid her way forward. "I'm fine. Are you guys okay? No, stay inside!" She faced him as he pulled the door closed behind him and started toward her. "What's wrong? Is Phoebe okay?" She sputtered and swept water out of her eyes. "What are you…doing?"

She might have backed up if she'd had time to think, if she'd taken a second to consider what she was seeing in his eyes, but it wasn't until he'd gripped her arms and hauled her against him, pressed his mouth against hers that she recognized fear. And worry. And…relief.

The storm raged around them. Through

them. In them. She heard a soft whimper escape and was stunned to realize it was she who had made the noise. His mouth demanded at first, drank her in, until eventually his lips softened and he lifted one hand to cup the side of her face. "I was worried about you," he murmured when the kiss ended. "Where have you been?"

"Uh, working." She blinked, uncertain what had happened. Uncertain what she was feeling. And she was feeling so much. So much more than she'd felt in…years. She closed her eyes as he pressed his forehead to hers, held her against him for a long moment. She tried to breathe easy, to calm herself down, but she inhaled the scent of him mingling on the wind, in the rain, and her mind was filled only with images of Hunter MacBride.

This couldn't be happening. Not to her. Not again. "I had to fix Lori's roof before the storm— Hunter." She lifted her face, pinned her gaze to his. "Hunter, I'm fine. I can take care of myself." That he'd worried about her should scare her right down to the tips of her toes, but instead, she accepted his concern as part of who he was.

"We were worried about you."

"*We* were?" She stepped back, letting the moment pass as she attempted to put some distance between them.

"Check out the window." He jerked his head back. "She's been standing on a chair watching for you."

"She was that close when the tree went down?" She didn't want to care. She didn't want to think about a little girl's fear or the fact that that little girl had been thinking about her. "She must have been so scared."

"She probably still is. You should come in and reassure her."

Kendall shook her head. "No." That definitely was not a good idea. She needed to rebuild that wall around herself, the wall that kept everyone, especially handsome men and their beautiful nieces, away from her heart. "No, I'm just going to go inside—"

"How?" Hunter followed her as she attempted to work her way around the tree that barred her access to her front door. "That's not budging without a chain saw, and you know it. And until it stops raining, you're out of luck. Kendall." She sat awkwardly on the tree, branches and twigs catching in her clothes, under her jacket. She could see deep gouges in the side of the house now, gouges that would need repairing. One of the smaller panes of glass in the window beside the door had been shattered. The water damage, hopefully, would be minimal. But that was where she was safe. That was where she wouldn't have to look at Hunter or Phoebe and be reminded of all she'd had. All she'd lost. All that could never be hers again.

"You can't get in there tonight." Hunter tugged on her arm. "You know I'm right, Kendall. Come on. Come with me."

She dug her fingers deep into the damp bark of the tree, wishing there was another option. She didn't want to know how Hunter and Phoebe lived their day-to-day lives. She didn't want to see a father and daughter curled up on the sofa, reading books and playing board games. She didn't want to bond over a roaring fire or hot soup or cuddle up against the storm. She wanted to just sit here, on this tree, and let the rain and wind take her away.

"Kendall." Hunter's hold eased. He stepped back, offered his hand instead. "Please."

Kendall looked over her shoulder to where

Phoebe stood in the window, her tiny nose pressed against the glass in between splayed hands. She couldn't do this. She couldn't spend endless hours looking at a little girl who reminded her so much of the future she'd lost when Sam died. The pain she'd felt when Samira had been killed. She couldn't…

She took a deep, shuddering breath, looked down at Hunter's hand.

And placed her trembling one in his.

"I KEEP STEALING your clothes."

"Seems that way." Hunter handed over a pair of sweatpants and a T-shirt, the quickest things he could find that might fit her. Despite the strength he'd seen in her, she appeared so frail, even more so now as she stood shivering in the small bathroom. If she'd thought the two jackets would help keep her dry, she was wrong. She was soaked right down to the skin. "Towels are on the shelf over there. Help yourself to whatever else you might need. Phoebe and I are going to make dinner. Having help means it'll be a while." He grinned and picked up the sopping coats. "So take your time."

"I need to c-call someone. Ab-bout the tree." Her teeth were all but rattling. "I d-don't have a cell ph-phone."

"Mine's right here." He left the cell on the counter and hefted the coats in his arms. "Oh, and before you start thinking about how to repay the favor, I'll appreciate it if you start a fire in the fireplace when you're done."

Kendall frowned at him after accepting the dry clothes. "You don't know how?"

"I know how." He shrugged and headed off. "Just not my strong suit." Something dropped out of the jackets. "What's this?" He bent down to retrieve the plastic container.

"Dessert?" Kendall gave him a tremulous smile.

"Brownies? My favorite. Thanks."

"Thank Lori Knight when you meet her. She made them."

"Will do." He saluted her with the treat and pulled the door closed behind him. He almost tripped over Phoebe, who was standing right outside. "She's fine, kiddo." Hunter caught her shoulder and turned her back to the kitchen. "Just wet and cold. What should we fix for dinner? A Calliope special?"

They decided a Calliope special was a kitchen-sink salad along with gooey grilled cheese sandwiches, one of Phoebe's favorites. The minutes ticked past in his head as Phoebe stood on her stool, meticulously cutting up a red pepper with her special-helper plastic knife. She paid as much attention to this task as she had those math problems. Into the bowl with the mix of arugula, kale and red-leaf lettuce went peppers and green onions and little heirloom tomatoes along with tiny broccoli branches and some shredded parmesan cheese. He pulled his desk chair over so there were three seats at the table, set the sandwiches in between two plates to keep them warm and had Phoebe clean up what he had begun to call her math lab.

She stacked her papers and notebook into a neat pile and set them on the edge of his desk, then picked up her copy of *Charlotte's Web* and placed it next to her dinner plate.

It was on the tip of his tongue to ask if she was enjoying the other books she'd picked up from the library, but now wasn't the time.

She hadn't screamed or cried, but he knew that tree falling in front of the house had scared her. It had to. That deafening boom had taken a few years off his life. He'd half expected to find the keeper house decimated when he rushed to the window. That the tree had just missed seemed both a miracle and a warning. A reminder of just how short life could be.

Seeing Kendall arrive just after the tree crashed had sent a surge of relief through him so hard it could have rivaled the midnight tide. Throwing caution out the window, he'd raced outside, wanting nothing more than to see her. Touch her. Hold her. And the moment he had, the moment he knew she was all right, there was only one thing left he needed to do.

He'd kissed her.

And possibly thrown the rest of his life completely off-kilter for the second time in less than a year.

The bathroom door creaked open, and Kendall stepped out, her bare feet stark against the dark-stained wood floors. "Sorry I took so long. I think I fell asleep." She started to push her hair out of her face, then seemed to remember she'd braided it and dropped her hand to her side. "I just hung the towels over the shower."

"That's fine," Hunter told her. "You want to eat first or get the fire started?"

Phoebe rubbed her hands down her arms.

"Fire it is," Kendall said without hesitation and walked over to the latched panel beside the fireplace. She ducked down and pulled out four solid pieces of wood as if determined to look anywhere but at him. Had one kiss, one impulsive move on his part, destroyed whatever progress they'd made? "I know you have plenty right outside the door, but this is much drier."

"I should have realized that's what that was. Great idea." He walked over, Phoebe right beside him, and they settled in to watch.

"My grandparents had one of these. As long as the wood is stocked, you don't have to go outside to get it. Makes for much nicer winter evenings, believe me."

"Where was that? The farm." Hunter drew Phoebe onto his lap when it became obvious she was determined to help. He locked his arms around her and rested his chin on her head, a sign to her that she wasn't going anywhere. She sighed and sagged back against him.

"North Dakota. Dad was in the service, so my mom and I spent a lot of time up there with them." Kendall stacked the wood, then crumpled up pieces of an old newspaper. "My grandfather didn't know what to do with a granddaughter, so he did what he'd done with his son and taught me about carpentry and construction. And baseball." She added with a surprising laugh, "I used to have a wicked slide into home."

Phoebe looked back at Hunter with something akin to wonder on her face.

Kendall struck a long match and lit the papers. They crackled and smoked and caught. Tiny flames licked up into bigger ones until the fire burned brightly. The orange-and-red flames illuminated her face and brought a healthy glow to her cheeks. "See? Nothing to it. But it's only when you have adult supervision, right, Phoebe?"

Phoebe nodded, then rubbed her stomach.

"I guess that means dinner is served." Hunter grunted as he set her down. "Hope you like salad and grilled cheese."

"I like them just fine." Again Kendall moved without really looking at him. "I called Frankie Bettencourt. She'll have volunteers out here to remove the tree as soon as the storm blows through."

"I've heard her name before. She's one of the firefighters in town, right?"

Phoebe tugged on Kendall's shirt, a surprised expression on her face when she pointed to herself.

"You've never seen a female firefighter before?" Kendall looked aghast when Hunter shrugged.

"We move around a lot and, honestly, haven't had much cause to interact with firefighters."

"I'm sure Frankie would be thrilled to give you a tour of the firehouse."

"My list of places to see and explore is growing exponentially," Hunter said as he retrieved the salad bowl from the counter. "Which reminds me, any chance I can get a look at the inside of the lighthouse?"

"Oh. Sure." Kendall shrugged. "I guess it should have occurred to me before, given your project." She sat back and watched as

Phoebe piled her plate high with salad. “So, um, you like vegetables, Phoebe?”

Phoebe nodded and smacked her lips.

“She has a salad with every meal.” Hunter set the plate of sandwiches beside the salad bowl. “Except breakfast. We decided that wasn’t working so well.”

Phoebe wrinkled her nose and shook her head.

Kendall let out a sound that sounded like a laugh as she reached for one of the sandwiches. “Grilled cheese is my favorite.”

“Ours, too.” Hunter shook a bit of dressing over Phoebe’s salad until she pushed his hand away.

Kendall cast him a surprised look, then glanced away as if she suddenly remembered she wasn’t supposed to be watching him.

“Do you still see your family?” Hunter sighed at the comforting feeling of the fire crackling behind his back.

“No.” Kendall barely flinched. “No, my dad died in Iraq during his third tour of service. My grandparents passed away soon after, and then my mom, from cancer, a year before I joined the army.”

"What about Sam?" Hunter had been wondering whether or not he should bring up the fiancé she'd only mentioned once. If he was already on thin ice with her, what did he have to lose by inquiring now?

"Sam?" Kendall's voice sounded a bit choked. "Oh, um. We went to high school together, then college. I tutored him in math, actually." Phoebe grinned at Hunter.

"What?" Kendall asked.

"We've just learned that Phoebe loves algebra," Hunter explained with a laugh. "So you're a math geek, too?"

"Math is logic," Kendall said as she plucked apart her sandwich. "There's a formula. You follow it. You get the answer. It might frustrate you for a while, but it never lets you down. Plus it looks like a foreign language when you write it all out. Like a secret code."

"You and Sam enlisted together, you said?"

She hesitated, and even Phoebe looked between them as if she didn't like the question.

"If you'd rather not talk about it." Hunter's expression held such compassion.

"I don't mind." Kendall cleared her throat.

"After all, I brought it up. The army offered what we both wanted, a solid future and a way to get it, and offer a contribution to others that Sam and I both felt was important. He was going to be a science teacher when we got back."

"And you?" Hunter asked.

The smile that curved her lips scraped against his heart. "I was going to be a mom."

He was about to respond, even though he wasn't sure what he would say. But she seemed lost in the memories and continued.

"He asked me to marry him the night after we made it through basic training. I was deployed with Matt's unit. Sam ended up being stationed a few villages away, protecting a school and other infrastructure being rebuilt. We emailed a lot. Video chats. He told the most awful jokes." Her laugh caught Hunter by surprise. "Just horrible. Those chats were a good reason I didn't completely lose it when he was killed. We never left anything unsaid. He knew I loved him. And I knew he loved me. And then he was gone, killed by a bomber who took exception to the new girls' school he and his team had just overseen being finished."

"He sounds like a good guy."

"He was." Now Kendall looked at him. Really looked at him, and he saw, for an instant, a flash of relief. "He would have been a good dad, too. The best." She continued to pick apart her sandwich but hadn't eaten a bite. Her arms might be all muscle, but she still looked too thin. "We always wanted a big family."

Phoebe shifted onto her knees and tapped the back of Kendall's hand, then pointed to herself.

"Phoebe, I think that's enough talking for tonight." Hunter should never have brought this up. Not now. Not without warning. And not having at least given Phoebe a hint of what and who Kendall had lost.

"It's okay." Kendall shook her head, as if trying to clear her mind. "Um, there was a little girl, Phoebe. Her name was Samira and she lived in this village my unit was trying to protect. She loved to read and make up stories, but most of all she loved to play soccer." Kendall squeezed her eyes. "She was the best player in the village, much to her brothers' horror. She and her family were ki—um, died. Just after—" Her voice broke.

Just after she'd lost Sam. "I put daisies on her grave. Daisies make everyone happy, she used to say."

"Kendall, that's okay, it's enough." Hunter grabbed hold of her hand and squeezed, held on tight when it felt as if she might pull away. "You don't owe us any further explanation."

"I know." Kendall blinked a few times and tipped her head back as if to stop the tears. "Maybe not talking about them is why it still hurts so much."

Phoebe tapped her fingers on the table one at a time. Hunter frowned, not understanding. But somehow Kendall did.

"She was nine," Kendall said. "And she had beautiful black curls, just like yours." She looked as if she wanted to reach out and touch Phoebe's.

In that moment, so much about Kendall made sense. Beginning with why, when she'd first seen Phoebe, she looked as if she'd seen a ghost. Because she had.

Phoebe's bottom lip trembled. She looked at Hunter, then jumped down from her chair and raced into the kitchen.

"I didn't mean to upset her," Kendall whispered. "I'm sorry. I shouldn't have said—"

"You didn't upset her." Hunter looked down to where Kendall continued to hold his hand; she squeezed as if doing so brought her some comfort.

Phoebe searched through one of the baskets they'd brought from Calliope's. The basket Calliope had promised would hold all they'd need for the weekend.

"What you got there, kiddo?" Hunter asked as Phoebe returned to the table, a small biodegradable pot cupped between her hands. She held it out to Kendall, tears pooling in her eyes. Kendall stared at the barely bloomed flowers, a collection of them: brilliant white daisies.

Phoebe set the pot on the table.

"Daisies make everyone happy."

Kendall's expression was unreadable until the first tear fell. She pulled her hand free of Hunter's and swiped her cheek. With one finger, she traced the petal of the largest stem, a soft smile curving her lips as she reached out and pulled Phoebe into a hug. "Thank you, Phoebe."

"Those are the flowers Calliope suggested

would look best in the window boxes. The ones she said would be strong enough to plant after the storm." Hunter could barely hear his own voice. "How did she—"

Kendall laughed, rested her cheek on Phoebe's head as she looked at him. "Because she's Calliope."

Hunter's heart twisted as he watched Phoebe cling to Kendall; she hugged her tight and copied the way she traced the flowers. His niece had managed to say all that was needed in just a few considered actions. Actions that, if he had to lay odds, might just have broken through the wall around Kendall Davidson's heart. "You know." Now he was the one who cleared his throat. "Someone brought us brownies for dessert."

"I love brownies," Kendall whispered.

"Yeah, well, we only get brownies when everyone finishes their dinner," Hunter teased her. "Family rule."

Phoebe climbed back onto her chair, picked up the salad tongs and dumped an over full batch of salad onto Kendall's plate, right on top of the remnants of the sandwich.

"I have to eat all that?"

Was it Hunter's imagination or had she actually whined?

"Every bit of it," he confirmed as Phoebe nodded. She pushed the bottle of dressing toward her. Then she returned to her own dinner as if nothing heart shattering had taken place.

"Well, since it's for brownies." Kendall sighed. She picked up her fork, and, after a quick look at Hunter, she dug in.

CHAPTER NINE

KENDALL PULLED HERSELF free of the fireplace-induced trance as Hunter quietly tiptoed out of Phoebe's bedroom.

"I think she's out."

"Stressful day." When was Kendall not the master of understatement. She'd taken refuge, physically and emotionally, in their temporary home. Curled up in the corner of the sofa, she sipped on tea she recognized as one of Calliope's special relaxation blends, recalling the one-sided conversation of a father putting his child to bed.

And somehow her heart hadn't shattered.

"Why *Charlotte's Web*?"

"Huh?" Hunter dropped onto the sofa beside her and rested his forehead against his hand. "Oh, that. It's the book Juliana was reading to her when she died. Doesn't matter how many other books we buy or which ones she thinks she wants to read, it always comes back to *Charlotte's Web*."

"Smart girl. Appropriate story, don't you think?"

Hunter shrugged. "I don't know. I haven't read it."

Kendall frowned. "All these months and you haven't read the book she's clinging to like a talisman?"

He dropped his hand and looked at her. "I've been a little busy."

"Sorry. Don't mean to judge." She sipped her tea. As she knew a bit about grief, she pressed harder. "Does she read it all the way through or just bits and pieces?"

"Uh." He leaned his head back. "Now that you ask, I think she gets to a certain spot and starts over."

Kendall looked back into the fire. "Maybe she stops where your sister did. Because finishing the book means having to finally say goodbye to her mother. Just a thought."

The silence stretched. "I hadn't thought about that," he said finally. "You think maybe I should push her to finish it?"

"No." Kendall shook her head. "I think you might try reading the rest of it to her, the way Juliana would have. Start from the beginning and go all the way through."

"She isn't too old for story time?"

"No child is ever too old for story time," Kendall said. "At least I never was. This might be a barrier she has to get over, but there's nothing saying you can't help her get there. What about school?"

"Is this some kind of therapy session?"

"Maybe." Kendall found herself grinning. There was something appealing about keeping him off-kilter—served him right since the second he kissed her, that was exactly how she felt. All these years, all the time she'd spent making sure no one got through, that no one wedged into her heart and expose her to another devastating loss, had been tossed aside by a single kiss from Hunter MacBride. "I've had enough of them myself to probably have earned a degree."

"Well, you seem to have taken it all to heart. And I bet you've been using it to help Phoebe, too."

"You look exhausted. You should get some sleep."

"Is that your way of saying you want me to leave you alone now?"

"No. And yes." How could this man read her so well? Maybe because the time they'd spent together had been quality… Oh, good heavens. Somewhere her former therapists were popping champagne corks. "The dishes are done. The place is cleaned up. You don't have any excuse not to go and get a good night's sleep."

"You did the dishes?" He leaned forward and looked toward the sparkling kitchen. "Thank you."

"It's the least I can do, as you've let me crash on your couch tonight."

"You can take my room."

"Absolutely not." She'd been waiting for this offer and answered him with her own rational argument. "I don't sleep for very long. And the second that storm clears, I'm going out to check the damage. You don't want me traipsing through here while you're trying to sleep. Or work." She motioned to his computer. "Speaking of which, how's the book coming along?"

"Butterfly Harbor's story is really coming together. I found a bunch of old books at the library, including one on the lighthouse itself. I had an interview with BethAnn Bromley a few days ago. Now, she's a character."

"That's true. I'd lay odds she has more information than most about this town."

"I've got a Mrs. Hastings and several others on my list for this week, and then I get to start snapping pictures."

"That's your favorite part, isn't it? What you can convey with a picture, no writer has ever evoked in me. Laughter, sorrow, grief or joy. You seem to have a knack for capturing it on film. Just raw, untouched, unfiltered emotion."

"If you've caught the true moment, you don't need to manipulate the image. Words can get in the way sometimes."

"Which is what you state on your website." She'd found her way online and lost track of the hours she'd spent looking at his photographs.

"Words are nice," he added. "Don't get me wrong. But I like the pictures to speak for themselves."

"That all sounds lovely. But that wasn't the book project I was talking about."

"Oh, yeah. That one." He looked over

at his computer and sighed. "I'm thinking maybe the fiction idea isn't such a great idea."

"Because you can't come up with an idea or because you're scared you will?"

Hunter rolled his head against the back of the sofa and looked at her. "Boy, you're tough, aren't you? We've gone days with barely a word to one another and then bam! All of a sudden you're calling me out on all sorts of things."

"Hey, you started it by kissing me."

That caught his interest, and he shifted to face her, linking their hands and bringing them up to his lips. Those amazing amber-accented eyes of his dancing as he watched her. "What did I start, exactly?"

"You know what you started." She would not give in. Not again. She would not surrender to that gravitational force that was Hunter MacBride and the smile that could heal any wound. "And it's not going to work. I'm damaged goods, Hunter."

"Damaged. Not destroyed."

"Obliterated," she corrected and, just to be clear, she set her cup down and mirrored his posture, eye to eye. Hand to hand. Knee to knee. There was no denying the attraction she felt for him—the first attraction she'd felt for any man since Sam had died, which made her even more leery of trusting herself. "I'm the last person you want to be involved with. And certainly the last woman who belongs around Phoebe. Don't go making a kiss into more than there ought to be."

"You mean I shouldn't be thinking how a white picket fence would look around this house?"

"That's not even remotely funny." But he'd made her heart stutter. "Let go of my hand." She tugged free, because the tingling of her skin was giving her goose bumps. "I appreciate that you were worried for me, but I'm not made for anything beyond friendship. With anyone. And even friendship is a stretch in most cases."

"You make it sound as if I'm planning on getting you down to city hall to have Gil Hamilton marry us."

Now she did shudder. "Heaven forbid."

Hunter's grin reemerged. "Was that a slight against Gil or marriage in general?"

"Hunter—"

"Tell me about these." He lifted his now free hand and stroked the side of her scarred face.

Now she caught his hand, which, as he re-twined their fingers, she realized was likely his goal from the start. "That's an ugly story you don't want to hear."

"Have you forgotten what I do, what I did, for a living? Where I've been? What I've seen?"

Again, she looked for something beyond understanding and compassion in his eyes, wanting to pounce on sympathy and pity. But he didn't give her that out. Near as she could tell, he wasn't giving her any out.

"Nothing you could tell me would shock me, Kendall. I've seen what war does to the human spirit, let alone the human body. Your scars represent a moment in your life, not a map of where you're going."

"Now who's getting therapeutic."

"Please, tell me."

Of all the events in her life, oddly enough perhaps, her scars didn't hold the most pain. Physically, the burn treatments and skin grafts had been hard to endure. But, honestly, they were no comparison to the pain she felt when she'd heard Sam had been killed on active duty, protecting the school when it came under attack. She'd known the instant he was gone. She'd…felt it. So by comparison, talking about her scars didn't bother her at all.

"There's nothing unique about what happened," she said finally. "A roadside bomb blew up and flipped the jeep I was riding in. The explosion killed most of our unit instantly. Matt and I were the only ones to survive. I'd been sitting closest to the gas tank and caught the brunt of the aftermath." She motioned to her face. "I think I was still on fire when Matt dragged me out, then subsequent gunfire hit his leg when he used his body to put out the flames. It's funny."

"What is?" Hunter trailed that finger down her arm, as if he could trace the scars beneath the sweatshirt she wore. Scars that reminded her each and every day that she was alive.

"Not funny ha-ha, but funny how our minds protect us from some things." And not from others. "I barely remember those first days. I was in and out of it so often, it's like I was never awake long enough to process the pain or the extent of what had happened. It was weeks after I'd been shipped home for treatment until I could finally begin to accept it. I don't know that I fully did until Matt wheeled himself into my room and asked me to take him dancing." The man who had lost the lower part of his leg was the one to push her toward healing.

She laughed now just as she'd laughed then. A laugh that had finally broken the pent-up emotions and had her and Matt crying and grieving over their fellow soldiers, their friends, their loved ones.

"I knew I liked that guy," Hunter said.

"These scars, I don't think of them much." She shrugged. "I used to worry that kids would be scared of me, but in an odd way, serving in Afghanistan, unlike other wars we've fought in—there's such an awareness of what happens or can happen to soldiers. It's an explanation that comes a lot easier these days, not even like when my father served. That said, I suppose it's a bit of a blessing to think that my parents never saw me this way. That's what worried me the most sometimes about going home, that my mom and dad would be hurt for me if I'd been injured. So." She shrugged, tried to push aside that thought. "I've never told anyone that before. Not even Matt." She brushed away the tears that escaped her control. "I miss them so much. And Sam, too."

"Do you have a picture of you and Sam?"

She shook her head. "Not with me. I have a storage unit back home in North Dakota. Where I have things from my grandparents and parents. I left it all there after the funeral. Asked the family lawyer to pack it all away. I wasn't ready. I'm still not. Even though that doesn't feel like my life anymore, you know? Or it's that I've lived a completely different one since then." She couldn't even carry a picture of her own fiancé. That's how weak she was. That's how...damaged she was. Even as the memories of Sam began to fade, she couldn't look at his photo. She didn't want to remember.

"You do realize that none of this is a turn-off, right?"

She couldn't help it. Kendall laughed. This man. Oh, this man. It would be so easy, so incredibly easy, to just let go of everything and surrender to what he was asking her to do. But that wasn't possible. She'd meant what she'd said earlier. She was damaged. Beyond repair. And no one, especially Hunter MacBride—let alone his niece—deserved to be saddled with her. "You're a good man, Hunter MacBride. And you make me feel…lighter."

"Always a good start." He lifted his hand to touch her hair, but she shied away.

"I meant what I said before, and I need you to hear me." She caught hold of him, held on tight. "I'm beyond the type of challenge you need. And while I know that sounds as if I'm playing hard to get, I'm not. I'm not capable of having those feelings for anyone anymore, Hunter. And to be perfectly honest, I don't want to." Because that meant risking the very tenuous hold on her new life. One she'd worked hard for. "But I might be okay being friends."

"I'm being friend-zoned?" Hunter groaned and dropped his head back, but not before she saw the flash of disappointment in his eyes. "You do know that's a death knell to a person's ego, right?"

"Oh, I think your ego can take it." She slipped off the sofa and picked up her mug to carry it over to the sink. When she turned, she found Hunter standing right behind her. He opened his arms and she stepped forward. She planted a hand on his chest to stop him even as part of her wanted to pull him closer.

Big mistake. Her fingers pressed harder until she felt the beating of his heart, the quick-time beating she knew was for her.

"If friendship is what you want, I'll take it." He dipped down slightly to catch her gaze. When she lifted her chin, met his challenge, he grinned. Before pressing his lips to hers. Not for long. For barely a breath. But long enough for her to lose hers. "But that doesn't mean I won't want to change your mind. Now how about you help me sort through my list of historic buildings in town so I can hit the ground running next week?"

"Sure." She patted his chest before he stepped away. "That I can do."

FOR THE FIRST time in weeks, Hunter slept. That deep sleep where everything inside him had a chance to reboot. Maybe it was the cathartic conversation he'd had with Kendall. Or maybe it was enough to know she was sleeping just outside Phoebe's bedroom, an unwitting sentry willing to turn his niece around should she attempt another midnight excursion.

With the sound of the wind and rain pummeling the carriage house, he dropped off, only to be awakened by the pattering of raindrops in what felt like the blink of an eye. He lay there, unmoving, for a long time, reacquainting himself with the laziness and relaxation that came after a good night's sleep. "Maybe I should call it the Kendall effect."

He pushed himself up, reaching for a T-shirt as he climbed out of bed. He scrubbed both hands through his hair, stifling a yawn as he crossed his bedroom, ready to encourage a typically sleepy and snuggling Phoebe out from under the covers.

He pulled open the door and froze. Phoebe wasn't only already up, she was dressed, bright-eyed and ready to conquer the still-stormy day. The blankets and pillow he'd given Kendall had been neatly folded and left on the corner of the sofa. The chill off the floor raced up his legs and had him shifting as he watched Kendall in the kitchen. She seemed to be assembling a collection of fruit to take to Phoebe, who was sitting at the kitchen table, cutting board and her own knife in hand.

Phoebe waved. Her smile plumped her cheeks, reaching her eyes.

"Okay, here you go. Oh, good morning." Kendall almost tripped on her approach to the table. Maybe it was the too-long, unrolled sweatpants he'd loaned her. Or maybe, given the surprise shining on her face, it was him. He was happy to accept option number two.

"Morning. What's going on?"

"Fruit salad for our pancakes." She scraped pineapple and bananas onto Phoebe's cutting board. "I can't guarantee perfection, but it should be edible."

"I'm sure it will be as soon as I've had my..."

"Coffee?" Kendall pointed to the pot. "It's already brewed." She returned to the counter and cracked some eggs into a measuring cup, set a skillet on the stove to heat. "Sleep okay?"

"Better than okay." She moved away, he noticed, when he scooted in beside her to claim his morning addiction. "You?"

"Better than expected." She wasn't lying.

The dark circles he'd become acquainted with seeing had faded a bit.

"Been up long?"

"A few hours. I hope you don't mind." She beat the eggs with a fork. "I was looking through some of those books you found at the library. The one on the lighthouse itself gave me a good feel for how the interior should be done."

"Happy to share." He reached around her and snagged a rogue chunk of pineapple. "A man could get used to this."

"A man shouldn't. You are looking at the extent of my cooking skills. And I'm talking about the eggs, not the pancakes. The storm's clearing."

"Is it?" Hunter walked around to pull open the door, stuck his head out. And came back in soaking wet. "Not from where I was just standing." He shook his head and sent water spraying over Kendall and Phoebe, who surprised him by giggling.

"The wind's died down, at least. I might be able to wiggle my way into the lighthouse and start taking some measurements."

"You mean you don't want to go traipsing

around town with me talking to residents about the good old days?"

"Ah, no. Besides, I'm on call to help Frankie and the chief with any repair work that needs doing around town."

"On call?"

"I'm on a list of volunteers with the fire department."

Of course she was. Was there nothing she couldn't do?

Hunter leaned against the kitchen counter and watched her. "Question. How can you be on call when you don't own a cell phone?"

"They just shine the bat signal in town." Kendall shrugged. "I have one of the radios from the sheriff's department. Matt calls me. Or Luke. Or whoever is around. Access to the radio is one of the reasons I need to get back into the house."

"I envy you, not being plugged in every second of the day on a cell. The darned things can be addictive."

"When blessings become curses. Hey, Phoebe, you done with those?" she asked.

Phoebe climbed off her chair and carried her cutting board over, offered it up. "Perfect. Thank you. Hunter, we have time before we eat if you want to get dressed."

"I guess I can't stop the day from starting, can I? Are we having toast, too?"

"Phoebe's chosen the menu so, yes. With Calliope's lavender honey." She motioned to the lavender gingham–topped jar sitting by the sink. "But hurry up. Before Phoebe and I finish it without you."

Phoebe giggled again.

KENDALL LET OUT a long breath once Hunter was back in his bedroom. Despite her determination to keep an emotional distance, the sight of him standing in his doorway a few moments ago, with his sleepy eyes and serious bed head, made her want to run her hands through his hair and kiss him good morning.

Despite the appearance of a well-organized breakfast chef, she was feeling off-kilter to say the least. She hadn't expected to sleep a wink, let alone more than five hours, longer than she'd slept in years, maybe. Waking up to find Phoebe sitting cross-legged on the floor beside her, back against the sofa as she read her book, should have paralyzed her.

Would have if she'd given in to the grief circling her from above.

But it was from above. The loss, that emptiness over Samira and Sam, was filling against her will. She didn't want to forget. She didn't want to move on, because moving on meant life was only going to smack her down again. But how could she turn her back on this little girl who so obviously needed her help?

What Phoebe needed was routine and hope. Both of which had been snatched from her six months ago. Hunter had gotten the ball rolling by showing her how much he cared and that he'd created a new life for himself by giving her a different life, one where there was a new adventure around every corner. Maybe it was time for them to…

Kendall had stopped the thought before it had time to settle. Nope. None of her business. They weren't hers. Phoebe wasn't her little girl, and Hunter wasn't anyone other than a friend she might listen to and steer in the right direction from time to time. Then she could get back to her own business. Her own job.

She glanced out the window to where the rain continued to fall. If only Mother Nature would get on board and leave Butterfly Harbor. She had a project to finish.

And a new town to find.

Phoebe tugged on Kendall's shirt, bringing her back to the present as the eggs sizzled in the pan. "What's that?"

Phoebe held up *Charlotte's Web*.

"Oh. You want me to read that to you?"

Phoebe nodded.

Hmm. "You know what? I think your uncle would really like to do that."

Phoebe's mouth twisted, and Kendall could read it on the little girl's face. She didn't believe that at all.

"Have you asked him?"

Phoebe shook her head.

"Maybe you should. Over breakfast. Just like you asked me, only maybe, out loud? He likes to do things that make you happy, Phoebe. And that would make you happy, wouldn't it?"

Phoebe nodded but still looked disappointed.

"I'll tell you what." Kendall bent down

so she could look Phoebe directly in the eyes. "You read *Charlotte's Web* with your uncle, and when you're done, I'll read one of your other books to you. How does that sound?"

Phoebe didn't answer. Instead, she pointed to the plant in the window that she'd given Kendall last night at dinner. "One of Samira's stories?"

"You, um, want me to read you something that Samira might have liked?"

"Yes, please."

"Um, sure. I guess I could do that." Kendall winced. She'd really walked into that one, hadn't she? "But only if you let your uncle read you *Charlotte's Web*." She held out her hand to seal the deal.

Phoebe scrunched her face, then accepted.

"Great. Now how about I put you in charge of the toast. I'm terrible with it," Kendall fibbed. "I burn it all the time. You good with that?"

She got another thumbs-up before Phoebe set her book down on Hunter's chair and went back to her chopping.

IF THERE WAS one thing the residents of Butterfly Harbor excelled at, it was coming together to get things done. Last year, the residents had brought a new food festival to town and then landscaped and refaced most of the distressed and abandoned homes in the area.

At Christmas, folks had put on one of the biggest celebrations ever seen when hometown girl Abby Manning had married celebrity chef Jason Corwin at the historic Flutterby Inn.

So it shouldn't have been too big a surprise that on this Sunday morning, post-storm, after Kendall had wedged herself through the broken window of the keeper's house for a change of clothes, she spotted a cavalcade of trucks and cars beelining for Liberty Lighthouse.

The panic swirled inside Kendall automatically. She may have made some progress over the last few months and perhaps more the last few days, but that didn't mean she was ready for…this. It looked like a parade of people advancing on her.

"Holy smokehouse pancakes, you really dodged a bullet, didn't you?" Abby called out. Abby Corwin, manager of the Flutterby, and resident pixie dust supplier, dropped out of her husband's car, her sneakered feet sinking an inch deep in mud. "Huh. Well. That's gross." She squelched her way over to Kendall's side. "Who would have thought you'd win for most damage in the storm?"

"I didn't know I was playing." Kendall couldn't help but frown. The sky hadn't only cleared, the storm had dragged a good dose of warmth behind it and bathed the town in unseasonable weather. She couldn't have asked for a better day to dispatch the tree and figured she and Frankie, and maybe one or two others, could make quick work of it. With this group, she'd be back inside in no time. "All of this wasn't necessary," Kendall told Abby, who stuck her finger and thumb in her mouth to whistle everyone over.

"Well, we weren't able to get in touch with you to warn you." Abby grinned in that way she had that prevented anyone from ever getting angry with her. "Alethea is going to be bringing the food truck around for lunch in a few hours. Jason's helping her get it stocked now. I don't think a day goes by I'm not grateful Xander's sister popped up in town. She's saved me ten times over and now Jason can relax a bit more. Oh, Holly's been put on booth rest—"

"Booth rest?" Kendall asked, darting out of the way as a uniformed deputy approached. "What's booth rest?"

"That's when Paige and Ursula allow her to come in to the diner but not to do any work. So she has to sit in a booth and fill saltshakers and ketchup bottles and wipe down menus. At least that was the plan." Abby frowned a bit. "I'm not sure she can fit in a booth these days. Those twins are growing every second. Do not tell her I said that," Abby warned.

"I wouldn't dare." Kendall couldn't stop looking at the deputy. He was tall-ish, not quite six foot, but his curly chestnut hair and lively brown eyes seemed oddly familiar. "Wow, is that Ozzy?" Kendall did a double take. It hadn't been that long since she'd seen the young deputy, had it? "I almost don't recognize you."

"All those carrots paid off." Matt trudged up behind him. "Kid's lost more than sixty pounds. He can almost outrun me now."

"A ferret can outrun you," Ozzy joked.

"Thanks, Kendall. Closest outlet?" He held up the industrial extension cord.

"I just installed an exterior one right at the edge of the tower." She pointed behind her. "Seriously, this is so unnecessary. I could have taken care of it. It's just one tree."

"More than that. Gil said we needed to install some safety fencing ASAP."

"Did he?" Kendall couldn't have been more surprised if Matt had shown up with a carnival troupe in tow.

"Word is he looked at our insurance policy on the place." Harvey Mills joined them. The older man had always reminded Kendall of her grandfather. Always ready and willing to pitch in and help. "Seems he can save a small fortune if we install it before renewal time."

"That's Gil, always thinking about the bottom line," Matt grumbled. "Which means our Sunday just got eaten up. But that's okay. Gives me a chance to check in with you. Kendall, you doing okay?" He drew her away once Abby darted off to help organize the fence crew and hand out safety goggles and gloves to those who would be cutting apart the fallen redwood.

"Yeah, I'm good." Kendall planted her hands on her hips and looked at busy activity around her. People, lots of people, swarmed about, offering smiles and waves as they passed. She waited for the surge of irritation, for the anger at feeling invaded, but nothing surfaced. "If all this pays off, I won't be off schedule more than a few days with the lighthouse."

"Right. Wouldn't want you to push back leaving, would we?" Matt quipped.

Guilt. The one emotion she hadn't anticipated feeling today, landed on her heavily as she glanced at her friend. "Matt—"

"Kinda sucked having to hear it from Gil, of all people. You really thinking of moving? I thought you liked it here."

"I do like it here. It's been great. It's just…" She glanced over to the carriage house as the door opened and Hunter came outside, Phoebe in his arms. They scanned the crowd. Her heart flipped in her chest, so hard and so fast she almost lost her footing. "It's complicated."

"Is it MacBride? I didn't pick up on any creep vibes from him. Did he do something? Say something…?"

"Don't be ridiculous," Kendall snapped. "If he had, I'd have taken care of it, but no. He's been great. They let me stay with them last night. When I couldn't get in here." She pointed to the house that had never felt as homey as the one Hunter had established within a few weeks.

"And you're okay with that? With Phoebe?"

"I wasn't." She cringed, was tempted to focus her attention on the ocean or on the growing pile of fencing being stacked by the cliff's edge. "It was hard at first, but then it was all right. She's not Samira." She'd told herself that hundreds of times since Hunter and Phoebe had first arrived, but she'd never once uttered the words out loud. Not until now. "Samira's gone. And so is Sam. Maybe I needed to be around Hunter and Phoebe to finally accept that."

"I am so sorry, Kendall." Matt reached out and laid his hand on her shoulder. He squeezed hard and she understood why. "All this time, all these years, and I don't know that I've ever told you how sorry I am."

"You didn't have to say the words, Matt." Kendall didn't hesitate to reassure him. "You stood by me every moment after. That said it all."

"Okay, you two look positively secretive over here." Lori came around the corner of one of the trucks. She'd traded in her typical maxidress for jeans and a T and tied her usually flowing hair up in a messy knot. Behind her came Sebastian Evans from Cat's Eye Bookstore and a tall, slender teen Kendall had seen around town. "Put us to work already."

"Actually." Kendall glanced over to where Hunter had sat down on the porch, clutching a nervous-looking Phoebe against his side. "I have a special project for you, Lori."

"Oh?" Lori asked.

"Yes. See that little girl over there? She's in need of some window boxes. Calliope sent the flowers. Now all they need is your special touch."

CHAPTER TEN

IT FELT AMAZING, Hunter thought, as he aimed and clicked his camera, to be documenting a community pulling together for a common cause. After years of photographing some of the worst kinds of horror, a zing of joyous excitement bounced through him like a pinball.

The two dozen or so people who spilled onto the property of the Liberty had divided into groups, more than half of whom were helping dig and set posts for the bright white crisscross PVC fence that would serve as a safety barrier for future visitors. Men and women, some of whom he recognized from around town, settled into an easy, organized collection of determined, almost jovial individuals. He caught a few sullen—or maybe they were just sleepy—teens, but also a few who were helping hand out safety equipment for the chain saws about to be put into action chopping up the enormous redwood.

Since Lori Knight was occupying Phoebe's attention, filling the empty window boxes hanging bare against the carriage house, Hunter was free to roam, capturing sweaty faces and wide-eyed grins.

"Do you want some water?"

Hunter turned and found Charlie Bradley, her broken-winged butterfly backpack slung onto her shoulders, two high pigtails sticking crookedly out of either side of her head. She held up a bag filled with bottled water.

"Hey, Charlie. Yeah, sure." He took one and cracked it open. "So they put you to work, too?"

"Yeah. Me and Simon—that's him over there." She dropped the bag long enough to point to a gangly-looking boy with big round glasses and a green superhero T-shirt handing out water from his own bag. "Our moms are on duty at the diner, so we said we'd come help. Are you going to want to see the caves I told you about?"

"I am, actually." Hunter stooped down, played with the lens on his camera before he aimed it at Charlie, who, as he expected, gave him an extra-wide gap-toothed smile big enough to fill the lens. "Now that's going to be perfect. How about next Saturday? I know you have school this week."

"We have half days on Thursday and Friday. We could go then. Simon can't, though. He goes to a smarty-pants school in a different town. I just go to regular school."

"Nothing wrong with regular school," Hunter told her. "I wish I could convince Phoebe to go."

"You mean she has a choice?" Charlie's mouth fell open. "That's not fair. How come?"

"Well." Hunter sat on the ground and bit back a smile when Charlie mimicked him. "See, Phoebe's mom, that was my sister, she and her husband died a little while ago. Phoebe was in school when it happened, and the police came to get her. She got really, really scared and now she doesn't want to go back."

"That's terrible." Charlie's eyes went wide. "And very sad. How old is she?"

"She's seven. She'll be eight in a few months."

"I'm gonna be nine on my next birthday. But that won't be until after Christmas. I'm sorry her mom and dad died. And I'm sorry your sister died."

"Thank you, Charlie." He could see she was. Oddly empathetic, this little girl seemed to be. "I appreciate that."

"Do you think maybe Phoebe would like a friend? I could be her friend. And maybe Stella and Marley can be, too. And Simon. And there's Kyle over there. And Mandy. She and Kyle like each other, but no one is supposed to know." She pressed a finger against her lips and rolled her eyes. "Older kids are so weird. They don't even want each other to know, but it's so obvious. They get all googly-eyed when the other isn't looking."

Hunter coughed to hide his laugh even as he felt his gaze pulled toward Kendall, who had suited up with the others and was revving up a chain saw. Everything inside him tightened, his breath hitching at the sight of her wielding that not insignificant piece of power machinery like a magic wand. When she sank the blade into the bulk of the tree, woodchips and sawdust flew up and around her, making her look like an odd fairy in the midst of casting a spell.

"It isn't just older kids," Hunter told Charlie then. "And in answer to your question, it would be great if you and Phoebe were friends. Even if you aren't the same age."

"Great. I'll go introduce myself again, and when she's done, we can hand out water together." She got to her feet and slung the bag over her arm. "Thanks, Mr. Hunter."

"Just Hunter is fine. Thanks again, Charlie."

Click. Click. Click, click, click.

He lowered the camera slightly as Kendall removed her hard hat long enough to wipe her arm across her brow, a now familiar smile breaking across her face. He could feel rather than hear her laugh as Matt Knight danced away to allow a group of younger men to push the cut disc out of the way.

He lost track of the time he spent, sitting on the barely there grass, feeling the dampness of the earth soaking into his jeans as he filled up roll after roll of film. When a butterfly, no, make that three butterflies, flitted around his hands, he froze. One settled on the edge of his lens, its wings beating slowly against the gentle spring breeze. "Calliope?"

"Close." Xander Costas came over and stood beside him. "Darned things have taken to following me now. Or maybe it's Stella." He pointed behind him as Stella ran toward Charlie, who was offering a skeptical-looking Phoebe a bottle of water. "How goes it?"

"Depends on what you mean by 'it.'" Hunter got to his feet and dug into his pocket for a new roll of film.

"Didn't realize anyone still used film," Xander said, then whistled when he got a better look at the downed tree. "Boy, that's a big one. They don't fall very often, but when they do—"

"They make a big bang. Believe me," Hunter told him. "Phoebe and I were in the house when it came down."

"I've been pushing for Gil to get the trees around here checked by an arborist. Maybe this will convince him."

"Kendall convinced him about the fence," Hunter told him. "Maybe you should have her ask him."

"Good idea. She is becoming a bit of a secret weapon. Speaking of a secret weapon, I wanted to talk to you about a job."

"Oh?" Hunter wound up the film, pulled it free, then loaded a new roll. How he loved that satisfying click when the cylinders caught. "Like I've told Kendall, I'm not much good with tools. I used to stink at building with Legos."

Xander laughed. "Nothing like that. I'm in the process of rebuilding Costas Architecture into Costas Architecture and Construction. We had a rough few years, and well, I'm taking things in a different direction now that I'm the one in charge."

"Okay." Hunter wasn't entirely sure what this had to do with him.

"The butterfly sanctuary is going to be my first major project in over a year. And, honestly, it's the first project I've ever overseen myself. I was thinking about hiring you to photograph the progress, create a story almost, of what happens along the way from start to finish. I thought maybe I could hire a video producer to turn it into a promotional bit for the website or a PowerPoint presentation… Actually, I'm not entirely sure what I'm thinking. Would you be interested?"

"Ah. Wow." Hunter blinked. "Maybe, yeah. Any idea how long the project is going to take?"

"We hope to have it done by migration season next year. Could be sooner. Not sure. I'm thinking of taking you on as an employee, maybe as one of my marketing consultants, which would be salaried, of course. I could guarantee maybe two years. More depending on what comes down the pipeline. I know you're used to traveling a lot, and there could be some of that. Depending on how this project turns out. I think we'd work well together."

Hunter wasn't entirely sure what to say. "Can I take a little time to think about it? I need to consider Phoebe and living arrangements and, well, some other things."

"Sure. We're officially breaking ground on Thursday. If you say yes, that would be your first day. We could get the before shots after the official ceremony."

Hunter chuckled. "That was Gil's idea, wasn't it?"

"The guy is all about showmanship and promotion." Xander shook his head. "Gotta believe there's a decent guy in there deep down. At least that's what Calliope keeps telling me. So, let me know by Wednesday?"

Three days to decide whether to put

down semi-permanent roots? Hunter found his gaze pulled back to Kendall, only this time, when he found her, he saw her watching him. When their eyes met, she smiled.

"You know what?" Hunter was tired of overthinking things. Once upon a time he used to live for the rush of spur-of-the-moment decisions. "I don't need time to think about it. I'll take the job."

IT WAS DIFFICULT, Kendall realized as she snatched a bottle of water out of the inflatable pool cooler, to find a bit of silent refuge. The initial shock that came with the crowd invading what was her usual bit of isolated paradise in Butterfly Harbor had worn off ages ago. About the time she sliced off her first hunk of redwood and looked up to find Hunter's gaze on her, which left her quaking in her work boots.

She tried to remember the last time a man had looked at her that way, as if she was the only light in an endless void. She'd smiled because she hadn't thought better of it. But now, with time to actually think about what was going on around her, she didn't have a choice and could recall nothing else. She needed some quiet, some peace. That would help sort out her feelings. If only for a few minutes.

Doing a quick survey of the crowd still busy at work, she found herself walking past the motor home and settling against the far side of the building. She slid down the wall, knees tight to her chest, where she could turn her head slightly and see the ocean beyond the cliffs. She drank her water in record time, closed her eyes and took a long, deep breath.

In the years since Sam and Samira had died, she'd found herself locked into an unbreakable circle of loss and grief. Reminding her over and over again that she was alone. It was as if her mind couldn't move beyond that worst day of her life.

Talking with Hunter about them had changed a lot, so much so that she wondered if she'd ever really grieved them properly. That perhaps all this time she'd been grieving the life she'd lost. The future, the family she'd been counting on.

The tears burned hot and thick in her throat, but this time she didn't try to stop them. She let them flow until they soaked her shirt, mingling with the sweat of determination to fix something. Make something, anything, whole again.

Something inside her had broken open these last few weeks, like an eggshell cracked in just the right spot. It wasn't just seeing Phoebe, a little girl who looked so much like Samira. Nor was it Hunter, who with his charming smile and easygoing attitude had drawn her out of her herself. It had taken both of them for her to find the courage to step back and see what her life could still be.

Kendall shook her head, squeezed her eyes shut and gritted her teeth as she tried to drag an image of Sam up from the depths of her memory. An image that no matter how hard she tried, became superimposed with that of another man. A man who had the unbelievable ability to make a bitter, angry woman like her laugh.

"There you are."

Kendall's heart did that little dance again, the one that had her glancing up into the tree-obscured blue sky. "Really?" She couldn't help but ask Sam, because only he would have such timing.

"Really what?" The next thing she knew, Hunter was sitting beside her, a camera that looked as if NASA had invented it clutched between his hands. "You talking to yourself now?"

"No." There it was. That irresistible urge to smile. How did he do that? "No, actually, I was talking to Sam."

"Ah."

Kendall watched him closely for resentment or irritation or an indication her talking about her dead husband offended him. But there wasn't a hint of any of that. If anything, his eyes brightened.

"You said he wanted to be a teacher."

"Grade school science."

"High school sweethearts, huh?"

"You really do pay attention to what people say, don't you?"

"Part of the job." Hunter shrugged, and stretched out his legs. He set his camera on his lap, and, like it was the most natural and normal thing in the world, he reached out and slipped his fingers through hers.

As if he were some sort of blast furnace, her entire body warmed. And in that moment she wondered if this man had the power to do the impossible and thaw her heart.

"Tell me something else about him."

"Sam?" His name came out like a croak.

"Yep. Tell me about the first time you met. No, wait. The first time you saw him."

"First day of freshman year of high school." The memory came fast, whooshing her back to the bustling halls, the sounds of slamming lockers, goading teases and the smell of palpable teenage angst. "He had his nose stuck in a book and was walking down the hall. He walked straight into a halfway-open classroom door." A bubble of laugher rose up and escaped. "Almost broke his glasses."

"Glasses, huh? A bit of a geek then?"

"Oh, he was king of the geeks. One of his books had slid across the hall and stopped at my feet. Stephen Hawking's *A Brief History of Time*." She still had that book. In that storage unit back home. "I hunted him down later that day, after he'd been to the nurse's office. Instead of thanking me, he went on this diatribe about how Hawking's theory changed his life and had I ever read it and if I did could he talk to me about it over lunch because no one else he knew had ever read it before."

"Hawking, huh?" Hunter chuckled. "Now that's a pickup line I've never thought of."

"I don't think he meant it as one, but it worked. I had stars in my eyes from that moment on. Pun intended."

Hunter smiled. "How long did it take him to ask you out on a date?"

"I asked him. If I'd left it up to him, it never would have happened." Kendall could still see the expression on Sam's round, bespectacled face as he'd blinked in confusion. "It took me a good few months, but I asked him to go ice skating with me. I might have fibbed a little and said I didn't know how."

"But you did."

"Of course," Kendall scoffed. "It was North Dakota. Most of us are born with skates on our feet. Sam was a transplant, by the way. He spent the first twelve years of his life in Florida. Man never did learn how to skate. I was going to teach him as soon as we got…home."

"You made the choice to go into the service together?"

"Absolutely. Both our dads were military.

It made sense and the army gave him a lot of options to put that brain of his to use. And he wasn't about to let me go without him. We decided we'd make it work." But it hadn't. Not in the end.

"He sounds like a nice guy."

"He was." Kendall nodded as some of the bitterness flaked away from her heart. "He really was. Thank you."

"For?"

"For asking about him. For listening. For..." She broke off, struggling for the right words. "Thank you for being my friend."

"I'll be anything you want me to be, Kendall Davidson." He looked into her eyes as he lifted their joined hands and pressed his lips against her battered knuckles. "Are you done hiding?"

"I haven't been hiding."

"Please." Hunter rolled his eyes in the same way his niece tended to. "Not that I blame you. That's a lot of people who turned up. But I'm hungry, and word has it Flutterby Dreams is sending a food truck."

"Flutterby on Wheels." Kendall laughed at his bemused expression. "Jason's latest brainstorm. Now that he has Alethea as an apprentice, he's putting her to use. And she's good. Really good. Maybe." Kendall pushed herself up and pulled him with her. "Maybe even better than Jason."

"Not possible." Hunter tightened his hold when she loosened hers. "Not that I've ever had the privilege of eating at one of his restaurants, but I have heard tell."

"You don't have any excuse not to while you're here. And you know a few people now with an in. You can eat there anytime you want."

"Great. When do we go?"

"Hold up." Kendall skidded to a stop, she'd caught a glimpse around the corner of three little girls huddled together. She motioned for Hunter to be quiet.

"It's too bad you can't come to school, Phoebe." Charlie Bradley's voice rang nice and clear over the crashing waves. "We'd have so much fun at lunchtime. We hang out at the library a lot. You could come with us."

A gentle tinkling of bells chimed in the air.

"Do you like my bells?" Stella Jones asked. "I just learned to do them myself. Calliope used to do them. I could do yours, too, if you want. But it would have to be next weekend because I get awfully busy with school."

"Are they..." Hunter pushed forward to get a better look at the girls. "Are they trying to con my niece into going to school?"

"With Charlie, anything's possible." Kendall bit the inside of her cheek.

"Your uncle says you're pretty smart," Charlie was saying. "I bet you're even smarter than Simon, and he gets to go to a supersmart school. Oh, there you go! See! The butterfly likes you!"

They watched Phoebe carefully cup her small hands around the insect and hold it up to the sky.

"Simon's school is for gifted students," Kendall explained. "From what I hear, he could be in the running to be a real-life supervillain genius. The kid was hacking computers just a few years ago. Luckily, his mother married the sheriff and put an end to his criminal reign. I think."

"I should have come here years ago. This place is ripe with story potential."

"Agreed."

"Hey, careful." Hunter caught her around the waist when she backed up into his space.

Kendall swallowed hard, gripped Hunter's shoulder as she found herself mere inches from him. "Sorry." Why did she always feel as if fireworks were happening whenever she was around him?

"Wouldn't want to invade the friend zone." Hunter smiled at her. A gentle hand came up to tuck a stray strand of hair behind her ear. "Thank you for telling me about Sam, Kendall."

All she could do was nod. She should move away. Before she forgot that bad things happened to people she cared about. Before he kissed her again. Before she kissed him. She licked her lips and tried to ignore how his arm had settled around her.

"That's not playing fair," he murmured as that hand shifted and he stroked his finger across his lips. "So when are we going to dinner?"

"Huh?"

"At the Flutterby. If I can find a babysitter for you know who, will you go with me?"

"Hunter." She would have closed her eyes, would have lowered her chin, would have pulled free if his face wasn't so fascinating. If she didn't want to say yes so badly. Now

Sam's face flashed before her—smiling, encouraging, happy. He'd been safe. From the beginning with Sam she knew he was safe, that he'd never hurt her. That he'd always be there when she needed him. Supportive, kind, staid Sam.

But Hunter? Hunter was different. Kissing Hunter was like walking in a lightning storm, charged, tempting and uncertain of what would happen next.

"I'll make you a deal," she managed and tried to ignore that his skimming finger almost created sparks against her cheek. "You find a Phoebe-approved babysitter, and I'll have dinner with you. But only if she's Phoebe approved. Deal?"

Hunter grinned. "Deal."

CHAPTER ELEVEN

HUNTER HAD BEEN staring at the cursor blinking on his laptop for the better part of an hour. The evil little digital gremlin was mocking him, demanding to know what made him think he could write a single word anyone else would want to read.

After Phoebe had gone to bed last night, he'd retreated into the motor home and developed the pictures he'd taken a few days ago. Those images, a good percentage of which featured Kendall, continued to spin in his head, bringing a smile to his face as he'd witnessed what made Butterfly Harbor so special to so many.

The fallen redwood had been hauled away in chunks. The new fence provided a protective barrier that eased a bit of Hunter's apprehension and he'd learned that you could find some of the best food around on four wheels. By the end of the day, many things had become clear: he and Phoebe had been welcomed into the community without a second thought, and Phoebe, finally, had made some friends. He didn't regret for a second accepting the job from Xander Costas. But if he was going to make the semi-permanent move to Butterfly Harbor, he had a lot of work to do. Beginning with getting this book proposal off his shoulders once and for all. If only he had a character, someone unique, someone different that people could relate to, perhaps be leery of, believe in. Someone like…

Movement out of the corner of his eye had him spinning in his chair. "Phoebe, what are you doing up?" He glanced at the clock. "It's only five in the morning."

She shrugged.

"Couldn't sleep?" Yeah, he knew the feeling. Every time he closed his eyes, all he saw, all he felt, was Kendall in his arms. Phoebe hugged a book against her chest, then held it out to him. "What's this?"

"Will you read to me?"

His heart twisted. "Of course. You want me to read *this* book?"

Phoebe nodded, but uncertainty hovered on her little face.

"Now?"

She nodded again, grabbed his hand and tugged him over to the sofa. Nonexistent book proposal forgotten, Hunter let himself fall into Phoebe's world. He sat down, a wave of love washing over him when Phoebe snuggled against him.

"You sure you aren't hungry? You want breakfast—"

She tapped her fingers on the book, shook her head.

"Okay, here we go." He flipped open the book and brushed his fingers over the note written on the title page. He cleared his throat. "'For my Phoebe. My best and brightest girl. I will always be right over your shoulder. Love, Mom.'"

Phoebe hiccupped and Hunter took a moment to wrap his arm around her and press his lips to the top of her head. "She loved you so much, kiddo." He squeezed his eyes shut to bank the tears. "So. Let's do this, okay?

"*Charlotte's Web.* Chapter One..."

WITH ONLY SOME of the paint she'd ordered for the lighthouse exterior waiting for her at the hardware store—she didn't want to start until she had all she'd need—Kendall busied herself evaluating the original hardwood floor of the Liberty. Her initial cursory inspection had led her to believe she would have to replace the planks, but now she was thinking she would only have to pull up maybe a dozen or so on each level. She had plans to visit a maritime salvage yard to try to find old ship wood she could cut to size.

Thanks to Hunter's hard work delving into the library archives, she'd been able to see photographs, grainy though they might be, of how the Liberty had looked more than a hundred years before. If she could restore it to that era, what great tourist appeal that might have. "Great. Now you're starting to sound like Gil."

She started toward the wrought iron spiral staircase, ran her hand around the rusted spots she'd be tackling soon. Boy, this place was going to look amazing when it was finished.

A knock on the door had Kendall calling out, "Yeah! Come on in!" She removed the pencil from her mouth when she saw Calliope enter, a gigantic, overflowing basket tucked in the crook of her arm.

Today's dress was the color of ripe oranges—not a color most people, especially redheads, could pull off, and yet the swirling dress suited her to perfection.

"Morning," Kendall said.

"Afternoon," Calliope corrected with a small smile. "Losing track of time again, I see?"

"Uh, yeah." Kendall frowned and walked over to the window that overlooked the carriage house. She hadn't seen a sign of Hunter or Phoebe this morning. "Afternoon? Really?" Was everything okay with them?

"Really. I hope you don't mind, but I brought all of you more food. I understand Phoebe is a big fan of vegetables? Stella filled me in last night."

"Kid's a regular rabbit." Kendall shuddered. "No offense to your bounty, but I can only eat so many carrots before I want to start hopping."

"Which is why I brought cucumbers and cauliflower this time. You know..." Calliope walked the perimeter of the room, drawing her finger along the wide mantel of the stone hearth situated against the wall that connected the tower to the keeper house. "I haven't been here since I was a girl. It's exactly how I remember it."

"I hear you told Hunter the legend. You don't really believe..." Kendall trailed off, remembering who she was talking to. "Never mind. Of course you do."

"The Liberty has helped many hearts find one another," Calliope said. "To make up for the one that was lost. I would think you of all people would understand that."

"Me of all people," Kendall repeated and got out her tape measure.

"Xander might have mentioned how happy you looked the other day. I'm sorry, not just Xander. I also spoke to Abby this morning and Lori when I stopped by the Flutterby. They had some very nice things to say about Hunter, as well."

"Well, sure, Hunter I can understand." The guy just radiated positivity, while she might as well have been the grumpy old lighthouse keeper from some scary black-and-white movie. "Don't read anything into it, Calliope. Really, it's nothing."

"But how is your heart feeling these days, Kendall?"

"My heart?"

"It's been heavy for a while. A long while." Calliope turned to her, inclined her head in that way she had that made Kendall suspect Calliope could see her soul. "I don't feel that from you anymore. You seem...lighter."

"Busier, maybe." Talking about Sam with Hunter was one thing. It was a safe topic with a built-in "don't cross this line." But she wasn't up to talking about her feelings with anyone else. Not even the perceptive—if not sympathetic—Calliope. "I have a lot to do before I move on."

"Ah." Calliope sighed. "So that's what I see hovering. You're planning to leave us, even though you don't want to."

"It's not a matter of want. And this isn't fair. I can't stay here, Calliope." She pushed the words out beyond the doubts she felt. "Things are getting too complicated. Too busy. Too—"

"Intimate?" Calliope finished for her. "Yes, building a new life, making new friends, falling in love again. I can imagine that's scary for you. No wonder you want to run away."

Anger sparked low in her belly. "I'm not running away." And she was *not* falling in love.

"Aren't you? Word is Gil wants to hire

you to restore more buildings in town. Structures that need a kind, understanding, logical touch. That would mean stability for you for quite a while, Kendall. And yet you haven't accepted."

"Because I can't stay." Why was she having this conversation? With Calliope Jones Costas? The only person she owed any explanation to was Matt, and even he had understood when they'd discussed it. Well, he'd mostly understood. And how had Calliope found out about that offer, anyway?

"You can do whatever you want to do, Kendall." If anything, Calliope's voice only gentled further. "But I wonder when this idea to leave first presented itself. If I had to put my finger on it, I'd say it was when a certain man and his adorable niece arrived in town."

"Now you're crossing a line. This is my business, Calliope. Mine." Kendall didn't want to lose her temper, but the irritation began to bubble. "I know what I need. And I know what I…don't." The door of the carriage house burst open and Phoebe raced out, black curls bouncing and swirling around her head, the bright yellow unicorn shirt she wore glowing beneath the sun. Kendall found herself smiling in spite of herself, wanting to laugh at the joy she saw on Phoebe's face as she dived onto the swing Kendall had made for her. And she gasped at the sound of the little girl's laughter dancing on the wind. The anger faded as her heart split into two. In the time it took her to breathe, she knew the truth. "I can't do this."

"Do what?" Calliope asked, a gentle hand coming to rest on Kendall's shoulder. "Love again?"

The idea of loving Hunter, loving that little girl, of opening herself up to the possibility of losing her, losing anyone again—it would end her. "Everyone I've ever loved has died, Calliope. And with such pain and violence they've left a hole inside me. My grandparents, my parents. My friends in the army. Sam." Her breath hitched. "Don't ask me to try to fill that hole, Calliope. Not when all I'll bring someone is excruciating pain."

"Oh, my friend." Calliope wrapped her arms around her and held on tight. "You've never brought me any pain. Irritation, perhaps. Annoyance, certainly. And having you here has helped Matt heal parts of himself he didn't realize were bruised. You've made a home here, Kendall. Whether you want to admit it or not. Lori needs you. Kyle needs you. Holly, Abby, Luke, Ozzy, they all need you, too, and those never-stay-put-for-a-minute seniors in the Cocoon Club who believe you're a remodeling genius.You're a part of this place now. Running away won't do anyone any good except prevent you from ever moving beyond your loss."

Her loss. It sounded so…selfish. As if she was the only person in the world who had ever lost someone she loved. She'd always worried what would happen to Sam if she had been killed; how could she not when they were soldiers fighting in a war? But never once had it crossed her mind to ask the opposite. Never once did she think she'd be the one left behind. And now, years later, she still couldn't see beyond that loss, a loss that thousands of people survived every day. Transformed forever, changed forever, but they went on. And they lived. Somehow, some way, they found a way to live.

"The universe doesn't put anything in front of us that it doesn't believe we can't handle," Calliope whispered. "It's not a coincidence these two people arrived when they did, Kendall. But not because you were ready, because they were. Yes, I believe these two can help heal wounds even you don't see, but have you ever stopped to think that maybe you could heal theirs?"

Tears choked her, and she shook her head. "Who would want me to—"

"Maybe there's been help from the beyond. It's time you accept that no matter how much you wish it to be otherwise, you are most certainly loved. Unconditionally. And there's absolutely nothing you can do about it."

HUNTER DIDN'T HEAR the knock on the door. From the moment he'd turned the last page on *Charlotte's Web*, he knew what he had to write. The idea, the character, had exploded, full bore, in his head and formed as he'd held a sobbing Phoebe in his arms.

Kendall had been right. His niece had been stuck, with half a broken heart hanging in the balance. Until she knew the rest of the story, there was no healing possible. He couldn't remember Phoebe ever crying this much. This deeply. This painfully. So painfully her agony had seeped into him. The tighter he'd held her, the more she'd sobbed, but eventually, the pain eased. Phoebe quieted, and she'd gone lax in his arms, still cuddled into him as if it was the only place she felt safe. He didn't know if she'd fallen asleep. It didn't matter. The minutes, the hours ticked by until she sat up, gave him a hug, then scrambled off to get dressed for the day.

"Wait!" Hunter bent down to pick up the book that had fallen to the floor. "Don't you want this?"

Phoebe froze, her eyes narrowing and then widening as her smile did. She pivoted and pointed to the bookcase next to his desk. Then she'd raced into her bedroom and closed the door.

And so he'd placed that book on the top shelf, between his own beloved copies of *Hitchhiker's Guide to the Galaxy* and *The Stand.* He'd fixed her scrambled eggs and sliced tomatoes, had toast and peanut butter himself, then, as she darted outside to play on her swing, he'd sat down at his desk.

And began to write.

His fingers flew over the keyboard, possessed by the idea of a woman who spent years mired in grief, blaming herself, cutting herself off from everything that had happened around her. A woman who threw herself into a life she'd never expected to live and with a child she never expected to have as the wind and rain and storms battered the home that by default, had become hers. The lady of Liberty Lighthouse sang to him, cried to him and settled inside him with an ease and satisfaction that soothed the swirling emotions he couldn't begin to sort through. He knew who she was; he knew how she felt. She was him. She was Phoebe. She was…

She was Kendall.

"Hunter?"

He jumped in his chair as her hand landed on his shoulder.

"I'm sorry." Her laugh lightened his heart. "You didn't answer when I knocked so I came on in. I hope that's— Oh!"

He leaped to his feet and swept her into

his arms, lowering his mouth to hers before he could think it through. Never mind the friend zone, she'd turned on every light in his darkened soul, and he was never going to stop trying to thank her for it. "I got it."

"Got what? Whatever it is, don't give it to me."

He was holding her feet off the ground, his arms tight around her waist as she linked her hands behind his head. She pressed her forehead against his, an odd and unfamiliar look of peace on her face when she whispered the question.

"The story. The character. It's there. All there. In my head. And it's because of you."

"I didn't do anything."

"You are so wrong. Do you know what Phoebe and I did this morning?"

She shook her head.

"We read *Charlotte's Web*. By the way, Charlotte dies in the end. Are you kidding me?"

Kendall winced, her lips twitching. "Oh, I probably should have warned you about that."

"No, no, you shouldn't have. It opened the

floodgates, Kendall. Phoebe, she's different. She's…happy. Look? She asked me to put it away. She's not going to drag it around with her anymore. She's moved beyond it. Just like you said she would."

"I suggested. There was no guarantee."

"Sure, but I'm not going to ask for everything at once. She cried, Kendall. She cried for her mom and her dad and everything in between. And then she ran off like a typical little girl, got dressed and went out to play." He kissed her again because he needed to. And because she seemed to need him to. "You are amazing."

"If you say so." She didn't look convinced. "Calliope is here. I think she might be plying Phoebe with more vegetables."

"Really?" Hunter sighed. "Why can't she like chocolate like every other kid? I guess maybe I'd best check and see what's for dinner."

They found Calliope stretched out on the ground beside where Phoebe was swinging back and forth, head thrown back, almost flipping completely over. Calliope was waving her hand gently as if conducting an orchestra.

"Careful!" Hunter warned.

"She's fine." Calliope lowered her hand, and Phoebe came to a gliding halt. "I was just telling Phoebe that Stella would like her, Charlie and Marley to come to a sleepover Thursday night. Since it's a halfday at school and Friday is a teacher's meeting, it seems ideal."

"Thursday night, you say?" Hunter slipped an arm around Kendall's waist and tugged her close. "That would mean she'd be ensconced with a babysitter."

Phoebe didn't look pleased with that phrase.

"That is exactly what it would mean," Calliope confirmed. "I hope maybe the two of you can find something to keep yourselves occupied. Maybe dinner and a night out on the town? They're having a run on Humphrey Bogart movies at the theater."

"Quick, favorite Bogie movie," Hunter asked Kendall.

"*The Big Sleep*," Kendall responded immediately.

"Oh, so close. *Maltese Falcon*."

"You're both wrong. It's *The African Queen*," Calliope said with a sigh as she pushed herself up. "Well, I'm off. Must get back to the farm. Xander asked if you'd meet him tomorrow at the sanctuary site, Hunter. Eight a.m."

"What for?" Kendall asked.

"I didn't get a chance to tell you. I've got a new job. Xander hired me to photograph the butterfly sanctuary build and maybe some other projects down the line. So it looks like we'll be sticking around Butterfly Harbor for a while. That sound okay to you, Phoebe?"

But he wasn't looking at his niece. He was looking at Kendall for some kind of hint, some clue as to how she felt about him, about them, sticking around.

"That's great news, congratulations." True to form, Kendall's words and expression refused to reveal her true feelings. Personally, he was beginning to love the idea; he'd never settled anywhere for long, and besides, if anything was going to tempt Phoebe into returning to school, it was seeing Charlie and Stella enjoying their days of education.

"Thanks. But eight in the morning? Um, yeah." He scrubbed a hand across his face. "I can make that work. I just have to figure out what to do with Phoebe."

"I'll watch her." Kendall's offer sounded more strained than he might have liked.

Phoebe gasped and launched herself off the swing, landing squarely in front of Kendall, a huge smile on her face. "Yes!"

"I don't know," Hunter hedged for fun and earned a glare from his niece. "You really want to do that, Phoebs? I might be gone most of the day. You'd have to be awfully good for a really long time."

"Phoebe never has to be anything more than Phoebe." Kendall reached out and brushed her hand over Phoebe's hair. "We'll be fine, won't we?"

KENDALL BLAMED CALLIOPE for the fact that she couldn't sleep. What had that woman done to her that she'd all but thrown herself into Hunter's arms and then offered to watch Phoebe during the day while he worked?

Not that Kendall could have talked to Hunter about it. How could she when, after Calliope had left, he had withdrawn back into the house to finish writing whatever he needed to submit to his agent. If he could just get that marked off his list, he told her, things would even out.

She hadn't been able to resist the excitement on his face when Phoebe had whispered something into his ear. Calliope had raised her face to the sun as if in silent thanks and then swirled off in a flash of color and a tinkling of bells.

But now, alone within the confines of the repaired keeper house, Kendall stared blankly up at the ceiling, counting her breaths, in and out. In and out. And wishing that darkness, that void she'd clung to for so long, would come back. She knew how to function with it hovering around her; now, she was in the unknown, both terrified and excited for what life might have in store.

She also couldn't contain the restlessness that had taken up residence, as if something wasn't quite right. Either with her or with Hunter or…maybe it was just her imagination. Throwing off the sleeping bag, Kendall rolled onto the floor, popping up despite the aching in her back. Might just be time for a new bed, she told herself. The thin mattress wasn't cutting it anymore. And actually, as she looked around, she realized the place could really do with some more furniture. Maybe a small sofa. Or a comfy chair to curl up in and read. Just a few creature comforts to make this place a bit more homey.

She checked her watch. Three a.m. Way too early to be working on the lighthouse without making a racket. But something called to her. Something warm and comforting and…outside.

Kendall pulled open the door and inhaled the welcoming, cool breeze. Barefoot this time, and forgoing Hunter's jacket she still had hanging on a peg in the kitchenette, she walked over to the scaffold. One hand wrapped round the solid piping, she hauled herself up. And climbed to the top.

If she'd needed any proof that Phoebe was one of the smartest children she'd ever met, she had it now. The instant she sat on the plank, dangled her legs over the side and stared up at the waning moon, her mind began to clear. And the heaviness around her heart began to lift.

"Is Calliope right, Sam? Did you send them here?" The wind kicked up and whipped her hair against her face. It was official. Butterfly Harbor had become her home. Why else would she accept Calliope's explanation and advice as truth? Her friend had a way of cutting through all the pain, all the junk, and pushing right to the problem.

In war, fear had been her constant companion. But not one that prevented her from acting, one that had served as a guidepost, an extension of her conscience that somehow kicked into overdrive. As a soldier she knew what had to be done. It was in her training; it roared through her blood. In an odd way, even in those moments after the accident, she hadn't given in to the fear. She'd embraced it. Wrapped herself in it, because once she did that, nothing else could hurt her. Fear, for her, became a kind of blanket of acceptance. What was she saying? Feel the fear and do it, anyway? Somehow a sniper's bullet seemed less terrifying than risking her heart again, but she was only now accepting what Calliope seemed to already understand: she was falling in love with Hunter MacBride.

CHAPTER TWELVE

KENDALL'S NERVES DIDN'T come close to settling the next day. She half expected her work to slow to a crawl since she'd volunteered to keep an eye on Phoebe, but Kendall soon learned the little girl was more than capable of helping with the smaller tasks.

Kendall took the time to explain what the different tools were, what they did and how things were set up. She made certain Phoebe wore her safety goggles at all times, since Kendall was never entirely sure what they'd be tackling next. Eventually Kendall had set her up at the tower with a small roller and her own tray of recently arrived paint. She also made sure Phoebe was wearing some of her older clothes, since no doubt the mess she'd make would be extensive.

Kendall was looking forward to finishing this exterior part of the project. The railing pieces that would line the tower walkway, or gallery, as she'd learned it was called, had been ordered, as had the new lantern, clock and double-paned wind-resistant glass that would encase both. She'd been studying the intricacies of lighthouse construction, right down to the number of recommended vents to the various lightning rods available.

Saturated paint roller in hand, Kendall made quick work of a good portion of the exterior well before noon. Phoebe, just as she was chopping her favorite vegetables, seemed to focus on the task at hand. When Kendall climbed down the scaffold to retrieve a new can of paint, she found Phoebe had exceeded her area and had moved under the scaffold, painting far more than Kendall had expected.

"This looks great, Phoebe." Kendall came along beside her as Phoebe ran her roller in the crisscrossing motion Kendall had demonstrated. "You good to keep going for a bit? Then we need to head into town and go to the hardware store. We could go to the diner for lunch if you want?" Kendall could count the number of times she'd eaten at the Butterfly Diner on one hand; she normally did takeout, but these next few weeks weren't about her, they were about getting Phoebe acclimated to this town and surreptitiously encouraging her to be with her new friends, and even go to school. "And I believe I owe you a trip to the bookstore. We made a deal, remember?"

Phoebe nodded, her paint-spattered face glowing with happiness. She pointed to the still-to-be-painted door of the lighthouse.

"You'll be done when you get to there?"

Another nod.

"Sounds like a plan." She then stopped. What looked like a whole community of butterflies flew by and up, up, up into the sky.

Kendall was awestruck and glanced over at Phoebe. "Did you see that?"

She looked up, but the butterflies had disappeared.

"Must be my imagination," Kendall grumbled. "Ignore me. I'll be back down in a bit, okay?" She grabbed a new bucket of paint and headed up the scaffold.

A little after noon, showered and changed into something more presentable, Kendall helped Phoebe clean up. They hunkered into the bathroom while Kendall tried to scrub the paint splatter off Phoebe's nose, which earned her a stream of little girl giggles that acted as an unexpected balm on her heart. They unearthed a collection of new T-shirts Hunter had been buying up for her and chose a bright blue one that stated she was a "little girl with big dreams."

She'd have thought the walk into town would be boring and the conversation one-sided, but Phoebe surprised her with efficient one- and two-word responses, each of which made Kendall feel as if she'd won some sort of prize. Because Kendall wanted Phoebe to feel more a part of the town, she took a detour to show her the yellow cottage where Charlie lived and the beautiful monarch butterfly stained glass window above the carved front door.

Phoebe made a C with one of her hands and pointed at the house just as a series of barks erupted from inside. Before they could move on, the door popped open and Paige Bradley came out, looking like the personification of sunshine and roses on what must have been a day off from the diner.

"Hello, you two." If Paige seemed surprised to see Kendall escorting Phoebe about, she didn't let on. "Perfect time for a break. I was just finishing up some paperwork for my nursing license. You ready for the big sleepover tonight, Phoebe?"

Phoebe gripped the hem of Kendall's shirt and drew closer. "Yes."

The three of them glanced down the street as Charlie raced around the corner on her bike, red pigtails flapping in the breeze. Phoebe let out a loud sigh, one that caught both Kendall's and Paige's attention but, both understanding that pushing the little girl wouldn't do any good, they only looked at each other in silence when Charlie skidded to a halt at the gate.

"Three-day weekend!" She straddled the bar and raised her arms in triumph. "Woohoo!"

"You'd never know she loves her teacher, would you?" Paige joked. "We were just talking about the sleepover, Charlie."

"It's gonna be so cool! Calliope's going to make a ton of popcorn and we're gonna watch movies and listen to music and dance and stay up all night long!"

Kendall had been around Phoebe enough to know that wasn't going to happen.

"I'm not sure Calliope is aware of that last part."

"What kind of sleeping bag are you bringing, Phoebe? I can't decide between my rock-star princess or the planets of the universe."

Phoebe turned slightly panicked eyes on Kendall, who only then realized neither she nor her uncle had asked what all was entailed.

Kendall offered what she hoped was a reassuring smile. "Well, I know how to pack for a night in the desert. Can't be much different, right?" She turned to Paige and mouthed, *Help me.*

"Charlie, maybe you could loan Phoebe one of your sleeping bags for tonight?"

"Sure. Yeah. You want the universe one? Then I don't have to decide."

Phoebe nodded.

"And I get to bring Tabitha. Calliope said, Mom. I asked. Tabitha's my dog. You haven't seen her 'cause she stays at the house when I'm in school but you can meet her now. You wanna?" Charlie asked Phoebe.

Phoebe nodded, but not nearly as enthusiastically as Kendall expected.

Charlie stuck two fingers in her mouth and whistled. Loud. "My dad taught me that."

A short, stout cocker spaniel came tootling out the front door. She circled Paige a couple of times before plopping her butt down beside her just as Paige clicked open the gate to let them all in. "Come on in and say hi. She's friendly. Just hold your hand out… There you go."

Phoebe giggled as Tabitha accepted her friendship with enough excitement to almost knock Phoebe to the ground. Kendall was smiling again. Her expression must not have been familiar to Paige, who did what Kendall could only describe as a double take. "You heading into town or home?" They moved away to let the girls play with the dog.

"Into town. We're going to do lunch at the diner, and then we are hitting the bookstore. And I guess we'd best check with Hunter to see if she has a sleeping bag for the future."

Phoebe glanced up and shook her head, her brow creasing in concern.

"She can always find one here. Charlie uses them to build forts in her room. And the living room. And the… Well, you get the picture." Paige turned to Phoebe. "Then you're all set. Calliope should have everything taken care of. Which means Kendall and your uncle can enjoy their date."

Phoebe's eyes went wide, and Charlie laughed.

Kendall rolled her eyes.

"Oh, right. Sorry." Paige laughed. "Your friendship time."

Kendall didn't believe for one second Paige had mistakenly mentioned her date tonight with Hunter. And if Paige knew, the entire town knew by now. Her months-long streak of flying under town's gossip radar had officially ended.

As Phoebe skipped by her side, Kendall wondered what the little girl was thinking. Should she say something about the date? Ask her what she thought? Did she want to know? Clearly overhearing the discussion with Calliope the other day hadn't made much of an impression, but Paige's comments had. Why? What had changed?

"So, Phoebe? Phoebe?" Kendall had to reach out and catch her arm before she skipped too far. "This date with your uncle, you know it's no big deal, right? It's just two, um, friends, having dinner together." Phoebe grinned in such a way that had Kendall doubting herself. “It doesn’t mean anything more than that.”

“Sure.” Phoebe shrugged as if it didn’t matter, but Kendall knew better. It mattered. It mattered a lot.

NERVES ATE AWAY at Hunter like termites at a lumber buffet. It wasn’t just because he’d sent his proposal to his agent; it wasn’t just that he had dived into potentially starting a new career, no, it was that in a few short hours, he’d get to be with Kendall. Not at the lighthouse. Not where little Phoebe ears were on high alert. Just the two of them alone.

Kendall. Funny to think a few short weeks ago he’d have worried about her roasting him over an open spit if he said or did the wrong thing. Funny how things changed.

Funny how the heart went in its own direction.

He’d been taken aback again by Butterfly Harbor’s outgoingness. The ground-breaking ceremony on the butterfly sanctuary was so full of goodwill that he’d felt it ricocheting around the soon-to-be construction site. The usual camaraderie that Hunter should have expected was there, even with Gil in the mix, who had wholeheartedly approved of Hunter's new job. Just as long as it didn't interfere with the still-in-progress project Hunter was determined to finish sooner rather than later. Gil's promotional book on Butterfly Harbor might have brought Hunter to town, but that was only the first step on this new life path, a path that would ensure stability and a good future for both himself and Phoebe and hopefully deal with his sister's in-laws' interference. They'd be hard-pressed to use his meandering career against him when he'd be staying put for a chunk of time.

He showered and changed and, much like a teenager going to his first prom, was ready well before the designated meeting time. He'd gone for the monochrome look: black slacks, black button-down, slim black tie. He'd called for a reservation for Flutterby Dreams, and requested a table with an ocean view—easily accommodated, according to Lori Knight, who answered the call at the inn.

He'd debated stopping to get flowers for her, but Kendall Davidson didn't strike him as the flower type, unless they were slightly wilting daisies. He reached over his desk and pushed open the window, breathing in the fresh evening air and looking into one of the half dozen window boxes Lori and Phoebe had filled. The once-empty wooden shells were now brimming with exploding colors, the white and yellow daisies interspersed with purple pansies and thick green ground cover to ensure a lasting season.

His and Phoebe's morning ritual had expanded to watering those boxes with the can Calliope had conveniently provided in the basket. The house, this house, was slowly becoming their home.

He heard Phoebe's pounding footsteps seconds before she burst through the door. She had in her hand a thick hardcover book with a bright emerald green spine with embossed gold lettering. She dived at him, and he hauled her up, already dreading the day she'd be too big to pick up.

"Let me guess. Someone got to go to the bookstore today." He held the book out to read the title. "*The Wizard of Oz.* Very cool. You going to start reading now or wait until after your sleepover?"

"She's going to wait," Kendall said. "We decided it was better for her to be with her friends rather than reading on her own, right, Phoebe?"

Phoebe nodded, but Hunter didn't think she was entirely convinced.

"You look nice." The surprise in Kendall's voice had him grinning.

"Yeah? Thanks. I have a date tonight. A first date." He nuzzled Phoebe's neck, and she broke out in giggles. His heart swelled. He didn't think he'd ever tire of hearing that sound. "And yes, I know. I'm early."

"Very." Kendall glanced down at her watch. "By about three hours. I was going to—" She pointed behind her, out the door to the lighthouse.

"Get some more work done before we go? That's fine. I'm going to get a jump on those photos I took today. I'll come get you in about two and a half hours, and we can drop off Phoebe on our way."

"Sounds good. I'll, um, see you later."

She backed out of the cottage with such an odd expression on her face. He followed, leaving Phoebe flipping through pages so fast she almost dropped the book.

Instead of heading for the lighthouse, Kendall was hurrying back toward town. Just before she was out of his sight, she began to run.

"I NEED YOUR HELP." Kendall was bent over, hands planted on her knees as she dragged in ragged breaths. She thought she was still in shape given all the physical labor she did, but the nine-block race to Frankie Bettencourt's cottage off Windmark Way had nearly done her in.

Frankie lounged in the doorway, grungy sweats and a tank top draping her body, a half-eaten ice cream bar in one hand. "What's up?"

"I need clothes."

Frankie snorted. "I don't have anything much different than—"

"Nice clothes. Something…not this." She waved her hand up and down her body now that her pulse was calming down. "Do not make me go all girlie on you, Frankie. This is humiliating enough. I have a date."

Frankie grinned. "Do you now? The hot photographer guy? Caught a good glimpse of him the other day when I was working on the fence. He asked you out?"

"Obviously, since I'm standing here begging you to let me look in your closet. This is the extent of anything I own."

"Everything you own fits in a duffel bag. Yeah, yeah. Come on." She stepped back and waved her in. "Just excuse the mess, please."

What mess? Kendall saw a well-lived-in home with knickknacks and mementos and photographs on the wall. Sure, there were a few filled laundry baskets on the sofa and the coffee table had a few more dishes on it than were in the kitchen sink, but nothing about this place showed Frankie to be a slob.

"How does he look?" Frankie steered Kendall to the back bedroom, then pushed her to sit on the mattress. Frankie stuck her ice cream in her mouth and flung open her closet doors. She tossed the now-empty stick into the trash can by the bed. "Other than good. 'Cause that's a man who always looks good."

"Have you ever met a man you didn't like?"

Frankie smiled over her shoulder and waggled her auburn-tinted eyebrows. "Nope."

"He's wearing black. All black. And a *tie*." And yes, Kendall admitted. He'd looked really, really good. "I don't want anything fancy. We're just eating at the Flutterby. I just don't want to look like this."

"Right. So color. Not too bright. Don't want to completely shock your system." Frankie sorted through the hangers. Kendall stared. Did most women own this many clothes? Her friend was right—everything Kendall owned could fit in her duffel. One of those things she'd learned in the army was to be frugal with space. "Blue's a bit too black. Hmm." Frankie pulled out a wrap-around dress in a rich, deep purple. "This could work. Try it on."

"What? Here?"

"Yes, here." Frankie handed the dress to her.

"What about shoes? I can't wear these." Kendall kicked out her legs to show off her boots.

"No kidding. I think I have something here that will work."

"No heels. I can't stand them, and besides, we're going to be walking."

"Wow. Someone save me from a woman who won't wear heels. Fine. Flats it is."

While Kendall swept her tank over her head and wiggled out of her jeans after unlacing her boots, Frankie dive-bombed her closet, crawling around and launching shoes over her shoulder like unaimed missiles. Kendall only had to duck twice.

"These!" Kendall caught a simple black ballet slipper, checked the size. "Might be a little snug."

"You never know. You've been walking around in those clodhoppers for too long. Let's see the purple dress."

Half an hour later, they decided on a simple flower-print dress with a high neck but a drape in the back that went just south enough for Kendall not to worry.

"What are you doing with your hair?"

"Brushing it." Kendall wiggled back into her clothes.

"Typical. Here." Frankie rummaged through the collection of hair bobs and such on her dresser and dropped some into a small cosmetic bag along with some simple makeup. "Take these. Leave your hair down, but clip it up on one side. Don't overdo it on the blush.

Keep it simple. Powder, eyebrows… Boy, if you have a few extra minutes, you should really tweeze—"

"No, I don't." And even if she did, she wouldn't surrender to Frankie Bettencourt and a pair of tweezers.

"'Kay. We'll save that for another time. Ah, lipstick. Let's go with a subtle pink. Nothing too glossy. Makes for weird kissing."

"There won't be any kissing."

Frankie looked offended. "Then what's the point? I bet he's a great kiss— Oh, ho! You already know that, don't you? I see that look on your face. Go, Kendall."

"There's no look, and stop that." Kendall laughed. *So this is what girlfriends are for.* No. Her heart pinched. This was what friends were for. "Thank you, Frankie. This means a lot."

"For me, too." Frankie gathered up the dress, shoes and makeup and headed out to get her a bag. "Just one request." She stopped Kendall on the porch before she left.

"Sure."

"Report back. I've been going through a serious dry spell lately, so I need to live vicariously through someone. Let me know how your date goes."

"Provided it goes okay, yeah. I will."

"Great. Have fun. And be safe!"

"Frankie!"

"Crossing the streets." Frankie went wide-eyed innocent, yet that twinkle in her eye was anything but. "Just enjoy and have a good time."

CHAPTER THIRTEEN

"WOW." HUNTER WOULD have fallen over at the sight of Kendall if Phoebe hadn't been holding his hand. He'd always thought her beautiful, even with all those sharp edges of hers, but the blue dress accented with a punch of white-and-yellow flowers softened her completely. He blinked. He'd always known she had legs, but he hadn't realized she had *legs*. Thank goodness she didn't dress like this every day, otherwise he'd never get any work done. "You look gorgeous. What do you think, Phoebe?"

Phoebe nodded and patted her hand against her heart.

"Thank you both." Kendall ducked her head and tucked her hair behind her ear, then she stopped, flipped the hair free again and laughed. "I'm sorry. I don't know why I'm so nervous."

"Because you're doing something you

haven't done in a very long time." Hunter held out his hand. "I'm nervous, too." But most of those nerves settled when she slipped her hand into his.

Phoebe jumped up and down, her book bag bouncing against her back.

"Shall we escort you to your sleepover, my lady?" Hunter bowed down to his niece, who giggled up at him.

"I hope she has everything she needs," Kendall said as she closed the door behind her and they headed down the hill to Calliope's farm. "Charlie's loaning her a sleeping bag. We weren't sure if she had one?"

"We don't. Not yet. But I'll add it to the list." His growing list. Sticking around Butterfly Harbor and accruing more stuff meant maybe he and Phoebe should be thinking about a larger place. He'd mention it to Xander. It was strange. He didn't have any second thoughts. No doubts. For the first time in almost a year, this felt like the right move. No question.

As they reached Calliope's, Phoebe was once again pulling on Hunter's hand. He was about to tell her to slow down when he saw three little girls race out Calliope's front door and head for the gate. Pigtailed, overall-clad Charlie, whimsical, ethereal Stella, and staid, practical Marley with her razor-sharp brown hair and equally sharp eyes. He let go of his niece and he and Kendall stepped back.

"Phoebe!" Charlie yelled before she popped open the gate and the group of girls surrounded her as if they were playing ring-around-the-rosy. Phoebe turned in circles, laughing until they all fell down.

"She's going to be just fine." Kendall squeezed his hand and leaned into his arm. He could hear the same tears misting his eyes in her voice.

"Okay, girls. Dinner's almost ready. Pizza's coming out of the oven." Calliope, barefoot as usual, headed over. "Phoebe, I hope you like veggies."

"Ewww." Charlie stuck her tongue out as Phoebe nodded.

"I thought so." Calliope beamed at her as she ushered the girls back inside. "Okay, you two. Off with you." She shooed Kendall and Hunter away as if they were pests invading her gardens.

A patrol car came up over the hill and

parked right in front of them. “Hold up!” A man in a deputy’s uniform climbed out with a neon-pink sleeping bag tucked under one arm. “Charlie! You forgot your sleeping bag.”

“Sorry!” Charlie ran over to her stepfather to retrieve it. “I was thinking about Phoebe’s and I guess I forgot mine. Thank you.”

“Not a problem. I had to stop for takeout, anyway.” Fletcher leaned against the hood of his car. “You must be Hunter MacBride. Fletcher Bradley.”

“Nice to meet you.” Hunter moved forward to shake his hand.

“Wait, wait, Phoebe, what’s wrong?” Stella cried as Phoebe raced back to Hunter. She buried herself in his arms, peeking out only slightly to look at Fletcher.

“Hey, hey. What’s this?” Hunter tried to pull Phoebe in front of him as her friends circled Calliope. “What’s wrong?”

Tears pooled deep in her eyes as her face paled. She just pointed at Fletcher, shaking her head.

“She was like this a bit with Matt,” Kendall remembered. “Phoebe, you have to tell us what’s wrong.”

"I can go," Fletcher said, but the concern on his face reflected Hunter's own fatherly concern. "If it'll help."

"No." It was Kendall who spoke as she bent down in front of Phoebe. "Phoebe, you don't have anything to be afraid of Deputy Bradley. He's Charlie's dad, remember? And he's a good guy. He's my friend."

Some of Phoebe's fear faded. She poked a finger against her heart, made a breaking motion with her hands.

"That's what she does when it's about her parents," Hunter told Kendall. "Kiddo, does Deputy Bradley remind you of that day? Are you afraid..." His voice trailed off as he began to understand. "It was a deputy who came to get you from school, wasn't it? They told you what happened to your parents?" Because he'd been halfway across the world taking photos at a refugee camp in Syria.

Phoebe nodded.

"Oh, Phoebe. They were doing their job." Kendall took hold of her and brought her close. "I know you were really scared. But you don't have to be here. The officers in Butterfly Harbor are safe, I promise. They aren't going to take you away."

"My dad wouldn't do that, Phoebe," Charlie announced. "If you don't believe Kendall, you can believe me. I wouldn't let him."

"Charlie, let them be." Fletcher held out his hand to his daughter.

But Charlie's words had broken through. At least somewhat—Phoebe had stopped shaking.

"Phoebe." Kendall spoke up. "You are a strong, smart little girl. I believe in you. So does your uncle. I bet everyone here does, too. You know in your heart that Deputy Bradley would never take you away from the people you love. And the people who love you. We'd hate for you to miss all the fun, but it's your choice."

Phoebe looked among the adults. Each second that ticked by was another twist in Hunter's heart. Times like this he missed his sister so much. She knew what to do in every situation; she always had. Especially when it came to her daughter. Finally, Phoebe took a step back, out of the protection of Hunter's arms, and walked right over to Fletcher.

He didn't move. He just looked down at her, and then Phoebe looked to where he and

Charlie were holding hands. Phoebe made a heart image in the air with her fingers, pointed to the two of them.

"That's right. He loves me," Charlie announced. "And he'd never ever hurt any of my friends. I promise, Phoebe. And I never ever, ever break a promise. Right, Daddy?"

"Neither do I. I'm sorry if I scared you, Phoebe. We protect the people who live here, and that includes you. Would you maybe like to come by the police station tomorrow? Charlie and I could introduce you to the other deputies so you feel more comfortable with us."

Phoebe nodded.

"And then maybe I can show Mr. Hunter the magic caves!" Charlie announced. "Can we, Dad? Can we?"

"As long as I don't have to go swimming this time, yes, that's a fine idea."

Hunter didn't hear much about the plans from then on. Part of him wanted to scoop Phoebe up in his arms and race back to the cottage, where she felt safest. Where he did. But that wouldn't do Phoebe any good. Kendall was right. She needed to confront the fears she had, face them head-on. The pride that swept over him as he'd watched Phoebe approach the deputy nearly took him under.

"All right, then." Calliope enveloped Charlie and Phoebe into a swirl of green and blue fabric to usher them toward the house. The instant Phoebe was back with her friends, Charlie, Marley and Stella linked their arms around her and led her inside. "We'll be fine," Calliope told them. "You may proceed with your date."

"Thank you, Calliope." Hunter didn't quite know what else to say.

"Never a dull moment around this town," Fletcher said as he removed his hat and slapped it against his leg. "Can I give you guys a lift to the Flutterby?"

"Are there no secrets in this town?" Hunter couldn't help but ask.

"Well, you're a bit dressy for the diner," Fletcher said. "And while Zane's pizza is stellar, it doesn't require a tie. That leaves Jason's place, which I'm on my way to, anyway, to pick up dinner for me and my wife. Calliope, I owe you for this."

"I will collect in my own time," Calliope said before she all but floated off.

"Well, my feet are killing me," Kendall said. "So we will happily accept the ride. Hey." She turned and placed her palm against Hunter's chest, right over his heart, and turned the kindest, most understanding eyes up at him. "You ever ridden in the back of a patrol car?"

"Ah, no." Hunter couldn't stop the chuckle that emerged, which broke the last of the fog hovering in his mind.

"Then allow me to show you how it's done. And at dinner, I'll tell you how I ended up in one on graduation night."

"YOU KNOW HOW there's something you've always wanted to do, you spend ages building it up in your mind and then you finally get a chance to do it and you worry if it's going to live up to all the expectation?"

"Sure." Although she had a difficult time recalling the last time she'd felt that excited about something. Culinarily satiated, Kendall leaned back in her embroidered chair and tried to hide her smile as Hunter polished off his crème brûlée.

"Expectations exceeded. That was phenomenal." He wiped his mouth on the sea foam–green cloth napkin and turned his attention back on her. "How was yours?"

"Good." She barely remembered tasting anything. Her nerves about tonight hadn't settled since she'd opened her door to find Hunter and Phoebe waiting for her. They'd abated a bit dealing with Phoebe's apprehension about Fletcher, something Kendall was kicking herself for not recognizing sooner. Problem solving was her comfort zone. Sitting across from a stunningly handsome and charismatic Hunter MacBride, wearing a dress for the first time since… Kendall cringed and shoved memories of Sam's funeral aside. Why couldn't she just relax and enjoy? Just for a few minutes, why couldn't she let herself believe in the good?

"Good? Kendall, come on." He reached across the table and slipped his fingers through hers. "That meal was spectacular."

"It was…food." She wished she could get excited about things like he could. Everything seemed to fascinate him; the world energized him, whereas she? Kendall shifted in her chair and tried to push a smile onto her lips. Kendall was just waiting for the world to implode.

"Ah, but it was almost veggie-free." Hunter's grin made her heart trip. "Phoebe would not have approved."

"No." Kendall finally found her laugh. "No, she would not have. Where does that come from, do you think?"

"Beyond the fact that my sister had a small container garden in the backyard, Phoebe and Brent used to play a game at dinner. Whoever ate the most vegetables got to choose the story they read that night. I don't know if you've noticed, but Phoebe knows her own mind when it comes to her books."

"I've noticed." One of the reasons she was surprised when the little girl had asked Kendall to choose one for her. "She and Mandy Evans struck up a bit of a friendship at the bookstore, I think. You know, in case you ever need another babysitter for her."

"Do you think I might need one again? Possibly to cover for a second date?" His thumb rubbed against the pulse in her wrist, making it difficult for her to breathe.

"Not sure. I'm not real great at this kind of thing."

"Well, I'm having a lovely time."

She ran a finger under the collar of the

dress. Was it choking her? It felt as if she was being choked.

"You don't think this is going well?" He inclined his head.

"Is it?"

"Why do you do that? Lower the bar so that no one can rise to it?" If he hadn't continued to stroke her wrist, she might have thought he was upset.

"Low bar means no one gets ahead of themselves. Assumes too much. That everything will always be okay. This isn't me, Hunter." She forced herself to look around the rather elegant dining room. The crisp white tablecloths, the glass jars filled with votive candles floating on water atop sparkling stones. Flatware that wasn't made of biodegradable plastic. Food cooked by a five-star celebrity chef. It was crowded but not packed, with more than half the tables filled with groups involved in relaxed conversation or couples needing no conversation at all. They all looked so happy. So normal. And she didn't fit. Not one little bit. "But this is you."

"Is that your way of saying we're opposites, Kendall? Because guess what?" He leaned across the table and lowered his voice. “I already guessed that.”

“Don’t make light of this, Hunter.” Tonight was a turning point. For both of them. And if he didn’t see that…

“That’s exactly what we should do. Kendall, what’s wrong?”

“I don’t know. This just doesn’t feel right.” The excitement that had propelled her to Frankie’s house only hours ago had faded into a swirling dread-tinged doubt that threatened to drag her under. “I’m not sure this is a good idea. You and me. Us.”

“Dinner with an ocean view? A night off from bedtime stories and dishes? Me, sitting across from a beautiful woman who clearly has no idea how I feel about her.”

Oh, she knew. Or at least, she suspected. That was part of the problem.

“Hunter—”

“How was everything?”

Kendall jumped at the intrusion of the young woman who popped up at their table, her long, dark curly hair pulled into a knot at the back of her neck. Her sous chef’s jacket was black, the smile on her face conveyed warmth and friendship.

"Hi, Alethea." Kendall snatched her hand back to hide in her lap. "You can definitely send our compliments to the chef. Oh, Alethea, this is Hunter MacBride. Hunter, Alethea Costas. She's Xander's sister."

"Guilty as charged," Alethea said with a laugh. "I heard the ribbon cutting went great."

"It had its moments," Hunter said without missing a beat. But he did shoot Kendall a look that let her know their conversation was not over. "I'm sure the feature in this weekend's paper will be entertaining for a lot of people. I was wondering if there's any chance I could get a look at the kitchen."

Kendall couldn't help it. Her lips twitched. He really had enjoyed his meal here.

"Sure." Alethea picked up the last of their plates. "Give me a few minutes to get caught up with clearing, and I'll let Jason know. Be right back."

"Should I leave you two alone?" Kendall teased. "You and Jason."

Hunter looked confused for a moment. "Oh. I guess I am coming off as a bit of a fanatic, aren't I? Juliana and I used to watch him and his brother on TV together. Growing up we could never agree on anything, but as adults, we found we both loved cooking shows. Being here, eating in his restaurant, it brings back some nice memories."

She should have kept her mouth shut. Something she could only identify as envy pricked at her heart. He'd lost his sister such a short time ago and he could already smile when he thought of her, and yet here Kendall was, years after her own loss, still trying to climb out of the despair.

"Does embracing what she loved help?"

"It does." She could tell with a mere look that Hunter understood exactly why she'd asked. "There's no time frame on grieving, Kendall. We move on when we can. I didn't have a choice, not when I had Phoebe to think of, to focus on. But that doesn't mean I don't have my moments. It does help, however, to have someone to share those memories with. And you can share with me. Anytime you want to talk about Sam, I'm right here. I'm not going anywhere."

"You aren't, are you." The statement came out a whisper, almost like a prayer. Was that what was holding her back? Was she worried that if she held on too tight, he and Phoebe would disappear? How could she have spent her adult life fighting against so much and yet find herself cowering at the thought of opening her heart again? "I don't want to feel this way, Hunter."

"What way?"

Someone else might have been searching for the closest exit. But Kendall sat stone still in her chair, her hands clenched into fists so tight she'd lost feeling in her fingers. "I don't want to be scared anymore. But there's so much about me that's wrong. I've made some breakthroughs since coming here and…meeting you and Phoebe. But I'm still not sure I have any place near or around you two." It hurt to be so honest, but he and Phoebe deserved that from her if nothing else. "This isn't great first-date talk, I know, but maybe it's best—"

"Maybe it's best if you give yourself a break." Hunter leaned his arms on the table. "Kendall, none of us is perfect. We all have a past, and we all have problems. Pretending like we don't is more damaging than admitting to them."

"You should try your hand at greeting cards."

"I'm not going to lie to you, Kendall. I have feelings for you. Feelings that, in all honesty, I've been waiting most of my life to have, and I don't want to walk away from them without seeing where they might go. What you see as faults, I see as strengths."

Didn't he understand? Didn't he see? "But Phoebe—"

"Who better for Phoebe to learn from than a woman who's been through hell and come out the other side? I hate to break it to you, but she already loves you. It wasn't just me she ran to tonight when she got scared. She ran to you, too. And you didn't falter. You didn't run away. You did what you always do. You stood. And you helped her face her fear. What more could anyone want in a role model?"

"I'm not a role model," Kendall said with a disapproving frown. "I think maybe your love of words is beginning to overtake your brain."

"And I think maybe it's time you realize that how you see yourself isn't how others see you." He stood up and walked around the table, bent down and pressed his lips against hers. Just for a moment, a brief, wonderful moment that chipped away at the remaining doubt and fear. "Let's take this a day at a time, okay? For now, let's just do that."

Kendall nodded, because any hope of words vanished under the emotions battling for control inside her. She wanted to believe a future with Hunter and Phoebe was possible.

But she also knew from experience, the moment she stepped into that new life, it would be pulled out from under her.

CHAPTER FOURTEEN

"THOSE CAVES ARE INCREDIBLE!" Hunter emerged from the opening at the shoreline damp with salty seawater and chilled to the bone, but both his soul and his camera were happy.

"They are when it isn't high tide," Fletcher told him as he tossed him one of the towels he'd brought. "And no, I won't bring you back to explore again then."

Hunter chuckled. "It's like you can read my mind. Maybe Charlie could play tour guide?"

"Over my dead body." Fletcher leaned over to look around the expansive outcropping of rocks to where Charlie and Phoebe were playing in the sand with Tabitha. "Most terrifying day of my life was when she'd gone missing and I had to go in there to rescue her. And believe me, that's saying something."

"If my notes are correct, you and your sister weren't born here, right?" Hunter wiped off his camera and stashed it into his bag.

"Lori and I came to live with our grandfather when we were pretty young. There were family issues." Fletcher shrugged as if trying to brush the memory aside yet didn't quite manage. "But there's something about this place. It heals you in ways you never expect."

"That I understand." It seemed odd to think or even say, but even as someone who had traveled the world, there were few places that brought him as much peace as Butterfly Harbor. "I'd really like to get the take on this town from people who have lived here the longest. I was thinking about maybe having a barbecue at the lighthouse, just an occasion for people to talk about the changes over the years, what Butterfly Harbor means to them. Do you think people would be interested?"

"Will there be beer?" Fletcher led the way back to the beach.

"What would a barbecue be without beer?"

"You do have the right attitude about that. I can help you make up a list, but maybe you'd best run it past Kendall first? She's pretty determined to get the lighthouse finished, and a big party might just get in her way."

"Good idea." Then again, a big party might go a long way in showing Kendall just how much people in this town had come to rely on her. And like her. He'd never met anyone in such a crisis of faith—both in herself and in her ability to exist in this world. "Hey, kiddo." Hunter held out his hand for Phoebe who raced over to him. "You done with your sandcastle? We should probably get you home—What?" He bent down when she crooked her finger at him. "What's going on?"

Phoebe grabbed his hand and dragged him to the sand, where she drew him a picture. When she was done, she turned expectant eyes on him. "See?"

"I'm going to need a bit more help, Phoebs." He dropped a hand on the back of her head and looked to Fletcher for an answer, but the deputy only shrugged. "Is this a building of some kind?"

"It's a school!" Charlie bounded over,

looking as if she'd buried herself in half the beach. "Phoebe wants to go to school."

Phoebe nodded and pointed to the building.

"What? Really? Are you sure?" The weight that had been pressing down on him for the last seven months released. "Why the— Wait. Never mind. I'm not going to argue with you. You're sure?"

After only the slightest hesitation, Phoebe nodded again and pointed to Fletcher as she stood back up.

"She didn't want to go back because she was afraid the men in uniforms would come and take her away. That she'd never see you again." Charlie slung an arm around Phoebe's shoulders. "But now that she's met the sheriff and all the deputies, she knows my dad would never let that happen. Right, Dad?"

"Absolutely," Fletcher said, his chest puffing with fatherly pride. "We would never do anything to scare you, Phoebe."

"So, um, school." Hunter scrubbed a hand across his cheek. "Okay. I can do this." He looked to Fletcher. "How do I do this?"

"Simple." Fletcher headed up the beach. "Follow me, I know where the school is."

They all laughed.

"Do we have a surprise for you!"

Kendall spun on the scaffold, a paint roller in her hand, and looked down at Hunter and Phoebe, both grinning up at her like loons. "I keep forgetting to put bells around your necks." Shaking off the jitters that still refused to leave her, she swiped the roller over the last patch of spackle and sighed. "I have my own surprise. It's done." She leaned back, just a little too far, to give Hunter his own small heart attack. "Now I can tackle the fun part."

"You mean this wasn't fun?" Hunter and Phoebe approached as she scaled down the side of the scaffold.

"Oh, it was. But up there." She pointed toward the walkway at the tippy top of the tower. "That's where the magic happens." Kendall caught Phoebe's gasp at the word *magic*. Clearly Calliope's influence. "And by magic I mean personality." Her work-booted feet hit the ground. "What's with the box? Phoebe, are you smuggling vegetables in here in bakery boxes now?"

"Nope. You'll see." Phoebe shook her head and pointed to the box.

"Well, if you insist." She set the roller onto the plastic tarp, wiped her hands on her paint-spattered jeans and pried open the lid. "Cupcakes. How cute. Are these from that new bakery in town? What are those? Little schoolhouses? And that one says Phoebe."

She looked at Hunter who grinned. "Phoebe wants to go to school," he announced in a formal voice.

"Really?" Before she thought about it, she dropped down and pulled Phoebe into her arms. "That's wonderful news! I'm so proud of you."

Phoebe giggled.

"Only one problem with the cupcakes," Hunter said as his grin faded.

"Is there anything ever wrong with cupcakes?" Kendall asked.

"They're carrot cake."

Kendall groaned. "Obviously they are. Speaking of which, I have a surprise for you." She took Phoebe's hand and led them to the side of the carriage house. "I know it's not much, but it's something to get you started. I talked to Calliope, and she's going to help you with some seedlings come next week."

The simple wooden box hadn't taken much to put together. With shortened sawhorses and a few bags of fresh dirt waiting to be piled into the drainage-ready container, Phoebe could start her own vegetable garden.

"Your uncle told me how your mom had a garden, and I thought maybe you could do with one yourself. What do you think?"

Phoebe's eyes filled. She kept hold of Kendall's hand but squeezed hard.

"This is a wonderful gift. Thank you, Kendall." Hunter wrapped an arm around her shoulders and brought her in close. He pressed his lips against her forehead and murmured, "It's perfect."

"Yeah, only one problem." Kendall sighed as Phoebe abandoned her to explore the collection of small gardening tools and the fabric tote Kendall had found at the hardware store. "Guess who's going to have to eat all those vegetables?"

"A PARTY." KENDALL stopped midchop and looked over at Hunter, who was watching the steaks grilling on the stove. "You want to have a party and invite half the town?"

"Not that many. Fletcher's making a list. Just a bunch of people who grew up here so I can get a feel for the experience. I'm making my way through the historical buildings and tourist spots. I want a personal story to attach to each. That reminds me, I'd like to include you when I talk about the lighthouse."

"Me?" Kendall's knife slipped, and she just missed her thumb. "But I didn't grow up here. I don't qualify."

"You're bringing the Liberty back to life. You qualify."

Unconvinced, she let that slide. "But a party? Here?" All those people around her space. Around her…home. That should worry her more than it did, right?

"Not much different than the tree cutting and fence assembly, right? Only this time we won't have to do any work. Next Sunday? And we could celebrate Phoebe going back to school."

Kendall glanced at Phoeb, who was hard

at work on her latest batch of math papers. Hunter and Phoebe had a meeting with the school principal Monday morning where they'd decide which teacher would best be suited to her, given Phoebe's continued shyness.

"That's your secret weapon, isn't it? Use Phoebe's schooling to get me to agree," she whispered.

"You don't have to agree to anything," Hunter said with a shrug. "Fletcher said he and Paige could host if we couldn't. But given as you've finished the exterior of the lighthouse—"

"I finished the painting. There's still a lot of work to do."

"But the scaffold can come down, right? And once we stash all your tools and stuff away, it makes for a pretty great barbecue area. I mean, talk about the perfect view."

"I really don't have any say in this, do I?"

"Sure you do. This is your home, Kendall. If you don't want to have it here, we won't. But it might be good for you. You know. To push you over the hump and away from becoming that grouchy old lighthouse lady."

"I'm not a grouch."

Even Phoebe looked at her for that comment.

"When did you become a master of passive-aggressive reverse psychology?"

"Not sure." Hunter glanced back at the calendar. "When did we get here, Phoebe?"

Phoebe grinned.

"Ha-ha." It occurred to her just how easy this conversation was. Something had happened to her. That solitude she'd thirsted for had faded; now she could barely tolerate the time she spent away from them. Instead of staring at the ceiling and counting the cracks, she counted the hours until she'd see Phoebe's smiling face across the breakfast table. Or hear Hunter's severely off-key shower singing. It had been so long, she couldn't be sure, but was it possible she was…happy? "Fine. You can have your friends over."

"Our friends," Hunter corrected.

"What do I have to do?"

"Nothing other than what I said. Just make the Liberty as presentable as possible. I'll take care of the rest."

"That doesn't worry me at all." But she

settled back into chopping and slicing cucumbers, zucchini, carrots and peppers for dinner.

After dinner and the dishes were done, Kendall puttered around trying to imagine where she could fit a child's desk in the living room as Hunter worked on his computer. Phoebe walked up behind her and tugged on her shirt.

"What's up?" Even as she turned, she knew. Because she'd been expecting this ever since they'd gone to the bookstore together. Phoebe held up the copy of *The Wizard of Oz* and pushed it into Kendall's hands.

"It's kind of late, kiddo," Hunter said without turning around. Kendall narrowed her eyes, wondering how he knew what was going on, then realized he was watching the two of them in the reflection of his computer screen. Clever man.

Kendall looked down at the book—the same edition as the one she'd hoped to give to her own daughter with Sam one day. She'd known at the time she bought it for Phoebe, she'd regret it. That merely seeing the tome would trigger that deep-seated ache. But that didn't happen. If anything, her heart thrummed with the promise of crisp pages and reading a story to Phoebe.

"It's okay." Her voice sounded strained when she spoke, but she took Phoebe's hand and led her over to the sofa. The way Phoebe jumped up beside her and curled into her felt as if the little girl was hugging her heart. She glanced up and saw Hunter watching them, the expression in his eyes unmistakable.

She smiled and turned her attention to the hardcover book.

Happiness, she thought, as she began to read, might not be such a bad place to be, after all.

"You have got to be kidding me." After a whirlwind of meetings and paperwork, Phoebe was attending her first official day at Butterfly Harbor Elementary, and Hunter had stopped at the diner for breakfast to catch up with his projects and schedule.

Mrs. Claypoole, the school principal, had been exceedingly impressed by Phoebe's reading skills, but it was her math skills that really caught the woman's attention. After discussing with three different teachers, they were going to take a specialized approach with Phoebe for the rest of the year, with some individual tutoring lessons in the hopes they could draw her out of her shell as well as address her advanced thinking in a couple of subjects. Thankfully, the student body wasn't a large one, averaging only fifteen students per teacher, which meant Phoebe could still be in the classroom with kids her own age, but have her own learning curve.

It also didn't hurt that Charlie, Marley and Stella had been waiting outside the school this morning to escort her inside. Hunter had stood back, a bit disappointed he wouldn't get to walk Phoebe inside, but proud as any father could be that she held her chin high and walked in surrounded by her friends.

"Bad news?" Holly Saxon asked.

Hunter glanced up and found the owner of the Butterfly Diner watching him. She was sitting alongside a table, a row of empty salt and pepper shakers waiting to be filled, unable to squeeze behind it given her very pregnant tummy.

"I don't mean to intrude." Holly held up her hands in surrender. "I just happen to be bored out of my mind, and the twins here are practice kicking like champs."

"It's fine." But everything inside him was saying otherwise. He'd wondered how he'd lucked out that Phoebe's grandparents hadn't continued to hassle him through their lawyer. He'd assumed maybe that last phone call, just after they'd arrived in town, had been enough to get them off his back and to abandon any notion of suing him for custody of Phoebe. He'd been wrong. Way wrong.

"You're about three shades whiter than the tile over there." Holly motioned to the black and white tiles and orange details that were the defining color scheme of the monarch-inspired diner. "You're among friends." She motioned to Paige and Abby, who had paused their wiping down empty tables. "Spill."

"Ah." How on earth was he supposed to say no? "It looks as if Phoebe's grandparents are suing me for full custody." Saying the words out loud felt like a knife in the heart. "They're claiming I'm an unfit parent and that given Phoebe's ongoing grief issues that

I'm not addressing adequately, she should be living with them."

"That's awful." Paige was up in a flash and snatching the registered letter he'd picked up at the postal annex just that morning. "Utter nonsense! Phoebe's one of the most well-adjusted kids I've been around."

"But she is still so shy and doesn't talk much." Doubt crept up his spine. Every decision he'd ever made about his niece, about their life, about her future, came flooding back at him. He'd always done the right thing, hadn't he? Letting Phoebe come to terms with her parents' deaths in her own time? Unless her own time had gone on too long and did more damage than good. As he'd seen with Kendall initially. He didn't want his niece going down that same road.

"Phoebe doesn't have to be a chatterbox," Holly said. "Sometimes I wish Simon would go radio silent. I mean, I love the kid to the moon, but some quiet would be heavenly."

"Said the woman bringing two more Simons into the world," Abby teased and tossed aside a wet cloth for a shake. "Sorry. One Simon, one Simonetta."

Hunter tried to smile.

"You need to show this to your attorney," Paige told him. "Get in front of this fast."

"I don't have one. I can't afford a good one, and the bad ones might make things worse."

"You can't handle this on your own, Hunter." Holly scanned the document and handed it over to Abby. "That's a big law firm. Even I've heard of them. You need someone with as good a reputation. Right, Paige?" Holly arched a brow at her friend and employee.

"Right." Paige snapped her fingers. "Be right back." She ducked into the kitchen, leaving Hunter feeling both dumbfounded and a bit nervous.

"Like I said, I can't afford—"

"Hunter, trust us," Abby told him. "And if what Holly's thinking doesn't work, maybe we can have Calliope whip up some of that magic of hers—"

Holly jumped in. "Let us see what we can do about a lawyer, Hunter. One step at a time."

"Leah's on her way. Hey. Relax." Paige laid a hand on his shoulder and squeezed. "You're part of Butterfly Harbor now, big guy. That makes you family. And if there's one thing we do, we look after each other."

KENDALL KNOCKED ON the door to the motor home before she pulled it open. The curtains were drawn, but Hunter didn't have the front light flipped on indicating he was developing film. Which meant he'd either forgotten to put it on, which she doubted, or he was hiding from her. "Hunter?"

She was anxious to hear how Phoebe's first day of school went and thought maybe the two of them could go and pick her up together. A step forward, she told herself. A small one, but one she wouldn't have even considered taking just a few days ago.

"Back here."

"Ooh, I finally get to see inside this place." She closed the door behind her. "What... you have got to be kidding me." Even in the dim light, the motor home was stunning. Leather driving seats, an expansive galley kitchen with polished redwood cabinetry. Two smaller chairs were to one side of the motor home, across from a small flat-screen TV. As she walked along the faux-wood floor, she saw that the space where a bed would have gone had been turned into a small darkroom, complete with a red lightbulb above the sliding accordion door. She got to the back partition and leaned inside, found him lounging on the double bed across from the smaller twin one. An official-looking legal envelope sat open on his chest. "Tell me again why you wanted to stay in the carriage house?"

She'd meant to tease him, but for the first time since she'd met him, she didn't see any hint of a smile or grin on his face. Or anything remotely connected to humor. The dread she thought she'd finally set aside dropped on her again. "What's wrong? Is it Phoebe? Did something happen—"

"Phoebe's fine."

But Hunter wasn't. That tone in his voice, the barely restrained anger tempered by resignation and frustration, didn't sound like him at all. She pointed at the envelope. "What's that?"

"That is Brent's parents about to suck every hope, not to mention, penny out of my life." He pinched the bridge of his nose. "They're suing me for custody of Phoebe."

"What?"

"And they're doing it here, in California, because that's where I've stayed the longest."

She didn't know much about custody laws. "You need a lawyer, Hunter."

"Got one. This morning, actually. Tell me something." He dropped his hand and looked at her as if he were a lost little boy with no idea how to get home. "Does anyone say no to the women in this town? Holly, Abby and Paige ganged up on me and hired Leah Ellis. I don't even remember saying yes."

"Good." Kendall nodded, relief sweeping over her. "She's good, Hunter. I mean, I've heard. She used to be a big defense attorney a while back, then changed to family law. People like her. People trust her. And she goes to the mat for her clients." If there were any other clichés she could pull out of her head, she needed them now. "Hunter, it's going to be okay. No one is going to take Phoebe away from you."

"What if it isn't okay?" Hunter only stared at her. "Kendall, I can't lose her. She's the most important thing in my life. She is my life."

"I know," Kendall whispered. All anyone had to do was look at the two of them together to see how much Hunter loved his niece. "And she's your last tether to Juliana. I understand that, Hunter."

"I know you do." He held out his hand and, with a heavy sigh, pulled her onto the bed beside him. "I'm going to fight them with everything I have, but it might not be enough."

"I have money." Kendall blurted it out before she even thought it through. "As much as you need. It's yours."

"Kendall—"

"I want you to take it. Please. It's just sitting there…" She took a deep breath. "It's money my parents left me. Sam and I were going to use it to buy a house once we got back." Instead, she'd barely looked at the account except to take Sam's name off it. "I haven't touched it. What did I need it for? But if it'll help—"

He pulled her to him and kissed her. One of those kisses that reached deep into her soul and brushed against her heart. She clung to him and sobbed against his lips.

"I love you, Kendall Davidson."

That he spoke with such intensity silenced

her to her core. She squeezed her eyes shut, absorbing not only the words, but also what they meant for her. For Hunter. For Phoebe. For all of them.

"You shouldn't," Kendall whispered. She knew what people could do, the dirt they could dig up. If Hunter was going to keep custody of Phoebe, he was going to have to present a consistent, positive picture of their life. And Kendall—with her past—was anything but positive.

He clasped her face between his palms. "I love you. For the first time in my life, I know exactly what I want, and what I want is Phoebe and you and me to be a family. Yes, you, Kendall. All of you. The good and the bad. The dark and the light." He kissed her again and didn't let her up for breath until she sagged forward and into his arms, the custody papers crumpling between them. "As long as you're by my side, I can do this, Kendall. Promise me you won't give up. Not on me. Not on us."

"I—" *I love you.* She wanted to say it. Needed to. Not only for him, but for herself, to step through that final barrier into the happiness and life she hadn't dared let herself dream of again. But she couldn't. Because she knew the moment she did, everything she hoped for would turn to ash.

"I promise, Hunter."

CHAPTER FIFTEEN

"THESE KIDS...IT'S like wrangling cats," Hunter muttered to himself. "Phoebe! Charlie! Simon! Marley! One more..." he mumbled. "There's one more, right." He snapped his fingers. "Ste-lla! Good gravy, I sound like Brando." He stuck his fingers in his mouth and whistled for the group of kids he'd innocently said he'd be happy to watch for the afternoon. He'd thought it'd be an easy way to spend a Saturday.

So far they'd eaten through his stockpile of food, played an almost-broke-every-window-of-the-carriage-house game of soccer and now they were scattered allover, of course, in an epic game of hide-and-seek that just might finally snap his patience.

He whistled again. "Yo! Guys! Time to get you all home."

Kendall, wearing her typical uniform of snug black jeans and a gray tank, her hair tied back out of her face, smiled at him in a way that set his heart on its side. Wait until he told her he had a list of houses he wanted to check out. Not that he was going to propose anytime soon. She needed time still, but that she was willing to admit her feelings for him and Phoebe, that she was going to stand by his side and fight for his niece, meant more to him than, well, most anything.

He would propose. But first he'd find a house in Butterfly Harbor that suited not only him and Phoebe, but Kendall, as well.

"Sorry, Mr. Hunter." Charlie came racing around the side of the house, the others hot on her heels. Phoebe brought up the rear, her pink shirt and jeans filthy from whatever they'd been doing. She'd never looked happier. "We couldn't stop until we found everyone. That forest back there is so dark even though it's still daylight. But the butterflies led us out."

Phoebe launched herself into Hunter's arms as all the kids gathered round.

"I've got some cookies and juice inside," Hunter said. "I think loading you all up on sugar before I take you guys home seems like a good plan."

"Cookies, yay!" Marley cried. Simon went first and opened the door for them.

Phoebe pointed to Kendall and the new state-of-the-art barbecue and smoker in the nearby clearing.

"She got a new toy." Hunter laughed. "It's for the party tomorrow. It's for cooking meat."

"But..." Phoebe frowned and looked over to her recently planted garden, which hopefully would sprout carrots, peas and potatoes soon.

"And vegetables, don't worry." He kissed her forehead and set her on her feet. The sound of tires grinding over gravel echoed in his ears. "You go on inside."

The town car that broke through the tree line spoke of wealth and privilege, neither of which seemed suited to visiting a lighthouse restoration project. Kendall joined him. "Who's that, do you think? Gil get a new car?"

"Gil would never hire a driver," Hunter said, his stomach pinching tight. "I've got a bad feeling about this."

"And here I thought I was the pessimist." Kendall wrapped her hand around his wrist and squeezed. "Relax. I'm sure it'll be fine."

The older couple that climbed out of the car nearly stopped his heart cold. "Or not. That's who I think it is, isn't it?"

Hunter took a long, deep breath. "Brent's parents. Eleanor and Stephen Cartwright."

"Do they always travel as if they are the king and queen of everyone?"

"Have I told you today how much I love you?" Hunter couldn't help but look at her.

"Maybe." She shrugged. "Don't worry. It's going to be fine."

"You trying to convince me or yourself?"

"Work with me, Hunter. Work with me." She bit out a smile as the two approached.

"Eleanor," Hunter said, wondering if that tight knot of hair on the back of her head ever gave her a headache. "Stephen. Welcome to Butterfly Harbor."

"We tried to call." Stephen Cartwright spoke with the authority of a man who had been running his mega–real estate corporation for more than four decades. "I take it you don't get reception out here in the middle of nowhere."

"Sure, I do." Hunter wasn't about to give him the satisfaction of putting down Butterfly Harbor. "But I was busy with the kids, so I turned it off. What brings you all the way out here?"

"Phoebe. We want to see our granddaughter," Eleanor said. She had a death lock on her yellow clutch, the same canary yellow as the skirt and jacket she wore.

"You could see her anytime. All you have to do is Skype."

"Skype requires conversation." Stephen angled his pointed nose down at them. "And we wanted to make certain you hadn't absconded with her after you received our letter."

"Phoebe communicates just fine. Not everyone has to be chatty or wordy or—" Kendall paused. "I'm Kendall."

"Yes, we know who you are." Stephen turned a sneering look in her direction.

Warning bells clanged in his mind. They knew about Kendall? How? Or perhaps the better question was why?

Hunter watched, amused as Kendall returned the expression and added a growl only he could hear.

"Where is Phoebe, please?" Stephen asked with a combination of snobbish pride and forced politeness.

"Inside with her friends. Phoe-be!" he called over his shoulder.

The door cracked open, and Phoebe poked her dark curl-covered head out. The light in her eyes faded the instant she saw her grand-parents. She slammed the door again.

"Smart kid," Kendall muttered. "I'll get her. Excuse me."

"I take it she's petrified of us because you told her about the custody suit," Stephen ob-served.

"Stephen, we need to keep this polite, please." Eleanor's eyes softened against the tears. "I'm sorry, Hunter. We only wanted to see her. It's been so long—"

"You could have seen her at any time, El-eanor." As angry as he was about the cus-tody suit, there was no mistaking the plea in her eyes. "I told you that at the funeral. And in response to your accusation, Ste-phen, Phoebe doesn't know about the cus-tody suit. I didn't tell her, because she's already petrified that someone could take her away from me. I didn't think it would serve any purpose other than to make her even more afraid of you."

"But why is she afraid of us?" Eleanor asked, a genuine look of confusion on her face. "We've never done anything to hurt or scare her. She's the only grandchild we have…the only one we will ever have. We love her. And we want her to have a good life."

"She has a good life. With me. And ask your husband why she might be afraid of you. Or didn't you tell Eleanor about your trying to buy me off the day we buried your son and my sister? The way you threatened me with financial ruin unless I granted you custody of Phoebe immediately. What was it you said? I wouldn't have a dime to my name and no judge would ever grant custody to a pauper. Phoebe was standing right behind you when you said that, Stephen. She heard every word."

Stephen flinched. Only a bit, but enough for Hunter to see he hadn't realized his granddaughter had witnessed his buy-off attempt.

"Stephen, how could you," Eleanor gasped as her husband went ramrod straight.

"I did what I needed to. It was bad enough Brent wouldn't let us into their life. I wasn't about to let someone like *him* raise my granddaughter."

"Funny. I was going to say the same thing about you." Hunter took a step closer to them as he heard the door open behind him. "One word about this custody fight to Phoebe and I will make you wish you never stepped foot in this town." He moved aside to allow Kendall to lead Phoebe over to her grandparents.

"Phoebe, you remember your father's parents, don't you?" Kendall was holding Phoebe's hand and he saw her give it a small squeeze.

"Hello, Phoebe." Eleanor dropped down and held open her arms.

Phoebe glanced at Kendall, who nodded. "It's okay. Your uncle and I aren't going anywhere."

Phoebe moved in and let Eleanor hug her.

"She's filthy," Stephen snapped.

"That's what happens when kids play. They get dirty." Hunter tried to keep the anger out of his voice when Phoebe jumped at her grandfather's accusation. "And she does play. With her friends. And in school." Phoebe turned back to Kendall and held up her arms.

"It's okay, kiddo." Kendall held her close. "I'm going to take her back inside."

Thank you, Hunter mouthed, then waited until the door closed behind them before he swung on his sister's in-laws. "You can leave now. You've seen her."

"She hates us." Eleanor's chin wobbled as tears pooled in her eyes.

"You've poisoned her against us," Stephen accused.

"No, I haven't. And she doesn't know you well enough to hate you, Eleanor. But just to stave off any other legal argument you might want to throw at me, she is back in school, and she's been evaluated as reading well above her second-grade level. Her math skills are significantly higher. Her teachers plan to set up a special program for her to make sure she keeps advancing. And before you ask, yes, we will be staying in Butterfly Harbor for the foreseeable future, since I've recently accepted a job in town." He knew all this and more was in the report Leah Ellis was preparing for the court, but it couldn't hurt to lob these details at them now. "We'll be renting or buying a house here in town. So if your plan was to use my, what did you call it, vagabond existence against me, you can forget it. I was just waiting until I found the right home for Phoebe."

"And what about that…woman?" Stephen spat.

"What about Kendall?"

"Stephen!" Eleanor placed her hand on her husband's arm. "Please, let's just go."

"That woman is unfit. Anyone can see that by looking at her. Those scars alone—"

"What?" Hunter moved in and stood toe to toe with him, the outrage inside bubbling over. "Oh, sorry. Do explain how scars she got defending this country as a soldier make her unfit for anything. Yes, please, let's debate everyone's character here, Stephen, because I promise you Kendall is going to come out on top of all of us."

"Stephen, enough. This wasn't our, or rather, my intention," Eleanor insisted as she pulled her husband away. "You have to understand, Brent was our only child. Phoebe is the one connection we have to him."

"It's the same for me, Eleanor. I do understand. Phoebe is the one connection I have to my sister." Sympathy for Brent's mother rose. "Stephen, you wanted to battle it out in court, let me finally give you what you want." He reached into his pocket, pulled out Leah's card and handed it to him. "My lawyer will be in touch."

KENDALL KEPT ONE eye on the kids scarfing cookies like a pack of renegade googly-eyed blue monsters and the other out the window. A quiet request to Charlie to distract Phoebe was instantly taken up as Charlie asked Phoebe to show her all the books she had.

Cartwright came across as an imposing man. Or he might have been to someone other than Kendall. She'd dealt with his sort before: privileged, entitled and so devoid of empathy that nothing was ever going to get through to him. The only thing men like Stephen Cartwright cared about was winning. He probably didn't even see a day beyond gaining custody of Phoebe, just so long as he could claim victory.

She wanted to be there, by Hunter's side, presenting a united front, but she'd seen something odd in Stephen's eyes when he'd looked at her—as if he could see directly through her. As if he knew all her secrets.

Kendall gnawed on her bottom lip. And she did have secrets. Secrets she hadn't shared with Hunter. Secrets that shamed her to the point of silence. She didn't put it past Stephen to have crawled around in the trash to try to dig something up. Or that he might have hired someone to do so.

When she saw Eleanor and Stephen drive away, that knot of unease loosened but didn't release. Not completely. "Guys, get your coats on. Time to go home." She rapped her knuckles against Phoebe's bedroom door before she headed outside.

Hunter had remained where he'd been, staring daggers at the taillights.

"Everything still intact?" It wasn't often she was the one struggling to find some humor, but she figured it was worth a shot.

"They're going to use everything they've got. I could see it in his eyes." That Hunter wrapped an arm around her and pulled her close eased the tension rolling inside her.

"I know. I saw it, too." For a moment, a brief moment, she leaned into him. Not to take comfort from him, but to give him whatever he needed from her.

"Something he said, about you." He frowned, tilted his chin down. "I'm afraid he's going to drag you into this."

"I figured." She wanted to sound casual, wanted to avoid going to the worst-case scenario, but that always seemed to be her default position.

"You're okay with that?"

"If it means you keeping custody of Phoebe, they can throw whatever they want at me." She laid her head against his shoulder and squeezed her eyes shut. The panic subsided and settled from a churning into a low-ebb tide. Every problem had a solution. And problems had always been Kendall's specialty.

SHE BEGGED OFF dinner at the diner with Phoebe and Hunter that night by claiming she had a last-minute consultation with a customer in need of cabinet repair. The duo had looked disappointed, but that lifted when she suggested Hunter and Phoebe pick up gelato on their way back to the Liberty for them all to have later.

Kendall trekked down the hill to the Flutterby Inn. Determined to get to the bottom of things, she headed inside and found Willa O'Neill manning the registration desk.

"Hey, Willa."

"Kendall. Hey! I can't wait for the barbecue tomorrow. I was so surprised Hunter invited me."

"Everyone's welcome. Besides, you're an expert on this town." Small talk was necessary for this mission, she reminded herself. "Hey, are a Mr. and Mrs. Cartwright staying here?"

"They sure are." Willa rolled her eyes. "She seems nice, but he's a bit of a—"

"Totally with you there," Kendall said with a nod. "Any chance you could call up and say there's a delivery for Mrs. Cartwright?"

"Oh." Confusion marred her brow. "Sure, I guess."

"Thanks. I'll owe you." Kendall moved across the room to pour herself a cup of fresh-brewed coffee while she waited.

A few minutes later, Eleanor descended the curving staircase. "You said there was a delivery for me?"

"Not so much a delivery as a message."

Kendall moved in before Willa got caught having to lie.

"Ms. Davidson."

Her stomach lurched. Sometimes she hated being right. "Interesting. I didn't mention my last name earlier, which means you already knew what it was." She had to give it to Eleanor. She looked neither surprised nor ashamed. "I think maybe you and I should have a talk, don't you?"

Kendall led the way outside to the memorial bench overlooking one of the prettiest views in all of Butterfly Harbor.

"It's beautiful here. I can see why Hunter likes it so." Eleanor wrapped a thin sweater around her shoulders.

"Seeing as your husband tried to buy him off to gain custody of your granddaughter, I thought I'd return the favor." Kendall sipped her coffee. "What's the price for you to drop the custody suit?"

Eleanor shifted slightly. "I had no idea my husband had done that."

"But it doesn't completely offend you, does it?"

"No." She turned grief-filled eyes on Kendall. "We went a lot of years without speaking to Brent. Which meant we rarely got to see my son after he and Juliana married. I'd hoped once Phoebe was born that might change, but..." She shrugged. "Where's your family, Miss Davidson? Or have you been using my granddaughter and her ward to fill an emptiness in you?"

Kendall had been expecting this tack, but it didn't lessen the blow.

She looked at Brent's mother, the tears she wanted to cry falling on the inside. "Actually, I did everything I could to avoid her. It didn't work. But I think because of her, finally, I'm close to being able to say goodbye to Sam and the future I thought I had with him. She's helped to heal me. Hunter has, too. He's a good man, Eleanor. And he loves Phoebe the way every child deserves to be loved. Don't take her away from him. Work it out. Visitation, maybe, or come here to stay awhile and get to know your granddaughter, but don't separate her from the only family she has left."

"She has us."

"No, she doesn't," Kendall said. "She never has. You can't force her to love you.

No matter how hard your husband tries. Ownership, custody papers—those aren't love. They're cruel when compared to the alternative. If you want Phoebe to have a good life, a happy life, then work to be a part of it. Don't force her to start over again for the third time."

Eleanor's grief faded and gave way to a sharp, assessing gaze. "I've read your history. Your medical files. You've had some issues in the past."

"I have." What was the point in denying it. "I suffered from PTSD once I was back from the service. I was also diagnosed with severe depression."

"And arrested for violent behavior."

"That's true." And she made no excuses for it. "It's difficult to adjust when your world is ripped apart. Or set on fire." She motioned to the scars on her face and neck. "You're worried I'm a danger to Phoebe."

"I am. We are."

"I've wondered the same thing." Kendall almost smiled at the surprise in Eleanor's eyes. "I love that little girl, Eleanor. And I love her uncle. Which is why I'm going to ask you one more time. What's your price?"

An eerie calmness seemed to descend over Eleanor. She smoothed perfectly manicured fingers over the sleeve of her pristine white sweater. "I can convince Stephen to drop the custody suit in exchange for liberal visitation with my granddaughter. But only if you aren't in the picture." She faced Kendall now, a glowing look of triumph on her face.

Kendall swallowed hard as her suspicions were confirmed. Stephen wasn't the one who Hunter had to be worried about. Eleanor was. Which meant she had to be kept away from Phoebe at all costs. "You want me out of their lives?"

"I do. The sooner the better." She sighed as if a weight had been lifted. "We'll be staying a few days, so that gives you time to think—"

"I don't have to think about it." Kendall dumped the last of her coffee out on the ground and gave Eleanor a withering look. "I'll be gone by the end of the week."

"KENDALL?" HUNTER KNOCKED on her door before he pushed it open. "Sorry I'm late this morning. I've got the steaks out and coming to room temp. Everyone should be here in about an hour or so and Phoebe is busy pulling weeds in the window…boxes." He'd stopped dead in the center of the room. "What's going on? You moving?"

Other than the few pieces of furniture, the single room was bare. A trash bag sat in the corner of the kitchen, filled to capacity. The few paperbacks that had been stacked on the floor by the bed were gone. Even the chipped mug that held her spoons and forks had disappeared.

She stood there, her back to him, unmoving.

"Kendall?" He approached and touched her arm. "What's going on?"

"I'm leaving."

It wasn't what she said but the way she said it that sliced through his heart. "What do you mean, you're leaving? You can't leave. We're just finding our way together. And besides, you have to finish the Liberty. So whatever joke you're playing—" He pulled her around and saw the duffel. A packed duffel. Everything she owned, everything she carried through this life, fit into one bag.

"It's not a joke, Hunter. It's time for me to move on." She swept past him and into the tiny bathroom. "I have a bus ticket for tomorrow morning, so I'll stay through the barbecue. Kinda have to. Not like you know how to operate that monster smoker out there."

"I don't care about the smoker. I want to know what's going on." He moved in front of her, determined to get her to stop long enough to explain. "You can't just leave, Kendall."

"Sure can. It's what I do best."

"It's what you used to do best. Come on, talk to me." A wave of panic as he'd never felt before washed over him. "You're serious. You're really leaving."

"You're smarter than you look." She smirked and pushed past him.

Hunter spun around, looking for whatever dimensional portal he'd walked through to find a Kendall he'd never met before. Not even the surly, hostile Kendall from the day he and Phoebe had arrived came close to this seemingly uncaring woman. "This isn't you. This isn't the Kendall I—"

"The Kendall you love doesn't exist," she snapped and stuffed whatever small toiletry bottles she'd found into her bag. "These last few weeks were a lie, Hunter. I'm not made for forever. I'm not made for even a fraction of that. I lied about my feelings for you so I could get close to you and Phoebe. Because being around you both lessened my pain. And now that pain is gone and I can move on."

He heard the words, but they didn't mean anything to him. "What's happened? Where is this coming from? Because this isn't the woman I've come to know these last few weeks."

"Maybe you're finally seeing beyond those stars to the real me. I'm poison, Hunter. I always have been. And the sooner you realize that—"

"You expect me to believe everything between us was a lie? Because I don't." He shoved his hands into his pockets and rocked back on his heels. Whatever was going on with her, hostility wouldn't fix it. "You're scared."

"Scared of what?"

"You're scared of being happy. Of taking another chance. Of worrying every day that something is going to happen to me or to Phoebe or to Matt or anyone else in this town you care about. You're a coward."

"That's right." She swung on him, eyes blazing. "I'm a complete and utter coward, and what kind of man would love a woman like that?"

"This one loves you. I love you, Kendall." He didn't know how else to say it, how else to convince her.

"Who you love doesn't exist. I'm a lie, Hunter. Whoever I was, whatever was left after that roadside bomb got buried in that grave back in North Dakota. I'm a ghost. And ghosts don't love. They don't love you and they don't love… Phoebe."

Hunter watched the color drain from Kendall's face. He spun around and found Phoebe standing in the open doorway. "Hey, kiddo." His heart slammed against his ribs. How long had she been standing there? What had she heard? "You done with the— No, wait, Phoebe!"

Kendall sank into a rickety high-back chair. "I'm sorry." The whisper nearly broke his heart. But he couldn't afford a broken heart. Not while his niece had had hers broken yet again.

"Sorry doesn't mean squat. I don't know what's going on, but if leaving makes things easier on you, then by all means run. But you'll never outrun yourself, Kendall. And you'll always be regretting what you've left behind. Phoe-be!" Racing after his niece, he didn't bother to glance behind him.

"SINCE HUNTER ISN'T TALKING, you going to tell me what's going on with you two?" Frankie sidled up next to Kendall at the smoker and twisted off the cap to a root beer. "Here. Take a slug."

Kendall shook her head. She knew her body well enough to know she couldn't keep anything down. Agreeing to Eleanor's terms had been gut-wrenching enough; confronting Hunter earlier today had tipped her over the edge. But it was seeing the utter betrayal and pain shining in Phoebe's eyes that had hollowed out her insides.

"I thought things were going gangbusters with you two." Frankie leaned against a tree and assessed her. "Now here you are, slip-sliding into that sullen mood of yours."

"How would you know about any of that?" Kendall asked and took her aggression out on the porterhouse steak sizzling over the low flame of the barbecue.

"Don't assume that the pretty package is all pretty. And don't use that tone with me. I'm not the one who messed things up with Romeo over there. What did you do?"

"I didn't do anything."

"Oh, so not true." Frankie took a long drink from her root beer. "Hunter's too crazy about you to screw up, which means you did something. Spill."

"No."

"Okay, fine. I'll ask him."

"No, don't." Kendall caught her arm. "Don't ruin the party, Frankie. It's… I'll work it out." Not that she knew how. Especially not with all these people swarming around the lighthouse. Pretty much everyone she knew in Butterfly Harbor had turned up, from Mrs. Hastings, Paige's across-the-street neighbor, to Sebastian Evans and his daughter, Mandy, who always seemed to be exchanging smiles with Kyle Winters when no one was looking. She saw Holly and Luke Saxon sitting on one of the benches someone had been smart enough to bring, while Abby, Paige and Alethea were playing a mean game of horseshoes. Frankie's twin brother, Monty, was discussing his newest nautical acquisition with Xander while Calliope flitted about, filling glasses with lemonade or margaritas depending on desires.

The kids who had become so familiar of late raced around as if they lived there, which, of course, they practically did now. The laughing and shouting and crying and goading should have been driving her back into her solitude, but it didn't. Instead she found the energy and affection among her friends to be soothing and comfortable.

"Hey. Earth to Kendall. Flip it."

"What?"

"Oh, never mind. Give me those." Frankie snatched the tongs and called over a few people to claim their steaks. "Go find him and work it out already. And would you please kick cranky Kendall to the curb? She's boring."

"Charlie." Kendall asked the little girl as she flew by, "Have you seen Phoebe?"

"Hunter said she wasn't feeling well. She's taking a nap in the motor home." Charlie pouted. "Bummer. 'Cause we need her for an even team. Is everything okay?"

"It's fine." No, that was wrong. She was wrong. She'd been wrong to confront Eleanor, and she'd been even more wrong to agree to her terms. She didn't want to leave Butterfly Harbor. She'd worked long and hard to make this place her home, and now that she could call it that, she wasn't going to give it up without a fight. But first she had to find Hunter and explain.

Hunter.

Kendall turned in circles, looking for him. She finally spotted him talking with Willa O'Neill. She couldn't stop looking at him. Didn't want to. Not now. Maybe not forever. Because she loved him.

"Time to eat crow. A whole big pot of it." She smoothed a nervous hand down the front of her shirt and headed toward him.

Willa smiled at her and went to speak with Calliope, leaving Hunter on his own. He wasted no time, once Kendall was at his side.

"You lied to me."

"I—um. I did." Did she admit everything in one big purge, or did she let him decide what she needed to say? "It's complicated, Hunter. And I'm sorry for earlier. Especially for Phoebe, but I had to—"

"You talked to Eleanor last night. That's where you went instead of going to dinner with us. Don't bother lying again. You stink at it, and besides, Willa said she called her down to the lobby for you."

"She did?" Kendall frowned. "Willa isn't a gossip. Why would she volunteer—"

"She didn't volunteer, I pressed her, because guess what?" He grabbed up her hands and stepped in to kiss her. "Because I know you, Kendall Davidson. And that even though you don't want to admit it, you love me. And you love Phoebe. You'd only walk away from us and your friends if there was a greater good being served. So, what was it?"

"I—"

"Hey, what's going on over here?" Matt, surrounded by his fellow deputies, asked. "Kendall, are you all right?"

"I'm fine, Matt." She held out her hand to wave him off.

"You tell me, you tell all of them, why you're going to skip town for good," Hunter insisted.

"You're what?" Matt, instead of standing behind her, circled around to join Hunter. "What the—"

"Kendall, why would you do that?" Lori moved in, as did the other partygoers as the din quieted. "This is your home. Why would you leave?"

"Because Eleanor and Stephen know about my past." What was the point of covering for two people who didn't deserve it? "It's bad, Hunter. Bad enough that I'm not the best person to be around Phoebe, even though I adore that little girl. They have my medical records, and know that I was arrested once, which I should have told you about though I didn't because I was worried that you'd be worried, but now they're going to use it all in the custody case—"

"Excuse me." Leah Ellis emerged from the crowd looking elegant and regal as always. Leah had reminded Kendall of one of those women who could tackle the world with one hand and knit an entire blanket with the other. Never a hair out of place, not even on a casual day like today, she was pressed and presentable for any court or possible suitor. "Did you say they have your medical records?"

"They must. She knows things." Kendall took a deep breath. "She knows about my time in the hospital. And about the depression. A court certainly isn't going to want me anywhere near Phoebe."

"You have got to be kidding me." Hunter stared at her as if he'd never seen her before. "Of all the ridiculous, harebrained—"

"Dude." Matt dropped a hand on his shoulder.

Hunter pulled Kendall into his arms and held her close. "We love you, you fool. The good and the bad. The darkness and the light, *remember*? More than that, we need you. Especially for this custody fight. The court has to see who her mother is going to be."

Kendall tried to talk, but her voice was muffled. And she laughed.

"What?"

"She said she can't breathe." Calliope moved in. "While this confession is no doubt good for the soul, might I ask where Phoebe is? I haven't seen her this entire time."

"She's in the motor home," Hunter said.

"No, she's not!" Charlie yelled from the open door behind them. "I just checked. She's gone. And so is her jacket and her copy of *Charlotte's Web*. I can't find her anywhere."

CHAPTER SIXTEEN

"We need to organize search parties," Sheriff Luke Saxon announced without missing a beat. "Ozzy, Fletcher…"

Kendall barely heard anything beyond *she's gone*. The past descended on her so hard and so fast her knees went weak. People scrambled in all directions while Hunter kept her tight to his chest, looking as uncertain and worried as she felt.

"We'll find her." It took Kendall a good few seconds to realize she was the one who had spoken. "We'll find her," she repeated, and this time she put her hands on the sides of Hunter's face and pressed her forehead to his. "I'll find her."

"I know."

Because she was looking into his eyes when he said it, she knew he was telling the truth. Because Hunter MacBride didn't lie. Not to anyone. And especially not to her.

Kendall could find Phoebe, bring her home. And when she did, she was going to hug that little girl until neither of them could stand it.

“Mom? Dad?” Simon Saxon dived for his ever-present school bag. “I have a map I drew the other day. I used it when we were playing hide-and-seek.”

“My little genius.” Holly grabbed hold of him and kissed the top of his head.

“Aw, Mom. Cut it out.” Simon shooed her away as he unfolded the pieces of paper. Everyone gathered around as Simon pointed out what was what.

“I need to borrow one of your deputies,” Leah Ellis said to Luke.

“What for?”

“To make an arrest. Where’s Hamilton? Gil, who’s on duty at the DA’s office this weekend?”

Gil had rushed over and pulled out his phone. “Ah, that would be Kevin Marshall. What do you need?”

“Charges brought against Stephen and Eleanor Cartwright. But I’ll settle for them being questioned first.”

“What kind of charges?” Hunter asked as Kendall committed Simon’s map to memory.

Charlie busied herself giving pointers about the various hiding spots as Frankie turned down the smoker and set the meat aside. "Question them about what?"

"We can start with illegally accessing a person's private medical file. Was that your military record, Kendall?"

Kendall nodded. "Yeah. I've only ever been treated at the VA."

"Excellent. Maybe Kevin can come up with a federal charge to really scare them. Time will tell. I'd like a record of it. Is that possible?"

"So long as the DA signs off on it, sure." Luke nodded. "I'll bring them in personally."

"Oh, please, let me come with you." Matt passed his drink off to his fellow deputy. "I will owe you for life."

"Fine," Luke agreed. "But we want this done by the book. No mistakes on this one. By any of us."

"What are you doing?" Hunter followed Kendall, who'd sprinted into the keeper house. She ripped open her bag and threw her belongings out, searching for her boots.

"I'm going to look for her. I bet I know where she went."

"Then fill me in along the way."

"No. You need to stay here in case I'm wrong. If someone brings her back and we're both gone, she'll be even more scared." Hunter stared down at her as she laced up her hiking boots. "Tell me I'm wrong."

"You're not. It's just nice to see this Kendall again. Do me a favor?" He bent down and kissed her. Hard. "Don't lose her again."

"I won't." This was what she was good at. Solving problems. Fixing things. And if anything ever needed fixing more than Phoebe's broken heart, she didn't know what did. She grabbed a flashlight, a baseball cap, then tugged on a jacket. "Give me your cell."

"Wh—ah, okay." He dug it out of his pocket. "You know how to use one of these?"

"You have one of those compass apps on here?" She tapped open the screen. "I need your password."

"Kendall."

"Hunter, please, don't argue with me. I need your password."

"Five three six three two five five. Kendall." He shrugged. "I changed it a few weeks ago. I'm a romantic."

"And a keeper. Okay." She tapped open the application. "Time to go find our girl."

KENDALL'S VOICE WAS raw by the time the sun set. Calling for Phoebe to respond seemed a lesson in futility. But into the forest between the Liberty and the ocean she went, down, down, down, into the darkness of the thick trees and rock formations.

Simon's map had been rudimentary, but she'd noticed one spot, the very highest spot that was far to the west. Far enough to the west she could only hope that area wasn't as close to the cliff line as she feared.

In the far distance she could hear the search teams calling for Phoebe, as well. They'd headed out in all directions, leaving Frankie and Hunter at the lighthouse along with Mrs. Hastings and Holly, who, despite Luke's pleas to head home, declared she wasn't going anywhere until Phoebe was found safe. Calliope, ever the voice of reason, also stayed behind with the children, urging them to be calm and send positive thoughts—and in Calliope's case a few flittering butterflies—into the universe.

The deeper Kendall walked into the trees, the louder the past roared in her ears. This was what happened when you cared about someone. That paralyzing fear, that dry mouth, can't-even-scream-because-it-would-hurt-too-much sensation.

In her mind, she heard the detonation of a bomb, saw behind too-wide eyes the flash of flame and smoke that had taken out her combat unit and left her smoldering among the wreckage. The suddenly quiet voices of the men she'd called brothers, voices she'd never hear again except in her nightmares.

Voices that guided her now as she kept the image of Phoebe in her mind. *Phoebe*, she told herself. Whose face no longer morphed into that of another little girl she'd loved. One she'd lost. She was not going to lose Phoebe, too.

She glanced down at the cell phone. She'd lost reception ages ago, and silently willed the little girl to hang on. That she was on her way. That she would spend the rest of her life making up for the betrayal of this morning.

Kendall shoved the phone into her pocket and clicked on her flashlight, arcing it up and around, down and about. There!

A flash of white light. Something in the shadows. “Phoebe?” Kendall called again and moved toward it.

Her flashlight flickered, sputtered and died. Kendall smacked it against a tree. “Stupid piece of plastic. I just replaced the batteries last week. What the—”

The shadow or white light flashed again. Kendall’s breath froze in her throat. Her entire body went cold as the light stretched and brushed against her, reminding her of a person. A lithe woman she’d only seen grainy images of in history books. “Liberty,” Kendall whispered.

The white light darted into the trees. Kendall ran after it, ran after her, ran so far and so fast she had to stop to catch her breath. And then she heard it.

What was that? Kendall tried to block out every other sound over the pounding of her heart. “Phoebe?”

A child’s sob rent the darkness.

Relief surged through her, drove her on, branches and twigs scraping at her face and catching on her jacket. Vines tangled around her feet as she tried not to trip. "Phoebe, it's me! It's Kendall. Make some noise. Tell me where you—" She skidded to a stop, grabbing hold of a tree to keep from toppling over the cliff's edge. Dirt and debris rained down into the ocean. "Phoebe." The sob she heard now was her own. "Oh, no, please."

The light exploded again, just in the distance and to the tall stack of rocks stretching up into the sky. And there the light settled, just above Phoebe's head.

"Phoebe! I'm coming. Stay there. Do not move!"

Kendall scrambled carefully along the path and climbed up the hill, gripping her cold and sore fingers into the rocks, up and up until she brushed against the fabric of Phoebe's jacket.

Phoebe sat there, arms stretched above her head, looking up at the silvery light shimmering around her. "Mama."

Kendall stopped breathing. Never in her life had she ever heard a more beautiful sound.

"Phoebe?" Kendall sat beside her, wrapping her arms around the little girl and pulling her securely into her lap. The battered copy of *Charlotte's Web* fell and tumbled into the ocean.

"Mama!" Phoebe cried and tried to dive after it.

"No. No, baby, you can't. It's not safe. We need you here." Kendall buried her face in Phoebe's hair, willing the little girl to understand. "I'm sorry about this morning. I didn't mean it. I didn't mean anything I said. I'm sorry, Phoebe. I'm so, so sorry." Tears obscured her vision as she glanced up and the silvery light began to fade.

But before it did, three beautiful monarch butterflies soared in a circle above their heads, then disappeared.

They sat there together, rocking back and forth against the growing chill, the two of them crying out their pain.

"Mama," Phoebe whispered.

"I know, baby. I know you miss her." And there was nothing she could do about it.

Phoebe leaned back, pointed to the sky, then just as her uncle had done in the past, she clasped Kendall's face in her palms and stared into her eyes. "Mama."

"I'm Mama?" Kendall asked on a sob.

"Oh, no. So much. So sweet. But I don't… I can't—"

"Mama." Phoebe's eyes narrowed. In that moment, beneath the barely there moon and the crashing waves, Kendall saw Hunter in his niece's face. And knew she'd found her home.

"Okay, baby." Kendall brushed her hair back and kissed her forehead. "For you, I'll be Mama."

"LOOK! KENDALL FOUND HER!" Frankie yelled to the crowd that had formed, the night binoculars still held up to her face. Most of the search parties had returned, and Ozzy had put out the call to town, bringing out even more residents to help.

Hunter sagged to the ground, the hope that had been keeping him upright surging out of him. "I think I might pass out." His mind spun from relief. Kendall had had the right idea the other day; clearly she was right and they needed to put a bell around Phoebe's neck. Matt threw an arm around his shoulder. "Hey, Frankie! Time to celebrate. Fire that grill and smoker up again!"

"One-track mind, that husband of mine,"

Lori muttered as she joined Calliope in helping Hunter to his feet. "I know now might not be the time, but I did hear the old Stedman place might be going up for sale. Seeing as the lighthouse will be open for business soon, you might want to take a look."

"An excellent suggestion," Calliope agreed. "Lots of land, and there's a large workshop for Kendall and her projects. And a lovely office overlooking the ocean."

"You guys are trying to sell me real estate *now*?" Hunter couldn't quite believe what he was hearing as they went on about the home's amenities and how it was the perfect place for a family. "Okay, stop. Enough. I'll take a look. This really isn't the time—"

"Told you it would work," Lori said to Calliope, who stepped back and waved her arm as Kendall, carrying a sleepy-looking Phoebe, stepped out of the woods behind the carriage house. "Kept you distracted for just long enough."

Hunter ran straight for them, and as Kendall let Phoebe down, he scooped his niece into his arms and squeezed. "Don't you ever, ever run away from us again, do you hear me? Running is never the solution to anything. Never. Right, Kendall?"

Kendall leaned against him and nodded, stroking Phoebe's hair. "He's absolutely right."

"I'm sorry," Phoebe whispered.

"I wanted to find Mama. And I did."

"You...did?" He was so confused. So tired. So...exhilarated, nothing was making sense.

"I think we've all found some closure out there. Now." Kendall bent down and, turning Phoebe to face her, zipped up the child's coat. "It's time to get this party started. An awful lot of people came to look for you, young lady. What do you say we go thank them?"

"Okay." Phoebe took a hold of both Hunter's hand and Kendall's.

Before the three of them headed to the place that had saved them all: Liberty Lighthouse.

EPILOGUE

Three months later

KENDALL BROKE DOWN the second last of the packing boxes and tossed it onto the pile with the others by the front door. Hands on her hips, she took a long, approving look around the onetime welding shop.

Lori's and Calliope's suggestion months before about the Stedman house and property being for sale had been the perfect solution. Phoebe had fallen in love with the place the moment she saw her proposed bedroom that included a bay window surrounded by large built-in bookcases. Hunter's new office, as promised, overlooked the ocean, which was close enough for them all to take walks along their own cliff's edge most nights after dinner.

As for Kendall's workshop, now home base for Kendall Construction and Refurbishment, she had everything she'd always been afraid of wanting.

Kendall walked across the cement floor to the office she'd created for herself. It wasn't anything fancy—a laptop computer, business cards, a schedule of jobs she had lined up well into the next year. She sat at the desk that had been her father's, one of the many pieces of furniture she and Hunter had brought back from their trip to North Dakota.

Some might have considered it an odd kind of honeymoon, but it was time to tie up all those loose threads of her life before Hunter and Phoebe. Before she'd arrived in Butterfly Harbor.

Thankfully, she'd kept her mother's antique writing desk, which was now in the front hall, her grandmother's china cabinet and a few other pieces that brought back fond memories of her childhood.

There was only one box left. The box sitting on the corner of her desk beside the framed picture of her and Hunter on their wedding day, with Phoebe, a rather spur-of-the-moment event that had taken place at the Liberty Lighthouse shortly after the job was completed.

With surprisingly steady hands, Kendall lifted the lid of the box. Sam's dog tags and military ID sat atop the collection of letters she'd mailed him—the letters they'd exchanged beyond the emails and the video chats. She sifted through them, pulling out the photographs and silly notes, setting them aside until she stopped.

Sam's officer's photo. Kendall's eyes misted as she looked at his smiling, handsome, glasses-clad face beaming through the lenses at her. "You'd like him," she whispered, tracing her finger across Sam's face. "You'd like him a lot." She would always miss him. Miss the boy she'd grown up with, the man she'd loved. But he of all people would have understood her need to move on. And that she could have a bright future with Hunter without ever forgetting Sam.

She slipped the letters and pictures back into the box and stored it in the bottom of the filing cabinet behind her. Kendall did one more pass through the workshop, made sure everything was in its place, before heading out and, with one more glance at the cabinet, managed a small smile as she closed the door.

"Phoebe! Charlie!" She headed up the path to the house, ducking around to the customized swing set she, Frankie and Kyle had built for the little girl as a wedding gift. She and Hunter had gotten presents. It only made sense that Phoebe should get something, too. "You two girls ready for dinner?"

"Almost!" Phoebe called as she soared through the air, leaning outrageously far back in the swing. Charlie, flying just as high, let out a laugh and Phoebe joined in. It lightened Kendall's heart.

A gentle tinkling of butterfly wind chimes from the patio behind her had Kendall looking over her shoulder. Kendall swore she heard the sound of laughter; another child's laughter, before it floated away on the breeze. "Samira," Kendall whispered as a trio of butterflies flitted into view. Her heart thumped, but the sadness and longing that had ensnared her for so long didn't descend as they once did.

"Did you see the butterflies?" Phoebe's excited words were like a balm to Kendall's soul. Kendall watched as Phoebe and Charlie raced past her to chase after the butterflies. "There were three of them. Did you see?"

Phoebe yelled out, huffing and puffing, but with a grin that stretched from ear to ear.

"I always see them, now," Kendall whispered and nodded, as she headed into the house through the patio doors. "Hunter?" She had to navigate the rooms since the unpacking and rearranging hadn't been finished yet. She found him in his office, sitting at his desk with his back to her. "Hey. Did you get anything out for dinner because I forgot to?" She knocked on the door frame. "Did you hear me? What's wrong?" She walked up behind him, leaned over his shoulder and peered at his computer screen.

"Nothing." Hunter's fingers went white around the computer mouse. "Yet."

"What do you mean, yet? Oh." She saw the email from Max, Hunter's literary agent, and felt her own nerves flutter. "I forget." Kendall slipped her arm around his chest and leaned closer. "Is it good news or bad that comes in threes?"

"I don't want to know."

"Come on, you have to face your fear." She reached over and covered his hand with hers. Together, they clicked to open the email from his agent. She could feel the tension in his shoulders.

The same sort of tension that had disappeared when Stephen and Eleanor Cartwright had dropped their custody suit in exchange for Kendall not pressing charges. Kendall had asked that they not get into trouble for having hired a private investigator to steal her medical records, even though she hadn't seen much remorse over the fact, or that Eleanor had tried to blackmail her. As a result, Hunter and Kendall felt it was better for Stephen and Eleanor to keep their distance until Phoebe turned eighteen and could decide for herself whether or not she wanted to have any contact with her grandparents.

The entire situation struck Kendall as just sad. But it was the only thing that was.

"Huh." Kendall scanned Hunter's email, unable to hide her smile. A smile she'd become more and more accustomed to since the night she'd found Phoebe on the cliffs. "I guess you're getting a book deal."

"Three books." Hunter sagged back in his chair. "They want a series. Off a single book proposal. Kendall, that just doesn't happen."

"All evidence to the contrary." She bent

down and kissed his cheek. "Congratulations, author. We can add that to our celebration today."

"Are we really doing this?" He spun in his chair and tugged her onto his lap. Pointing to the unorganized room, he said, "It's been a lot for us to take on. Newlywed homeowners. Phoebe back in school. You getting your business license—"

"Kendall Construction and Restoration Inc., at your service."

"And now a book deal, too?" This time, he kissed her. "You are definitely my good-luck charm."

"Mom! Dad!" Phoebe burst into the room and practically slid into a heap at their feet. "Charlie says we're invited to Calliope's tonight for dinner cause Holly and Luke are coming with the babies. Everyone's gonna be there. Can we go? Please! Sebastian is going to be there with a new litter of kittens from the shelter. Can I finally get a kitten, Daddy? Or maybe two? Sebastian says two is better than one. That way they'll always have someone to play with like when I'm in school and we don't want them to get bored. Please?"

Hunter looked to Kendall and she gave a

small nod of approval. She sighed, leaned back in his arms.

"Honestly?" Hunter said, with good humor in his voice. "I think the only thing missing from our lives is a cat. But just one!" Phoebe didn't seem to take any notice, though, since she'd already run off and started yelling for Charlie. "Shoot."

Kendall laughed. "It's like you can read my mind."

"We're going to end up with two kittens, aren't we?" He caught her chin in his fingers and brought her mouth to his.

"Yes," she murmured happily. "Yes, we are."

* * * * *

Other great titles in the
Butterfly Harbor Stories
miniseries include:

The Bad Boy of Butterfly Harbor
Recipe for Redemption
A Dad for Charlie
Always a Hero
Holiday Kisses

Available at
www.Harlequin.com today!

And don't miss Frankie's romance,
Under the Mistletoe,
coming in November 2019!

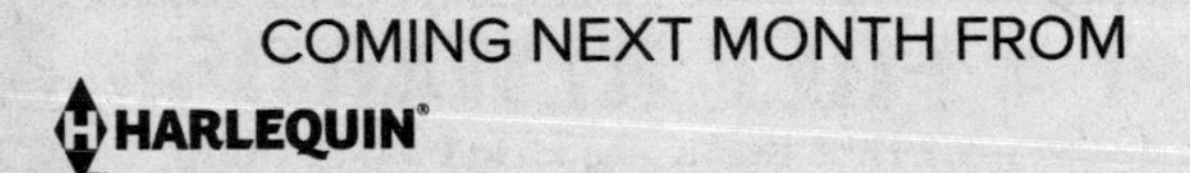

HEARTWARMING™

Available October 8, 2019

#299 RESCUED BY THE PERFECT COWBOY

The Mountain Monroes • by Melinda Curtis

Hiring down-to-earth Zeke Roosevelt as nanny for her twin boys seems a no-brainer to Sophie Monroe. Zeke figures the "easy" job will tide him over until he realizes he can't keep his eyes off Sophie!

#300 A RANCH BETWEEN THEM

Sweet Home, Montana • by Jeannie Watt

When Brady O'Neil accepts a job caretaking a ranch, he never dreams he'd have to share the place with his best friend's sister, Katie Callahan! Or that he'd have to guard his heart all over again...

#301 KEEPING HER CLOSE

A Pacific Cove Romance • by Carol Ross

Harper Jansen likes her quiet life and doesn't appreciate former navy SEAL Kyle Frasier turning up on her doorstep insisting he's been hired to protect her. She tries to avoid him, but has to admit maybe she doesn't really want to...

#302 AFTER THE RODEO

Heroes of Shelter Creek

by Claire McEwen

Former bull rider Jace Hendricks needs biologist Vivian Reed off his ranch, fast—or he risks losing custody of his nieces and nephew. So why is Vivian's optimism winning over the kids...and Jace?